I0599735

Back To You

LAKE CITY SERIES
BOOK ONE

JASMINE AHMAD

Copyright © 2025 by Jasmine Ahmad

All rights reserved.

No part of this book may be reproduced in any form or by any electronic or mechanical means, including information storage and retrieval systems, without written permission from the author, except for the use of brief quotations in a book review.

The characters and events portrayed in this book are fictitious or are used fictitiously. Any similarity to real persons, living or dead, is purely coincidental and not intended by the author.

To all the survivors of domestic violence—to those who have fought battles no one knew about, to those who have endured immense loss and still found the strength to persevere. I see you. I feel you. I am you.

To Mima y Abuelo, Te extraño.

To Amir, thank you for loving me exactly as I am.

Author's Note

Dear Reader,

Thank you for picking up this book. While I hope this story brings you joy, connection, and maybe even a few tears, I also want to acknowledge that certain topics in this book may be difficult for some readers.

Content Warning:

- Emotional & Physical Abuse - References to past domestic abuse (not depicted in real-time but discussed by the character).
- Grief & Loss - Death of a loved one, discussions of past loss.
- Chronic Illness - Representation of Lupus, including symptoms, struggles with self-care, and the impact on daily life.
- Mental Health: Anxiety and trauma responses.

I encourage readers to take care of themselves while reading.

My goal is to tell stories with heart, complexity, and healing—I truly appreciate you being here.

Con mucho amor,
    Jasmine

Playlist

1. A Puro Dolor - Son by Four
2. I Miss You, I'm Sorry - Gracie Adams
3. Neptune - Sleeping at Last
4. Ghost (Acoustic) - Jonah Baker
5. Kiss Me - New Found Glory
6. Te Extraño - Xtreme
7. Invisible String - Taylor Swift
8. Until I Found You - Stephen Sanchez
9. My Tears Ricochet - Taylor Swift

Prologue

MARIANA

The day I should have been the happiest was the day my life stopped feeling like my own.

Today would have been Andrew's and my wedding anniversary. Instead of marking another year of a marriage that, if I'm being honest, never quite felt right, I'm here—at his funeral.

I stand in front of the mirror, tugging at the sleeve of my white blouse, willing the fabric to stretch farther down my wrist. The nearly faded bruise stares back at me, a sickening reminder of everything I've buried—everything I still refuse to let surface.

My fingers tremble as I smooth the cuff over my skin, a ritual so ingrained that I don't even think about it anymore. Hide it, cover it, protect him—even now, even in death.

The bathroom is silent except for my breath, too shallow, too fast. Beyond the door, voices murmur—hushed whispers, quiet sobs, the rustle of tissues.

They are grieving. They are heartbroken. They miss him... I should miss him, too.

I press my hands against the sink, gripping the cool porcelain edge, and force myself to breathe. My reflection wavers, distorted by the moisture in my eyes. I blink hard, refusing to let the tears fall.

I don't even know who they would be for—the man I lost, or the man I had to survive. The thought makes my stomach twist. Because I *did* love him...once.

Andrew had been my safe place once upon a time. He had been the man with bright blue eyes who made me laugh, who kissed me like I was something precious, who whispered promises of forever against my skin.

The man who held my hand and told me I was the best thing that had ever happened to him. The man who got down on one knee and made me believe in us. That's the man I crave.

The one I still find myself searching for in memories, in old photographs, in the quiet moments before sleep, when my mind betrays me. But that man is long gone—in his place, there is only cruelty.

Hands that once cradled my face in tenderness became weapons, gripping too tight, shoving too hard. A voice that once whispered, "I love you", turned sharp, cutting through me with insults that burrowed under my skin like glass shards.

The change was slow, like a storm rolling in on a clear horizon. At first, it was just a tone in his voice, a look in his eyes, an unexpected moment of silence where warmth used to be; then came the control, the accusations, the outbursts that left me shrinking smaller and smaller, afraid of saying the wrong thing, of being the wrong thing.

The first time he grabbed my wrist too hard, he apologized — held me afterward, kissed my hair, told me he didn't mean it.

By the time he stopped apologizing, I had already learned to pretend it didn't hurt. Even now, even here, I find myself swallowing the truth, keeping it locked away where no one else can see it—because it's easier that way.

A soft knock at the door startles me. "Mariana?" A voice, gentle, hesitant, filters through the wood. "It's almost time."

Time. I straighten my spine, adjusting the collar of my blouse, making sure my sleeves are in place. The bruises are hidden; the truth is buried. I take one last look in the mirror, at the woman who mastered the art of pretending. Then, I step out of the bathroom.

The church is packed—rows of black, heads bowed, hands clasped together in sorrow. Faces blur together—family, friends, people who think they knew us, people who think they knew him. I walk forward, the weight of their gazes pressing down on me like a vice. The whispers start as soon as they see me.

"She looks so pale."

"She must be devastated."

"They were so in love."

I want to laugh, I want to scream, I want to run. Instead, I stop in front of the casket.

Andrew's body is still, his skin pale and waxen. His light brown hair is neatly brushed to the side, his lips pressed into a peaceful line. Peace...the thing he stole from me, and yet, in death, it's the only thing he has left.

I stare at him, my hands clasped tightly in front of me to keep from shaking. I should feel something. More than this. More than just...confusion. More than the exhaustion that sits heavy in my bones. I squeeze my eyes shut, and for a second, I let myself pretend.

I imagine him opening his eyes, those bright blue eyes that used to make me feel safe. I imagine him smiling at me, brushing his fingers over my cheek. For a moment, I let myself believe in the man I loved, in the life we should have had. The life he ruined.

A tear slips free, and I don't know if it's for him or for me. Because now that he's gone, I don't know who I'm supposed to be.

For so long, my life has revolved around surviving him. The apologies, the justifications. The careful, measured steps I took to avoid setting him off. The excuses I made, the lies I told myself, the silence I forced upon myself. If he's not here... who am I, without him?

Someone steps up beside me, offering their hand. Automatically, I take it, gripping tightly. The pressure sends a dull throb through my wrist, through the bruise I've hidden beneath my sleeve—a reminder.

This is why I won't tell them, because I don't want to ruin their memory of him, because it's already hard enough for them, because they need to believe he was a good man. And maybe, in some ways, I need to believe it, too. I take a deep breath and finally turn to face them.

It's showtime.

CHAPTER 1

Mariana

I t's been six months since Andrew died. Six months of playing the grieving widow, mourning her perfect husband—when that couldn't be further from the truth. I loved Andrew. At least, I thought I did.

We met on a Friday night at a dive bar, the kind with sticky floors, a jukebox that only half-worked, and a bartender who poured heavy. I'd had a few too many drinks and was belting out Whitney Houston's 'I wanna dance with somebody' on the stage. When I stepped down, Andrew walked right over, flashing a cocky smile.

"I hear you're looking for someone to dance with. I'm here to make your dance dreams come true."

I guffawed—the line was ridiculous. But there was something about the way he delivered it, with confidence and charm. So I danced with him that night. And the rest was history.

Now that I know who he really was, I wish that I could go back to that night and stay home. At first, he showered me with love. So much attention. He was everything I thought I wanted. Constant gifts and endless compliments always made me feel like the only girl in the world. I was so damn naive. I should've known that something was off with him when he kept pushing for marriage before we'd even been together for a year. I loved him, but I wasn't ready. I kept holding off.

Eventually, he convinced me—a small courthouse wedding, just my mom and his parents. And that's when everything changed.

At first, it was little things—wanting me home by six every night. I thought it was sweet. He wanted to have dinner with me, right?

We didn't live together until after the wedding. I claimed I wanted to be traditional, but the truth was, I liked having my own space. The first night I got home late from work, he was furious. I was confused. I had texted him—told him I was meeting a client after hours. I work in event planning and also make dessert tables for clients. This client could only meet after work, so I stayed.

That was the first night he slapped me.

I was in complete shock. Even now, thinking back, I still don't understand what I did wrong. I should've left. I know I should have. But he was so apologetic. Swore it would never happen again. And I wanted to protect our marriage. I took our vow seriously, for better or worse. Little did I know, the 'worse' would drown out the 'better'.

After that night, he was great...for two months. Then, slowly, his controlling behavior started creeping back in...or maybe he had never changed at all. He became possessive and obsessive. I felt sick if I left work even a minute late, never knowing how he'd react. He checked my phone constantly and accused me of cheating. Later, I found he'd actually been following me, trailing my car to make sure I was where I said I'd be.

And still, I stayed.

I don't believe in divorce. We had to make it work—no

matter the cost. And it did cost me. My confidence, my mental health, and my friends—sometimes, I was sure it would cost me my life.

His control turned to cruelty. His words turned to fists. And there were days I wasn't sure I'd make it out alive.

Now, six months after his death, I still can't believe I outlived him.

During our five-year marriage, I endured so much at his hands. I prayed every night for the strength to leave, but it never came. I hate that I was so weak that I clung to the love I once had for him, hoping it would be enough to keep me going.

My body felt battered every day. I thought the bruises, the exhaustion, and the pain were just part of surviving him. But in that sterile hospital room, with the IV lines in my arm and a doctor's careful voice telling me I had lupus, I realized I had been fighting two battles. One battle was visible; the other was hidden in plain sight.

Andrew was the picture of perfection during my time in the hospital and for a while afterward. He held my hand, whispered promises, and kissed my forehead like he meant it. I let myself believe it. I let myself hope, and that hope became the cruelest lie of all. I thought maybe this was the pivotal moment he needed. Maybe this would change him, make him remember the man he used to be. I couldn't have been more wrong. Because monsters don't turn back into men.

Still in bed, I roll over to shut off my alarm, groaning. I'm not ready to get up yet. Mornings can be tough on my body, but I have to get up—I can't miss this meeting again. My client is planning her daughter's quinceañera, and we've already rescheduled a couple of times because I wasn't feeling well. I'm excited to help bring her vision to life, but first, I just need my body to cooperate.

Slowly, I push myself out of bed and wrap myself in my

favorite thick wool cardigan, slipping my feet into my Taylor's Version slippers. Feeling cozy, I head to the kitchen and reach for my cafetera—I literally can't even begin to think about functioning before my cup of Café Bustelo.

With a piping hot coffee in hand, I stare out the floor-to-ceiling windows. It's raining again—shocker. Leaning my forehead against the glass, I close my eyes, letting the soft rhythm of the rain calm me. I take a deep breath, the rich aroma of coffee filling my senses.

My fingers find my wedding ring, and I start to twirl it absentmindedly. I don't know why I'm still wearing it. Maybe it's because taking it off feels too final. Maybe because I'm not ready to let go—even if I already have in every way that matters.

I should feel devastated, and I am. Andrew was once someone I thought I'd spend the rest of my life with, but he changed, and that changed me. I'm sad that his alcohol abuse led to his death. I'm sad for his family that they'll never see or speak to him again. I'm sad that our life together was one big lie, not only to everyone else but also to myself.

I have so much sadness...but I also feel relief. And that relief feels like the deepest betrayal.

I glance at the large clock on my wall—shit—I need to get ready if I'm going to make it to my meeting on time.

Placing my empty mug in the sink, I rush to my room and throw on my ripped jeans, an oversized flannel over a white tank, and my white Converse. Too rushed to fuss with it, I leave my long, wavy chocolate-brown hair down.

Grabbing my keys from the dish by the door, my phone starts ringing. Mom. I groan, hesitating. Do I answer or just shoot her a text saying I'll call later? I pause for a beat, then sigh and pick up. If I don't, she'll just worry. Ever since Andrew's death, she's been hovering more than usual. Throw in my lupus diagnosis, and she's turned borderline overbearing. I know she means well; she's a great mom, but I just want to feel normal again—like the person I was before Andrew, before all of this.

"Bendicion, Mami. Cómo estás? I say, trying not to sound like I'm in a rush, even though I am.

"Estoy bien, mija. Cómo estás? Estás demasiado delgada en esa foto de Instagram...estás comiendo bien?," she says, voice laced with concern.

I bite my lip. I know she means well, but I wish she wouldn't comment on that. I take a deep breath before responding.

"Don't worry, Mom. I'm fine. Yes, I'm eating. I've lost a little weight, but I promise I'm okay."

"Okay, okay, mamita. You promise to tell me if you're not okay, right?"

"Yes, Mami—te lo prometo."

"And you've been keeping up with your medicine? And that stretchy exercise the doctor said could help with your pain?

I laugh. "Stretchy exercise? You mean yoga? Yes, I go whenever it fits around my client meetings. And I take my meds every day—I even set an alarm on my phone.

"Okay, good. I'm happy to hear that," she says, sounding relieved.

"Was there something you needed, Mami?"

"Nada, mamita. I just wanted to check in on you, make sure you're okay. Tonight's dominoes night with the girls from bingo, so I wasn't going to be able to check in before bed."

I smile despite myself. Mom means well. I know that, and maybe I need her hovering more than I want to admit.

If there's one thing my mom loves, it's playing dominoes. Before my dad passed away, Friday nights were theirs—dominos, alcapurrias, flan, and Hector Lavoe playing from their radio.

Hearing that she's playing again makes me so happy. After Papi passed, she couldn't even look at a domino set. A love like theirs comes around once in a lifetime. She was shattered after his stroke took him, her grief swallowing her whole.

When he died, she became everything people expect me to be right now—a walking ghost. A heart in pieces, too broken to exist. I wish I felt that way. I wish this were normal. I wish I had a love like theirs. But I don't. I didn't. And I don't think I ever will.

"That's great, Mami. I'm glad you're having a girls' night. Just don't play too hard, okay? I know you guys like to play for money, and if you put in all your effort, you'll wipe out their bank accounts." I say, humor in my voice.

Did I mention my mom is a champion domino player? Sweet little Lucia turns into a ruthless competitor the second she picks up a tile. Before moving to Lake City, Colorado, she grew up in Puerto Rico, where domino tournaments in the park were a big deal, and she was undefeated.

That's how she met my dad—going head to head, and of course, she beat him. Every time he tells the story, he grins and says she slapped down the winning domino with a sharp *clack*, leaned back in her chair with her arms crossed, a smug grin on her face as the whole table erupted in laughter. Then she smirked at him and said, "Ay bendito, papito, pa' esto hay que tener talento, y tú... bueno, mejor suerte pa' la próxima." He swears that was the moment he knew she was going to be his wife. He always loved how competitive she got when they played games.

But if you ask my mom, she'll say he really fell for her after tasting her pastelillos.

Pastelillos have a golden, flaky crust and can be filled with all kinds of things, the most common being carne molida—bursting with spices, garlic, olives, and onions. She swears that after his first bite, she saw it in his eyes. He was in love.

And honestly? I believe her. No one makes pastelillos like my mom. I guess the saying, "The way to a man's heart is through his stomach," rang true for my dad.

My mom's laughter pulls me from my thoughts, and she says, "I can't make any promises, mija. Ya tú sabes, I can't go too easy on them!"

I can picture her smile as she says this. She's probably standing at her kitchen counter, her signature cup of coffee in hand—black, with one packet of Sweet'N Low. Like me, my mom is a small woman, barely five feet tall, but she packs a punch. She's the perfect mix of hard and soft, firm but fair.

She was always clear about the rules of the house and about the expectations she had. But not once did she ever make me feel like I couldn't turn to her. No matter how badly I screwed up—and believe me, I've made plenty of mistakes— she was always there.

She's been there for everything, every crush, every heart-break. She'd laugh with me, cry with me, and spend nights teaching me how to cook. We've had more game nights than I can count, and of course, I can't forget the evenings we spent watching telenovelas with crackers and cafecito, dipping them in just the way she likes.

She truly is my best friend. I couldn't dream up a better mom even if I tried. I swallow hard. So why have I hidden so much from her?

I just don't want to break her heart. And I guess...I don't see the point in rehashing the past. Andrews gone. He's never coming back. He can't hurt me anymore.

Maybe if I don't talk about it, if I don't turn it into some-thing bigger than it already was, I can pretend it never happened.

Maybe then, I can finally move.

11

I sit at my desk, sketching the cake my client envisioned for her daughter's quinceañera. I love event planning, but my favorite part is when I get to create beautiful desserts. Tapping my pen against my sketchbook, I glance around my office. Pictures of my friends from back home sit on my desk, a framed photo of my parents hangs beside my degree, and a small Puerto Rican flag rests beside my jar of pens. I miss them all so much.

When I moved to Seattle, I was seeking out adventure and change. I didn't think I'd feel this alone. But after Andrew and I married, he made sure to pull me even further away from everyone. Before I knew it, calls home became rare, and messages went unanswered. Leaning back in my chair, I take a sip of my now-cold coffee and wince. I'll have to microwave it for the third time today.

After my morning meeting, I've been running around making sure every event I'm planning has everything it needs. One thing about me? There won't be a damn thing missing to ruin anyone's event—not on my watch. I wish I had more dessert clients, but that's not where the real demand is. So, instead, I plan weddings, birthdays, baby showers, and even corporate events—whatever people need. And I'm good at it. But baking? Creating something beautiful with my own hands? That's where my heart is. Cakes, cupcakes, croissants, macarons—I love making it all.

The joint pain from my lupus makes baking harder than it should be—most days, more than I care to admit. But if I had the chance? I'd spend every day covered in flour and sugar, lost in the rhythm of creating something beautiful.

A light tap on my door pulls me from my thoughts. I look up to find Josephine, the owner of Glamour & Grace Events, standing in the doorway. "Time for lunch," she says, flashing a friendly grin.

I've been working for Josephine for seven years now. When we met, I was 24—wide-eyed, lost, and stuck bartending while Andrew pressured me to quit. I walked into my interview with no experience, just the argument that bartending had trained me to handle people and keep them happy. She took a chance on me when she didn't have to, and I swore I wouldn't let her regret it.

Over the years, she's tried to build a friendship with me, but I always kept her at a distance. Andrew hated the idea of anyone knowing too much about our lives, so I made sure to keep everyone at arm's length. Before I get the chance to speak, she beats me to it,

"I'm not taking no for an answer today, Mari. We're going to lunch. You've been killing it all day, and I promise you, that sketch can wait."

I look up. Her arms crossed, and her left eyebrow was raised. Yeah, she means business. She knows I'm a total workaholic.

That promise I made years ago? I meant it. Every single day since I stepped through these doors, I've busted my ass to prove she was right to take a chance on me. Even now, seven years later, I can't turn that part of me off. It's just not who I am. When I commit to something, I give it everything I have.

I sigh heavily. "I really, really wanted to finish this sketch so I can send it over to the client for approval."

"You have time, Mari. Everyone needs to eat—including you. Now get your ass up. I'm starving."

The hostess ushers us inside, the scent of garlic, oregano, and freshly baked pita bread immediately wrapping around me like a familiar embrace. We shake off the rain, close our umbrellas, and place them on the stand by the door, droplets slipping from the fabric and pooling on the tiled floor.

I slip off my jacket, the warmth of the restaurant a stark

contrast to the damp chill outside. As I settle into my seat, I take in everything I love about this place. The food is to die for, but it's the warmth of the atmosphere that keeps me coming back.

The white and blue walls, reminiscent of the Greek islands, are adorned with framed paintings of Santorini sunsets and fishing boats bobbing in sapphire waters. Grape leaves and olive branches weave through wooden trellises overhead, casting delicate shadows against the ceiling. Small potted herbs—basil, rosemary, and oregano—sit on the windowsills, filling the space with a fresh, earthy aroma.

Every table is dressed with crisp white linens, a single candle flickering at the center, its soft glow reflecting off polished silverware. The gentle hum of traditional Greek music plays in the background, the faint strumming of a bouzouki and melodic voices weaving through the air like a comforting lullaby.

Waiters glide between tables, balancing platters of sizzling souvlaki, golden spanakopita, and steaming bowls of avgole-mono soup. The sound of laughter and clinking glasses blends seamlessly into the ambiance, making the place feel both intimate and lively.

As a foodie and an event planner, I live for a beautiful atmosphere—the perfect balance of aesthetics and experience. That's why I come to Mykonos Taverna at least three times a week.

Across from me, Josephine watches me, contemplative. This is how people have been looking at me for the last six months—waiting for the breakdown that isn't coming.

"How are you?" she asks.

"Fine. I'm doing fine." My voice is steady.

She narrows her eyes. "You've said that word so many times, it's lost all meaning. Are you sure you're fine, Mari? I know I didn't know Andrew very well, but I want you to know I'm here for you. You don't have to go through this alone."

These are the moments I dread. The moments I try to avoid. How do I say I feel relieved my husband is dead without sounding like a monster? She doesn't know our history. She wouldn't understand.

"I really am doing fine, Jo." I keep my tone warm and grateful. "Thank you for everything. Not just in the last six months, but in the last seven years. Losing Andrew was hard —of course, it was. But every day, I get a little better. A little more at peace with this new chapter of my life."

I offer her my warmest smile, hoping it conceals my hidden truths. She isn't fully convinced. I can see it in her expression. I'm not the grieving widow people expect. But she respects my privacy enough not to push.

The waiter sets our food down, and I exhale in relief. It was a perfect, much-needed interruption. The smell of souvlaki makes my mouth water, and I take my first bite.

I guess I was hungrier than I thought.

After work, the rain finally stopped, so I walked home. I love taking walks after it rains—it's like the world has been rinsed clean. The air is crisp against my skin, cool and fresh. But as I near my building, something feels off, like the world has tilted just slightly out of place.

The clicking of my shoes against the pavement pounds like a drumbeat in my ears. My heart slams against my ribs. My breath feels too shallow, like I can't pull in enough air. I don't know why I feel like this. I just do. Something's very wrong. Was it the food? Am I coming down with food poisoning? Is it my lupus? Is something happening to me?

I quickened my steps, and my condo building came into

15

view. I just need to get upstairs. The doorman greets me, but I barely hear him over the rush of blood in my ears. I manage a quick, distracted hello before racing to the elevator. The ride is agonizingly slow. Every stop, every ding feels like torture.

Upstairs, I take a few steadying breaths. My clothes feel suffocating, so I strip them off, kick off my shoes, and pin up my hair. I walk to the kitchen, splash cold water on my face, then pour myself a glass of wine.

I sink into the couch, taking a long sip. My heartbeat slows, but the feeling lingers.

Something is wrong.

And then my phone rings—shattering everything.

CHAPTER 2

Mariana

I step out of my car, the crisp autumn air wrapping around me. After the call about my mom, I packed whatever I could and drove straight here. Home. Lake City, Colorado.

The scent of damp leaves lingers in the air, and trees stretch overhead, their canopies glowing in shades of gold, copper, and burnt orange.

I've always loved autumn here. Not just for its beauty, but for the way the town comes alive—the annual harvest festival, pumpkin carving contests, the farmers' market brimming with fresh apples, homemade jams, and warm, flaky pies. It doesn't get better than that.

Sometimes, I wonder why I ever left. I tell myself not to dwell on regrets, but some days, they sit heavy on my chest, impossible to ignore. Life in Seattle was supposed to be better. Easier. But looking back at the last few years, I can't help but wonder...What if I had just stayed?

When Hilda called and told me my mom fainted during game night, my heart sank. She wouldn't give details—just that my mom had fallen ill and needed to come home. Fast. I've known Hilda my whole life—more like a Tia than a family friend.

She was the first person my mom met when she moved here from Puerto Rico, and they've been inseparable ever since. She owns Ink & Paper, my favorite bookstore—and really, the only bookstore in town.

I've spent countless hours there, curled up with a book, losing myself in different worlds. Reading has always been an escape for me—my own personal movie playing in my mind, A break from the chaos of life.

Before heading to the hospital, Hilda asked me to stop by. So I do. The moment I step inside, the bell chimes softly, and I breathe in the familiar scent of aged paper and ink. God, I missed this.

I spot Hilda weaving between shelves, likely expecting another customer. But then she sees me. Her eyes widen, her lips part in surprise, and before I can say a word, she rushes forward, wrapping me in a hug so tight, I feel like a child again.

I sink into her warm embrace, breathing her in. "It's good to see you too, Tía. I've missed you so much."

Being here, wrapped in Hilda's arms, I realize just how much I've missed her. The warmth, the familiarity. God, I need to get it together before I start sobbing in the middle of this bookstore. Being away from home has been harder than I ever let myself admit.

"Don't you ever leave for that long again!" Hilda scolds, squeezing me tighter. "We've all missed you, especially your mom," Her voice dips into something softer. Sadder.

I sigh, guilt gnawing at me. "I know. I should have been around more. I can't believe it's been this long since my last visit."

"That's because of your no-good husband; may God rest his soul. He never wanted to be around us." Her eyebrows furrow.

"Hey! That's not fair. He loved coming here. He just worked a lot. And he missed me when I traveled too long."

The words leave my mouth before I can stop them. Once again, I'm defending him. I don't know why—why I still fall into the role I played when he was alive. Why is it easier to protect his image than to admit the truth? Maybe because if I agree with them, I'd have to face the real question. Why did I stay? And I don't have an answer for that.

I can't do this right now. I can't keep pretending that Andrew was something he wasn't. So, I latch onto the only thing that matters. "What's going on with Mami? What exactly happened?"

"I told you already, Mari. We were playing dominos, and she was kicking our asses, when out of nowhere, she got up to make another margarita and fainted. We rushed to her, and I called an ambulance. She's still in the hospital now."

My stomach twists, my patience fraying. "Okay, but what is actually wrong with her? Why did she faint?"

Hilda crosses her arms. "You'll have to talk to her about that."

"I'm talking to you."

Her expression sharpens, a warning in her eyes. "Watch that tone. She wants to talk to you directly, and I'm going to honor her wishes."

I exhale sharply, forcing myself to back down. I know I pissed her off now, but I'm scared. She hasn't told me anything, and I just want my mom to be okay. After losing my dad, the thought of losing her terrifies me.

I know I won't win this fight. So instead, I say, "I'm heading to the hospital."

Hilda softens. Without a word, she pulls me into another hug, squeezing tight, like she knows I need it. I cling to her warmth for just a second longer before pulling away.

I don't know what I'm walking into at that hospital, but I know one thing—whatever my mom has to tell me, I'm not ready for it.

∾

The moment I step through the hospital doors, my stomach lurches. The air feels thick, suffocating, pressing in on me from all sides. Memories slam into me. The last time I was here was when my dad died. When a stroke stole him from me. When my world shattered in an instant.

The walls close in. The sharp sting of disinfectant mixes with something metallic—blood, I realize. The scent clings to the back of my throat, making my stomach churn. The beeping monitors, the harsh fluorescent lights, the muffled voices of nurses—it all crashes over me like a tidal wave.

Cold sweat trickles down my back. My vision tunnels. I bend over, hands gripping my knees, forcing in shaky breaths. Please don't throw up. Please don't throw up. I whisper the words over and over, a desperate prayer to my body to keep it together. Minutes pass before I can stand straight again, before I can force my feet to move toward the front desk.

"Umm...Hi, I'm here to see my mom." My voice comes out uneven, my nerves pressing at the edges.

"Mari?? Oh, sweet girl! It's good to see you!"

I blink, my focus shifting to the woman behind the desk. Maria. One of my mom's friends.

"Hi, Maria. It's good to see you too." I roll my lip between my teeth. "How's my mom? Is she okay?"

Maria's smile falters. Her lips press into a thin line. My stomach drops.

"She's in room 204, sweetheart. Get on over to her. She'll be so happy to see you."

~

I walk into my mom's hospital room. It's small, simple. A single bed sits in the center, its rails raised on either side. She's asleep. I rushed over, grabbing her hand. It's cold and clammy.

"Mami? I'm here."

Slowly, her eyes flutter open. "Mija? Oh, Mariana. I'm so glad you're here."

"Of course, I'm here, Mami. I came as soon as Tía Hilda called. I was scared out of my mind."

"I'm sorry I scared you, Mija." She gently squeezes my hand.

"No, Mami, don't be sorry! Just, please, tell me what's going on. I'm losing it over here."

She tries to sit up but is too weak, so she lays back down.

"Mari..." She takes a slow breath. "I love you so much, Mija. You're a good girl. A good daughter. Papi and I have always been so proud of you."

"I love you too, Mami, But you're scaring me. Please. What's going on?"

She exhales, her face lined with exhaustion. "For the past year, I've been feeling sick. Bloating, stomach pains, so tired all the time. I figured it was just age. My diet. I didn't think it was a big deal."

"Okay...?"

"One day, I felt awful, and Hilda convinced me to see a doctor. I went to see a gastroenterologist, but they couldn't figure it out. I saw specialist after specialist, until, finally, a gynecologist ran more tests—pelvic exams, ultrasounds, bloodwork, and then a biopsy. She stops.

21

I grip her hand tighter. "And what did they say, Mami? Why are you sick?"

We're both crying when she finally says it.

"Mija, I have stage 4 ovarian cancer."

At that moment, my world caves in. The air is sucked from my lungs. Her words don't make sense—they can't be real. Cancer? No. No. No.

My hands shake as I grip the side of her bed, as if holding onto it will stop everything from spinning. "Why didn't you tell me sooner? Why am I finding out like this? I could have been there for you! You know I would've dropped everything to be with you."

She strokes my cheek, her own tears spilling over. "And that's exactly why, Mija. You lost Andrew. You're mourning. I wanted you to take care of yourself. I didn't want you to worry about me too."

"You're my mom. Of course, I'm going to worry about you." My voice cracks. "How could you keep this from me? I deserved to know. I deserved every second with you, and you stole time from me."

"I'm sorry, my love. I'm so sorry."

I wipe my face with the back of my sleeve. "What's the plan? What are they doing for you? How do we fix this?" My voice is desperate now. Pleading.

She squeezes my hand. "There's no fixing this. I've been doing chemotherapy since I was diagnosed. They removed as much of the tumor as they could, but it's spread, Mija."

My heart shatters.

Once again, in this very hospital, my world is breaking into pieces. We're holding onto each other, sobbing. She's not going to make it out of this. I know that now. But she won't go through it alone. I'm staying. For every moment, every breath, every second—I'll be here.

I'm moving home. For good.

~

After spending the day with my mom, I finally headed to my childhood home. The moment I step inside, I'm hit with the scent of home. Not just the scent itself, but the years of love and warmth baked into the walls. The faint traces of garlic, sofrito, and fried plantains still linger in the air, as if my mom had just stepped out of the kitchen, a wooden spoon in hand, ready to tell me to taste something.

There's the familiar scent of black coffee, robust and earthy, a staple in our mornings together. It's as if every meal she's ever made is still woven into the walls, clinging to the air like a warm embrace.

I shut the door softly behind me and take slow steps into the living room. The house feels frozen in time—exactly as I remember it, yet impossibly different, like I don't fully belong here anymore.

I stop at the photo wall, the collection of frames my mom has carefully arranged over the years. My fingers brush lightly over a picture of her and Papi on their wedding day—him in a sharp black suit, her in a lace gown, eyes full of love. Next to it is a picture of me as a baby—chubby cheeks, wild curls, toothless grin. Another frame holds a photo of my mom's family in Puerto Rico, all gathered outside my grandmother's house, faces sun-kissed, frozen mid-laughter.

A lump rises in my throat, my vision blurring as tears prick my eyes. My dad's gone. Now I'm going to lose my mom too. It isn't fair. It isn't fucking fair. I thought I had more time.

I sink onto the big red couch, the same one I curled into as a child when I was sick, when I was sad, when I just wanted to be near my parents. The worn fabric is soft beneath my fingertips, filled with years of memories.

The memories flood in, wrapping around me like a heavy blanket. The dance parties we had right here in the living room, music blasting from my dad's old stereo, my mom twirling me around as we laughed until our stomachs hurt.

The smell of onions sizzling in a pan, my mom teaching me how to chop vegetables without slicing my fingers, showing me how to roll out dough for empanadas, and scolding me when I tried to eat the filling before it was ready.

The time I broke her lamp, hurling a ball across the room and watching in horror as it shattered into a million tiny pieces. I swore I could fix it before she got home. I swore she wouldn't notice. She noticed.

The time I broke my arm, daring myself to jump from the ottoman to the couch, convinced I could fly. The hard smack of the floor, the sharp, white-hot pain shooting through my arm. My mom, frantic, rushed me to the hospital, holding my hand the entire time, whispering in my ear, "Mija, I've got you. You're okay."

I close my eyes and let out a slow, shaky breath. I hit the jackpot with my parents. They loved me fiercely, without hesitation, without limits. My dad worked himself to the bone to make sure we never went without. My mom held us together, the glue that kept our little family whole. When my dad died, I wasn't sure how I was going to get through it. Now, I don't know how I'm going to do this all over again.

A chime pulls me from my thoughts. I glance at my phone —A text from Anna.

We met when we were four. I was shy; she was fearless. When Tommy, the class bully, shoved me down and stole my toy, I just sat there and cried. But Anna saw.

"Hey! That's not yours, give it back!" She stormed right up to him and shoved him to the ground. "And say sorry while you're at it!"

After he mumbled an apology, she turned to me and declared, "We're best friends for life now." And that was that.

Even after I moved to Seattle, we stayed close—constant

texts and endless phone calls. Until Andrew. He pushed me away from her, from everyone. He never wanted her to visit.

I opened the text. I already know what it is going to say.

ANNA

My mom told me she saw you today. How are you feeling? She told me what happened. I'm so sorry, babe. I'm here for you, always.

MARIANA

Thanks, An. I'm still in shock. I can't believe she's sick, and I can't believe it took her this long to tell me. I'm trying not to be mad at her, but I wish she would've told me sooner!

ANNA

Totally understand. I'd be pissed if my mom or dad didn't tell me they were sick. But I guess she was trying to shield you from the pain, especially considering what you've been dealing with.

MARIANA

I'm not fragile. I didn't need protecting. Andrew's death has been hard, but she's my mom. I deserved to know.

ANNA

I get it. I guess with Andrew, and then the lupus—everyone was scared about how it might affect you. I'm sorry. Why don't we meet for lunch tomorrow? I've missed you a ton.

MARIANA

Sure, yeah. We can have lunch before I go see my mom at the hospital.

ANNA

Sounds good. See you tomorrow.

I toss my phone aside and press my arm over my face. This day has drained everything out of me. I haven't unpacked yet. I don't have the energy. I curl into the couch, wrapping myself in the throw blanket from the armrest. Sleep takes hold.

CHAPTER 3

Mariana

I'm rushing into the restaurant when my heels break, and I nearly face-plant onto the floor. Because, of course. Why is it that when you're already late, the universe has to throw one last humiliation for good measure?

I hit snooze on my phone so many times this morning that it just...gave up on me. By the time I finally dragged myself out of bed, I was already late to meet Anna, so I threw on the first thing I could find and sprinted out the door.

Now, I look and feel like a complete disaster—limping, off balance, frustration bubbling under my skin. Then I see her.

Anna is sitting at our table, her dark eyes lighting up as soon as she spots me. Her black hair, once long and flowing, is now cut short just below her chin. She's wearing small gold hoop earrings, a red crop top, loose-fitted jeans, and sneakers —effortlessly cool, just like always. God, I've missed her.

For a second, I hesitate. It's been too long. Too many missed plans, and too many ignored texts when I was caught up in someone else's world. A flicker of guilt twists inside me, but before I can dwell on it, Anna is already up and running toward me. I don't even have time to think—I hobble forward, one heel in my hand, and then we collide, wrapping each other in the kind of hug that makes everything else disappear. We hold on tight, and suddenly, we're laughing and jumping up and down like we're teenagers hanging out in our old bedrooms.

For months, our only constant has been our Thursday night FaceTime calls. No matter how many texts went unanswered or plans fell through, we always had that. But, despite all the FaceTime calls, there's nothing like this. Nothing like having her right here, yet beneath the joy, there's an ache. Because deep down, I know why it's been so long.

Andrew always talked about the importance of family, of surrounding ourselves with people who love and support us. I used to believe him. I used to think he meant it. But what I learned, far too late, was that he didn't want me to have those things—he only wanted me for himself.

At first, it was subtle—a comment here, a disapproving look there. Little things that made me second-guess the people I loved. Until, one day, I looked around and realized he had pushed every single one of them away, and I hadn't even noticed until it was too late. The people in my life weren't a support system; they were a threat.

I swallow hard and squeeze Anna just a little tighter. When we pull back from the hug, I realize we're both crying.

I laugh, swiping at my face. "Look at us, tontas, crying in front of everyone."

Anna cups my cheeks, studying me like she's trying to read every emotion running through me. "Mari, I'm so sorry. I'm here for you, okay? Whatever you need."

I nod, tears slipping down my face.

I'm so grateful for Anna. No matter what, she's always stuck around. Through every high and crushing low, she's been my anchor. Friends like her are rare, really; she's more like the sister I never had but always wanted.

When Papi died, it was Anna who sat beside me in that suffocating funeral home, her hand wrapped around mine, steady and unshakeable. She was the one who spoke to the funeral director when Mami and I couldn't find the words, the one who made sure we ate when grief hollowed us out.

When she found out what Andrew was doing to me, she was there. She didn't scream or curse at me for staying, though I know she wanted to. Instead, she sat with me in silence, waiting for a moment when I was ready to talk. She begged me to leave, tried to make me see that love wasn't supposed to hurt, that it wasn't supposed to leave me questioning my own worth. But when she realized I wasn't going anywhere, she didn't walk away in frustration like so many others did. She stayed. The only one who knew—the only one I let in, while I kept the truth buried from everyone else, including our families.

She called me, even when I stopped answering. She sent texts every morning, sometimes something simple like Good morning, other times longer messages reminding me that I deserved more than the life I was living. When I wouldn't respond, she'd send voice notes instead, her voice gentle but firm, telling me stories about her day, slipping in reminders that she loved me, that she wasn't going anywhere.

She mailed me care packages, little things she knew would make me smile. A book she'd just finished and needed me to read. A candle that smelled like the vanilla chai lattes we used to get in high school. Once, she even sent me a box of my favorite pastries, packed carefully with ice packs and a note that simply said, For when you need a taste of home.

She made sure that no matter how many times Andrew tried to convince me that I had no one, I knew the truth. He could push and pull and manipulate all he wanted, but he would never erase her.

And now, with Mami's time slipping away, I know she's

going to be here again, helping me through all the pain that comes with knowing that I'm about to lose her. Anna has never wavered. She's my constant, and I love her for it.

The waiter stops by, and the first words out of Anna's mouth are, "Mimosas! And keep 'em coming, please."

She flashes me that wicked smile—the same one she always had when we were kids, right before she talked me into doing something guaranteed to get us in trouble with our parents.

"Last time we had a keep 'em coming kinda day, I ended up with a tattoo," I say, raising an eyebrow at Anna as the waiter walks away.

"And what a beautiful tattoo it is!" she huffs, arms crossed over her chest like she's still defending her decision all these years later.

We each have the word 'Promise' inked on the side of our pinkies, a permanent reminder of the vows we made to each other long before adulthood tried to pull us apart.

We got them on my 21st birthday. Anna had turned 21 three months earlier and insisted we had to go all out for mine. And by "all out," she meant bottomless margaritas, standing on sticky bar floors, and, of course, a spontaneous trip to a tiny tattoo shop down the street.

I can still hear her voice in my head, slurring slightly as she held up her pinky and said, "We've made so many pinky promises, Mari. What if we made one that never goes away?" It had sounded profound at the time, and maybe it still was.

The next morning, when my mom saw it, I thought she was going to blow a gasket. People are always surprised when I say she still expects me to ask for permission—even as a full-grown adult—but I just tell them it's a Latiné mom thing. Besides, I know it's just because she cares.

Anna tilts her head, watching me carefully now, her playful smirk softening into something gentler. I know that look. She's debating whether to bring them up.

"So..." she begins, drawing out the word like she's testing the waters.

A prickle of anxiety creeps up my spine.

"Do you want to talk about anything? Andrew? Your mom?"

My stomach twists.

Do I want to talk about them? No. Not particularly. Should I? Probably. But I don't even know what to say. My heart is wrecked—so much has happened in such a short amount of time, and I have no idea how to get through any of it.

I exhale slowly. "Can the right answer be that I want to stay in bed and do nothing?"

Anna grins, leaning back against her chair. "Sure! But that's not like you, so it would have a lot of people worried. Including me."

She's not wrong. For as long as I can remember, I've been on the go—always moving, always chasing the next thing, never letting anything hold me back.

But now, I wonder if I've just been running. Running from the past. Running from the things I don't want to feel. Running so hard for so long that I never stopped to ask myself if I was actually getting anywhere. And right now? I just feel tired. So damn tired.

"True. I definitely don't want to talk about Andrew, and honestly, I'm not really sure what to say about my mom." I exhale, staring down at my hands. "A part of me knows this is real and happening, but another part of me is still in denial. And I'm so damn mad that she waited so long to tell me. But at the same time...I kind of get it. I don't know. My feelings are a mess right now."

Anna nods, her gaze steady, like she's absorbing every word. "All of those feelings are completely fair and valid. You've gone through a lot in a very short amount of time. It

31

makes sense that you're feeling conflicted." She pauses, like she's choosing her words carefully. "But you know Lucia loves you so much. She'd do anything for you. I'm sure she just didn't want to add to your pain."

I sit up straighter, my chest tightening. A familiar frustration flares in me, and I part my lips, ready to argue—she has to stop trying to protect me from everything. But before I can get a word out, Anna lifts a single finger, stopping me in my tracks.

"I'm not saying what she did was right," she says, eyes locked onto mine. "I'm also not saying what she did was wrong. If I were in her position, I honestly don't know what I would have done. But I do know that she believes she did the right thing, even if you disagree. And while I think you should allow yourself to feel all of it—be angry, be sad, hell, schedule a full-on ugly cry—I also know you. You want to make every moment with her right now count. So let's lean into that feeling. Let's make these last moments special."

I sit there quietly for a moment, letting her words settle over me. She's right. I know she's right. My mom has never done anything without the best of intentions—especially when it comes to me.

I swallow hard. "You're right. You always know what I need to hear."

Anna flashes me a grin, "I got you, girl. You can always count on me to get you back on track." Her laughter is light, but the weight in my chest lingers.

"Anyway," she says, shifting gears, "How did Josephine react when you told her you were moving back to Lake City?"

I sigh, rubbing my hands over my face. "She was sad, of course. I feel bad that I left without giving her enough time to find my replacement, but she understands. After losing my dad and then Andrew dying...she knows I need to be here with my mom. I'd never forgive myself if I stayed and something happened."

I leaned back in my seat, unease settling in my stomach. Leaving Seattle was the right choice. The only choice.

Anna reaches across the table, squeezing my hand. "I get it, and I know you're probably tired of me saying this, but…" she exhales, voice softening, "I am so sorry for everything you're going through. I know there isn't a single thing I can say to take away your pain, but please, please remember that I'm here. Don't shut me out, and don't try to handle everything on your own. Everyone in Lake City loves you and your mom. We want to help in any way we can."

I nod, a small smile tugging at my lips. This place, these people, my home…Sometimes, I wonder why I even left Lake City in the first place. We're a small town, but we love each other fiercely. When something happens, we show up.

Anna must sense my need for a change of subject because she launches into a story about her students. She's a middle school teacher, which means she has an endless supply of ridiculous stories to keep me entertained. "One of my kids actually tried to convince me that a dog ate his homework," she says, rolling her eyes. "Like, really, kid? That's the best you got?"

I laugh. "People are still using that excuse?"

"Oh, but it gets better," Anna smirks. "We live in a town with, what, 300 people? Everyone knows everyone. And I know for a fact that this kid doesn't even have a dog."

I burst out laughing. "Did you call him out?"

"Of course. But because I'm the best teacher ever, I gave him a chance to make it up. And then I reminded him that I know his mama, so he better not ever lie to me again.

"That poor kid." I shake my head, still grinning.

Anna grasps dramatically. "Poor kid? Poor me! This is the level of nonsense I deal with every single day."

I roll my eyes, but it feels good—letting myself laugh, even if just for a moment.

"Oh! I forgot." Anna perks up. "Tomorrow, I need to head over to Ink & Paper. Hilda's holding onto some books for my students. Want to come with me?

I nod, warmth spreading in my chest. "Definitely. I love that place."

CHAPTER 4

Sebastian

I'm leaning against one of the trucks in the firehouse, surrounded by the guys, my uniform soot-stained from this morning's drill. It's been one hell of a morning.

Cap simulated a warehouse fire for our drill, complete with thick smoke and controlled flames. I had to lead the team through the dark and smoky space, practicing search and rescue maneuvers, and crawling on our hands and knees to stay below the smoke.

The heat was intense, and now, standing here in the aftermath, I look like hell. The guys are all laughing as I tell them how Libby called me again to get her cat out of a tree.

"I swear that cat waits until I'm about to start a 3-day shift to put me to work," I say, shaking my head. "I walk over to the tree, and the damn thing jumps right on my head! I didn't even have to climb up. Just landed on me like it was planned."

My friends burst into laughter, shaking their heads.

"The cat has it out for you, man," Mateo says between chuckles.

"Right?" I run a hand through my hair. "I'm telling you, she does it on purpose."

The clock on the wall catches my eye, and my stomach drops. Shit.

"I almost forgot—I gotta head out," I say, already pushing off the truck.

"Forgot what, Seb?" Andres asks, raising an eyebrow.

"Picking up Maya from school. I promised I'd bring her back here for a bit."

Maya's my six-year-old niece and, hands down, the coolest kid I know. She's been begging me to come back here every day, and I finally caved. Her mom, my sister, Analyse, is a teacher at the elementary school, and since I wanted to spend time with Maya, I offered to pick her up for a few hours.

Luckily, we live in a town where nothing ever really happens, so it's easy to bring her here. If the alarm does go off, Hilda runs right over to grab her. Ink & Paper is right across the street, so she hears the alarm before the rest of the town does.

Everyone in this town looks out for each other—it's just how things are. Hilda has always been there, part of the background of my life, and she always will be. She's watched me grow up, just like the rest of the town, and at this point, she's just as much family as anyone else.

Andres claps me on the shoulder. "Well, you'd better get going then. Can't leave our girl waiting."

When Maya was born, we all fell in love with her instantly. There was no hesitation, no question, she was ours. She had a whole firehouse of uncles before she could even hold up her head, a team of men who would drop everything for her, no questions asked.

The first time Analyse brought her to the station, she was just a few weeks old, wrapped up in the softest pink blanket, with a tiny fist curled near her face. We all crowded around, this group of rough, soot-covered men turning into absolute mush at the sight of her. And from that moment on, she had us.

Birthdays, school plays, scraped knees—we were there. We taught her how to ride her bike in the firehouse lot, chasing after her while she wobbled on training wheels. We let her sit in the trucks, honk the horn, and pretend to be just like us. She's got an entire army behind her. And if anyone ever dares to mess with her, well...let's just say they'd regret it.

Her dad walked out before she was even born. A fucking scumbag who didn't want to be in her life. I was furious when it happened—furious for Analyse, for Maya, for the fact that this coward of a man couldn't see what he was leaving behind. So the guys and I stepped in, and promised we'd always be there for her and Analyse. A promise we all intend to keep.

Analyse is strong, she always has been, but even the strongest people need a village. And whenever she needs help, one of us steps in. No hesitation. If she's running late at school, we pick Maya up. If Maya wants to play soccer in the park, we take her. When she wants pancakes for dinner, there's always one of us willing to cook them. She's our girl.

I adjust my gear, about to head out, but Mateo smirks. "She's got you wrapped around her little finger, huh?"

I nod. "That girl owns me, and she knows it."

Mateo laughs. "You, man? She's got us all wrapped around her finger."

I point at him as I head toward the locker room. "You know it."

Maya's got an entire firehouse of uncles looking out for her. And me? I'd do anything for that kid.

Hopping into my truck, I feel a buzz of energy. Maya's face always lights up when she comes to the firehouse—it's one of my favorite things to see. It reminds me of myself as a kid.

But unlike me, she has zero interest in being a firefighter, even after I told her girls can be badass firefighters, too. No,

Maya's got bigger plans; she wants to be a ninja clown—clown by day, ninja by night. She says she wants to make people laugh and protect them. I gotta give it to the kid; she's got her priorities in check.

By the time I pull up to her school, she's already spotted me.

"TÍO SEB!! You're here!"

She's running full speed, her backpack bouncing behind her, arms stretched out like she's about to take flight.

"Of course I'm here, Maya," I say, crouching down to catch her as she crashes into me. "I told you I would be, and I never break a promise to my best girl."

"Are we going to the fire station now??" she asks, tilting her head and hitting me with her best puppy eyes.

I chuckle. "You bet we are."

I lift her into my car, strapping her into the booster seat I always keep for her. "Ready to see some fire trucks.?"

"Yes! Yes! Yes!" she bounces excitedly, and I can't help but grin. Her happiness is infectious.

Pulling into the station, I already see Mateo and Andres running around, getting everything ready for Maya's visit. Their laughter and shouts fill the air—it's like watching a bunch of big kids at recess.

The second I park, Maya bolts out of the car, heading straight for the kitchen. Her delighted squeal echoes through the station before I even make it inside.

I jog in after her, ready to make sure she has a day she'll never forget. But the last thing I expect to see? A goddamn waterslide. A giant waterslide. The guys really did go all out.

Standing back, I watch as Maya runs straight into Mateo's arms. He swings her up onto his shoulders like she weighs nothing, laughing as he carries her toward the waterslide, where Andres and a couple of the other guys are waiting,

I throw my head back, laughing. I was planning to give

Maya a fun day at the firehouse. But this? This is next-level. With a grin, I take off after them, ready to join in on the chaos.

Maya is happily sleeping in one of the beds in the station, the sugar crash hitting her like a ton of bricks. There was nothing better than seeing her excited—shoving spoonfuls of ice cream in her mouth, laughing like a little maniac, chocolate smeared all over her tiny face.

She looks so much like Analyse—the same long, curly brown hair, tan skin, and those big brown eyes. Of course, she'd birth a carbon copy of herself. I glance down at my phone, re-reading Analyse's last text:

> Be there in 5. Have her ready.

Yeah, that didn't happen.

I look back at Maya, curled up like a little burrito, her tiny hands tucked under her cheek. How the hell am I supposed to wake her up when she looks this peaceful?

Not even five minutes later, I hear the familiar sound of tires crunching on the gravel outside of the station. Analyse steps out of what she proudly calls her 'mom car'—a white SUV that, despite her protests, is covered in stray crayons and forgotten snack wrappers.

She's got a cup of iced coffee in one hand, sunglasses on top of her head, and an expression that tells me she already knows I let Maya fall asleep.

"Where's my girl?" she asks, scanning the station.

I grimace. "Uh...in the back. Sleeping."

She crosses her arms, tilts her head back, and sighs.

"Seb! I told you not to let her sleep. Now she's gonna wake up with more energy than the Energizer Bunny himself."

39

"I know, I know. But come on, have you seen her? How can I say no to anything she wants? She's basically my boss." I say, trying to keep a straight face.

Analyse snorts. "That kid knows exactly who to go to when she wants something and, of course, she's cute—she's her mama's twin."

She takes a sip of her iced coffee, eyes flickering around the station before landing back on me. Then, too casually, she asks, "Where's Mateo?"

I narrow my eyes. "Why?"

Analyse shrugs, adjusting the lid on her coffee. "Just wondering."

I cross my arms, giving her a long, skeptical look. "If I had to guess? Probably off being an idiot somewhere."

She snorts, then quickly hides it behind her cup—but not fast enough. That catches my attention. I squint at her. "Why do you care where Mateo is?"

She rolls her eyes. "I don't. Just making conversation."

I don't buy it. Analyse hates Mateo, always has. Says he's reckless, immature, a walking red flag. Which is why it's weird that she's asking about him all of a sudden.

Before I can push, she sighs dramatically. "Seb, please. Mateo is your headache, not mine. I was just wondering if he was off ruining some poor girl's life again."

I make a mental note to keep an eye on that.

"Alright, Alright. Let's get your kid."

I head to the back of the station, stepping into the dorm-style room. Rows of identical metal-frame beds stretch across the space, each one neatly made—except for Maya's.

Her blanket is pulled up to her chin, her wild curls splayed across the pillow. I place a hand on her shoulder and gently shake her awake. Not gonna lie, I'm a little scared. If she's anything like her mom, I need to prepare myself for a major attitude.

She stirs, blinking sleepily before letting out a long yawn.

"Tio? Is it morning? She mumbles, scrunching up her nose and covering her eyes.

"No, but your mama's here to get you."

Maya groans and rolls over, pulling the blanket over her head. "Okay, tell Mama she can come back in the morning. Nighttime is for sleeping."

I bite back a laugh. Yep. Just like her mom. I tug the blanket back. "Princesa, Mama's waiting, and she's gonna be really mad at me if I don't get you to her."

Maya sighs dramatically. "Fineee. But only so she won't be mad at you, Tio."

"I appreciate that, kid."

She rubs her eyes, then looks up at me. "Tío Seb?"

"What's up, princess?"

"Can we go get more books tomorrow?"

Seeing her tiny face light up at the thought of more books? Yeah, I'd take her every single day if I could.

"Let me ask your mom. If she says yes, I'll take you to Ink & Paper."

Maya launches into my arms. "Thank you, Tio!!"

Analyse was right—she does know exactly who to go to. And she always will.

CHAPTER 5

Mariana

I'm sitting in one of the green velvet seats at Ink & Paper, my hands wrapped around a warm cup of coffee that I grabbed on my way here. I take a slow sip, praying the caffeine will finally give me the pep I need after another night of no sleep.

Glancing down at my watch, I see that it's already twenty past ten. I told Anna I'd meet her here at ten, but I guess she's running late. No complaints from me—I'll gladly take this time to browse the romance section. Let's see what new books Hilda has on the shelves.

After about twenty minutes of browsing, I realize that Anna is now forty minutes late. That's not like her. A little late? Sure. But this? It kind of freaks me out.

Just as I'm reaching for my phone to call her, the door bursts open. Anna storms in like a bat out of hell, hair flying, sweater slipping off one shoulder, her eyes wild as she scans the room. She's normally so put together. But today? She looks like she's been to war and back.

I immediately walked over to her, placing a hand on her shoulder. "Hey, are you okay?"

"Omg, Mari! Do I look that bad?"

I grimace. "Welllll...I can honestly say that you've looked better."

She chuckles, then inhales deeply before pulling a clip from her purse, hastily brushing the hair out of her face and twisting it into place. "I had the most insane morning," she says, her voice still breathless.

I gesture toward the small couch facing the window. "Do you want to sit? What happened?"

As I gently push her down onto the couch, she exhales and shakes her head. "I don't even know where to begin."

"Start anywhere."

"You know how my mami and papi went back to Colombia to be with my abuelita while she's sick?"

"Right, yeah. And then your mom came back while your dad stayed. They said he'd be gone for a few more months."

"Yeah, well...it's been a few months. And when I asked last night when he plans to come back, they kept evading the question. And today? I found out why I couldn't get a straight answer."

I sit forward. "Wait, why?"

Anna stares at me, her expression expectant, waiting for me to connect the dots.

I frown. "No. Is your dad not coming back? What about your mom? He wouldn't just leave her here without him."

"You're right. He wouldn't leave her here."

I open my mouth, then close it. My brain is working overtime trying to put the pieces together. Maria and Jorge are inseparable. They grew up together, childhood best friends turned high school sweethearts. They've always been perfect for each other.

Jorge staying in Colombia made sense. His mom was sick. But moving there permanently? Without Maria? That doesn't make sense. And then, like a lightbulb flicking on, realization crashes into me.

"No." I gasp.

"YES." She yells back.

"Your mom is moving to Colombia to be with your dad."

Anna lets out a long groan, dropping her face into her hands. "Yes."

I sat back in my seat, stunned. I guess it shouldn't be shocking; they've always talked about moving back one day. I just didn't think one day would be now. Ay bendito, pobre Anna.

She's just as close with her parents as I am with mine. I know this is hitting her hard. She used to joke that if they ever moved back, she'd go with them. Wait a minute...

"You're not moving too, are you??"

Her head snaps up. "No, no. I'm staying."

Thank God. If she had really wanted to move, I'd support her—wholeheartedly. But selfishly? I don't want her going anywhere. I've lost so much already, and the idea of not having her in the same country as me makes me feel sick.

Reaching over, I grab her hand and squeeze it. "I'm sorry. This sucks. It feels like everything is changing."

Anna sighs, nodding. "It does. It does suck. And I can't even be mad at my mom because, of course, she wants to be with her husband. And, of course, my dad wants to be with his mom while she's sick. It all seems perfectly logical in my head. But in my heart? It feels completely unfair."

She lets out another breath, then shakes her head. "And to top it off, I dropped my phone in the sink while the water was running and got personally attacked by Libby's devil cat."

I blink. "Excuse me?"

She deadpans. "Mari, that thing is not a cat. It's a demon in a fur coat."

I lost it. Laughter bursts out of me.

Libby's cat is a nightmare. Anyone who gets too close suffers—one swipe of her claws and you're marked for life. So we've learned to keep our distance. We keep our eyes to ourselves, and she keeps her claws to herself. Well...except for two other people.

If Anna and one other unlucky soul are even in the vicinity of Libby's cat, she attacks. No warning, No hesitation. Just pure, unprovoked violence.

"What happened?" I ask, already bracing myself.

Anna throws her hands in the air. "So, I see that the devil cat is out, and like a good neighbor, I decide to bring it back to its rightful owner." .

"Anna, you didn't!"

"I did! I was just trying to help!"

"You know what that cat feels about you!"

She clutches her chest. "I did nothing to her! She's a psycho! Anyway, I tried to gently coax her to come with me, but in true devil cat fashion, she refused." She mimics reaching out her hands dramatically, then reenacts the moment with a full-body shudder.

"So, like an idiot, I picked her up. And the SECOND she's in my arms? She hisses at me and scratches both my arms. I fall. Fall, Mari, to the ground. And then? I watch this little hellspawn scale the tree like freaking Spider-Man. And now here I am." She waves a hand over herself.

I bite my lip, trying, and failing, not to laugh. "Wait. So... you just left?"

"I sure did. I was not about to get my eyes scratched out, Mari!"

"But what about the cat?"

"Oh, don't worry. I called her best friend to come get her out. I left as soon as he arrived." She smirks.

I gasp. "You didn't!"

"I did! It's fine, he'll be okay." She laughs, then runs a

45

hand through her hair. "Sorry I look like shit. It's been one hell of a morning."

I shake my head, smirking. "You literally saw me yesterday with a broken shoe; trust me, there's zero judgment coming from me. Besides, somos hermanas. You and me until the end, babyyy."

Since both Anna and I are only children, we've always said we're sisters, not the family we were given, but the family we chose. She's always been meant to be in my life, which is why it was so hard for me to keep her away when I was in Seattle.

Looking at her now, it's hard not to think about the girl I used to be. The one who let herself stay in a relationship where she was constantly choosing someone who never really chose her back. The one who hid pieces of herself from the people who actually loved her. I don't want to be that girl anymore.

We both stand and head toward the counter where Hilda is sitting, lost in a book. Her grey hair hangs loosely, framing her soft, round face, and she's smirking. She must be reading something smutty.

I'll never forget the book that led to my sexual awakening at fourteen, Forever by Judy Blume. Not exactly smutty, but it was the first time I read about characters having sex.

And the real revelation? The idea that some guys name their penises things like Ralph. That alone had me avoiding boys at school... at least until my sophomore year.

After that, I started smuggling smutty books from Hilda's shelves, hiding them beneath the loose floorboard in my room. She always left them lying around, and since I basically lived at Ink & Paper, I'd sneak one into my bag, devour it, and swap it for another.

Now, at thirty-two, I can buy my own books, and thank goodness for discreet covers. Because I cannot tell you the number of times I turned tomato-red putting down two handfuls of books with half-naked men on the cover at the checkout.

We reach the counter, and Hilda looks up, closing her book with a knowing smile.

"Hi girls. Anna, you're here for the books for the kids, right?"

"Hi, Hilda. Yup! They're getting antsy now that spring is here, and summer break is right around the corner. I'm hoping this will keep them engaged."

"You got it. Twenty-six copies of Holes by Louis Sachar coming right up." She stands, making her way to the back room to grab the books.

Leaning against the counter, I glance at Anna. "Holes? I loved that book as a kid. That's a great pick."

"Yeah, I want to do an in-class read-along, and then, when we're finished, I'll let them watch the movie as a treat."

I grin. "Okay, world's greatest teacher, I love that. Remember when we were kids, the rush of excitement when we saw the teacher rolling the TV into the classroom?"

Anna throws her head back, laughing. "The best days! Now, my kids won't get that, but they will get the excitement of seeing me put the movie on the projector."

"Not the same, but still iconic."

Hilda finally returns, balancing a large box of books in her arms. Just as she's about to hand them to Anna, the doorbell chimes. A little girl runs in, her sneakers skidding against the hardwood floors.

Something about her feels... familiar. I can't quite place it. Then, I hear footsteps behind her.

A man steps inside. And the second I look up, all the air whooshes from my lungs. My fingers tighten on the counter. A jolt of recognition shoots through me, sharp and unforgiving. My stomach clenches, my heart thudding against my ribs as my brain scrambles to catch up with what my eyes are seeing.

I know that face.

I know that face.

Oh my God.

Sebastian. My first love. My first everything.

He comes strutting into the store like he owns the entire damn world. Broad-shouldered, commanding, and looking even better than the last time I laid eyes on him. Gone is the boy I left behind all those years ago. The Sebastian standing in front of me now is all man.

Six foot four of pure strength and confidence. His tawny brown skin, deep, warm, and smooth as caramel, glows under the soft shop lighting, like the sun has permanently kissed every inch of him.

His thick, dark brows are just as expressive as I remember, always framing those intense, soul-piercing chocolate brown eyes—eyes that used to look at me like I was the only thing that mattered in the world.

His hair, once a little unruly, is still dark and wavy, but now it's got this effortless, perfectly imperfect look, like he just ran a hand through it and somehow it fell into place, messy in a way that makes me want to run my fingers through it.

And that jaw, strong, angular, dusted with the perfect amount of stubble. I used to run my fingers along it, feeling the slight roughness beneath my touch, loving the way he'd smirk when I did.

Instinctively, my eyes drift lower. He was always athletic, but now? Now his body is all hard muscle and smooth control. His broad chest fills out his shirt, the sleeves straining just slightly around his thick, sculpted biceps. His shoulders? Massive. Powerful. I swallow hard.

As if he feels my eyes drinking him in, I see his biceps flex slightly, a subtle movement, but I don't miss it. My heart skips. I haven't seen him since our high school graduation.

We had been together since sophomore year. Inseparable, in love, convinced we were forever. But I was leaving, and Sebastian was staying. He had his dreams, and I had mine—and no matter how much we loved each other, I couldn't ask him to wait.

So I broke his heart. I broke my heart.

I could have given us one last summer. One more season of midnight walks on the beach, tangled limbs in the backseat of his car, his heartbeat steady beneath my palm, his lips whispering my name like a prayer, but I thought it would be easier this way.

That giving ourselves the summer to heal would be better than dragging out the inevitable. I'll never forget the way he looked at me that night.

One second, he was smiling, hopeful, talking about our future. The next? His entire face shut down. It was the first time I had ever seen Sebastian cry. And it was all because of me. God, it shattered me. But I told myself I had done the right thing. I had to believe that.

And now, looking at him? Looking at the little girl by his side? It seems like I was right. He got the life he wanted. The family, the stability, the happiness. And if breaking his heart back then led him to this, then it was worth it. Even if seeing him now makes my own heart ache as if I never left.

"Seb!" Hilda calls out, waving Sebastian over.

Oh God. My brain instantly screams at me to do something. Hide, vanish, evaporate into thin air. I grab the box of books, lifting it slightly, angling myself behind it like it might block me from view.

He walks over, the little girl already darting toward the kids' section. She grabs a few books and plops herself down onto one of the teddy bear-shaped chairs, completely in her own world.

"Hey, Hilda. Anna." His voice is the same. Warm, deep, confident. Then he turns toward me. And freezes. His eyes widen just slightly, the shock unmistakable before he quickly masks it. Like seeing me after all these years is nothing. Like I'm nothing.

"Wow, Mari. Hey, it's been a long time. How've you been?"

I swallow. My throat feels like sandpaper. "Great. Good. Fine. I've been fine."

Sebastian's lips twitch, his dimple appearing. "Well, I'm glad you've been great, good, and fine. Hopefully, mostly great."

Kill me. Just kill me now.

My heart races as I try to gather my thoughts. There's too much I see when I look at him. Too many thoughts. Too many what-ifs. Get it together, Mariana. What is wrong with me right now?

I lean back slightly, trying to play it cool. "Is that your daughter?"

He opens his mouth, but before he can answer, Hilda jumps in. "No, sweetheart, that's his niece, Maya. Analyse's little girl!"

I jumped a little at her voice, completely forgetting that she and Anna were even here. A wave of relief washes over me before I can stop it. His niece. Not his daughter.

"Oh! Your niece?" I say, my voice too high. I clear my throat. "That's great. She's adorable. How old is she?"

"Six. First grade. Although if you ask her, she'll say 'almost seven.'"

I glance over at Maya, now lost in a book. "Looks like she's a bit of a bookworm."

Sebastian chuckles. "Not a bit. A huge bookworm. Kinda

reminds me of someone." He leans in slightly, his voice dipping just enough to send a shiver down my spine. "Are you still a bookworm, Mariana? Still into those smutty books?"

Oh. My. God.

Heat creeps up my neck. I cross my arms, forcing out a casual shrug. "Guilty. What can I say? Hot girls read."

Anna snorts. Hilda coughs to cover a laugh. Sebastian just grins, slow and knowing.

Turning to Anna, he nods toward the box of books. "What's in the box, banana?"

I forgot he always called her that. Not Anna Banana, just Banana. She always said she hated it, but I think she secretly loves it—the way he teases her like the big brother she never had.

Anna smirks. "Books for my kids at school. Actually, since you're here, can you carry them to my car?"

Leave it to Anna to put him to work the first chance she gets.

"Yeah, sure." Sebastian grabs the box from the counter, and he and Anna walk out of the store.

The moment he's gone, My heart finally slows. My lungs unclench. I can breathe again. Sebastian Garcia. The first boy who stole my heart. The one I never truly got over.

And now, I'm back home, and I have to face him again. Over and over.

In this small town, there's no escaping him.

God help me.

CHAPTER 6

Sebastian

After placing the box in the trunk of Anna's car, I step back and rock on my heels. Hands in my pockets, I ask, "So Mariana is back, huh?"

Mariana was the last person I expected to see today. And yet, the second I laid eyes on her, something inside me shifted. Like a sharp pull deep in my chest, a muscle I forgot existed suddenly reminding me it was there.

It's the sort of feeling I wasn't prepared for. The kind that knocks the air from your lungs, that makes time stutter for just a second too long.

She looks... different. The same, but different. Older, stronger. There's a confidence in the way she carries herself now, something steadier, more certain. Like she's seen the world, walked through fire, and come out of it sharper. The wide-eyed dreamer I once knew is still there, but now? She feels untouchable. Like a force of nature.

And damn, she's more beautiful than I remember. Her long brown hair still cascades over her shoulders, but now it holds subtle waves, framing her face in a way that makes her look softer and more untamed all at once.

Her olive skin still glows, but there's something richer about it now, like she's been kissed by faraway suns, like she carries pieces of places I'll never know.

Her curves? Fuller, more defined, moving with a grace that makes it impossible not to notice.

And that look in her eyes? That's what gets me the most. They still hold the same deep brown warmth, the same fire I fell in love with all those years ago. But now, there's something else there too...something heavier. A weight, a story I don't know yet.

More like the version of her I was always afraid she'd become—the one who didn't belong here anymore. The one who outgrew this place. The one who outgrew me.

Anna plays with the ends of her hair, avoiding my gaze. "Uhhh, yeah, she just got back from Seattle."

"Cool. How long is she staying?" I ask, trying to sound casual. Trying not to sound like I care.

"She moved back, Seb. She's here for good. Her mom isn't doing well, and she wants to be here for her."

I blink. "Shit." I knew her mom was sick, but I didn't know how bad it was.

Lucia was like a second mother to me. It was serendipitous, the way Anna met Mariana first, and then somehow, I followed right after. Our parents moved here from Puerto Rico looking for a better life, and in us, they found community. Family.

When Mariana and I started dating, Lucia welcomed the idea with open arms. I think our moms secretly prayed we'd end up together. Maybe I did too, but people change, and what we want changes.

I don't hate Mariana. I never have. I understood why she left. I knew she wanted more. Our parents left everything behind so we could chase bigger dreams, and she did.

I just wish I hadn't fooled myself into thinking she'd stay.

If I had faced the truth earlier, maybe I could've saved myself from a hell of a lot of heartbreak. But I don't regret it. I don't regret her.

Anna's voice pulls me back. "Yeah...Mari is acting like she's okay, but you know how she is."

I sigh, running a hand through my hair. "She puts up a brave face, but inside, she's hurting."

"Exactly. So be easy on her, okay? She's gone through a lot this year."

That's right. Her husband recently died. Her husband. The words taste wrong, even in my head.

For years, I tried not to think about it. About her, with someone else. About her life moving forward while I stayed here. When I first heard she was married, I felt a hundred things at once. Anger, regret, something sharp and bitter that I never wanted to name.

But in the end? I just wanted her to be happy. Fuck. First, she loses her husband. Now, she's losing her mom. My heart breaks for her.

I'm just standing here, useless, wishing I could be the person she used to turn to. I clear my throat. "You don't have to worry about me, Banana. I'm not going to give her a hard time."

"Good—because I will kick your ass if you do."

I laugh, shaking my head. "Noted."

Anna smirks, then shifts gears. "So, about these kids... want to let them check out the fire trucks?"

I nod, welcoming the change in topic. "Say the word, and I'll rally the guys."

She hugs me, and I return it, but my mind is still somewhere else. Mariana is back. And no matter how much I tell myself things have changed, that she's changed, one thing hasn't.

The second she walked back into my life, my heart knew exactly where it still belonged.

∽

Later that night, I finally made it home, dead on my feet. I throw myself onto my bed, ready to call it a night, until a loud knocking echoes through my house. I groan, dragging myself out of bed and pulling on a shirt.

Please, for the love of God, don't let Libby's cat be stuck in a tree again. I don't think I have it in me to deal with that little demon right now.

I yank open the door, expecting to see Libby looking frazzled and begging for help. Instead, I get Andres and Mateo. Grinning. Holding a pack of beers. Looking far too pleased with themselves. Just my luck.

I narrow my eyes at them. "I think you made a wrong stop. This isn't your house."

They exchange a look before Mateo says, "That attitude right there? That's exactly why we're here."

I sigh. "So, I take it you heard. But there's no need for this. I'm fine. Just tired."

"Yeah, yeah, yeah, whatever you say," Andres says, already pushing past me.

Mateo claps me on the shoulder as he follows. "Let's pop open these beers and watch the game."

I exhale sharply, debating whether I should just kick them out. But at this point, it'd take a bulldozer to get them off my couch. I really need to get one of those ring cameras so I can start screening my visitors.

The Rockies vs. Mets game is on, but I'm barely watching. My mind keeps drifting. Mariana. I wonder if she's okay. How she's handling the news about her mom. If she's thinking about me. If seeing me today did anything to her. Did it catch her by surprise the way it did me?

Did it make her heart race the way mine did? Or did it mean nothing?

Mateo sets his beer down with a thunk and turns to me. "Alright, let's cut the shit."

I blink, tearing my gaze from the screen. "What?"

Mateo leans forward. "You know why we're here. We know why we're here. So let's just talk this shit out before your brain explodes from how much it's overthinking right now."

"Mateo—" Andres warns.

"What? So we beat around the bush now? Is that it?" Mateo gestures between the three of us. "We've known each other forever. Why are we pretending like this isn't driving him insane?"

I roll my eyes. "I don't know what you're talking about. You two invited yourselves, remember?"

Andres gives me a pointed look. "Come on, man."

I scrub a hand over my face. "Fine. Mariana is back. There, I said it. Happy?"

Mateo smirks. "Ecstatic. So... how'd it go?"

I frown. "How was it supposed to go? We said hi and went about our day. I helped Anna put some books in her trunk, and by the time I went back inside for Maya, Mariana was running out and toward her car."

That memory sticks with me. The way she bolted out of there like she couldn't leave fast enough. That shouldn't bother me. And yet...

"That reminds me," I continued. "We're gonna help Anna out with her students, give them a ride on the truck, all the bells and whistles."

Andres leans forward, rubbing his hands together. "Nice. The next generation of firefighters. Name the day, and we'll be there."

Mateo waves him off. "Yeah, yeah. But back to Mari. What happens now that she's back?"

I stare at him, brow furrowed. "What do you mean, what happens? Nothing happens. She's back because her mom is sick."

Andres sighs. "Yeah, we heard. That's tough."

"Exactly." I take a swig of my beer. "So she's back home. Nothing new. Nothing is changing."

Andres and Mateo exchange a look.

I narrow my eyes. "What?"

Mateo leans in. "Come on, bro. It's us. We know all about your history with that girl. You've been down bad for her for ages, and now she's back and you're telling us you're just gonna do... nothing?"

I scoff. "Down bad? What the hell are you talking about?"

Mateo crosses his arms. "You're telling me that after all these years, after how wrecked you were when she left, you don't feel a single thing now that she's back?"

"We were in high school," I say, forcing a casual shrug. "She broke up with me. We both moved on. There's nothing more to it."

"Uh-huh," Andres mutters, clearly unconvinced.

I lean back, sighing. "Look, we'll probably not even speak again. Especially judging by the way she ran out of Ink & Paper today. I'd say chances are high she's gonna be avoiding me."

I say it like I don't care. Like it doesn't bother me that she ran. But deep down, I find myself hoping that isn't true. I can't get the image of her out of my damn head.

She's a smoke show. Always has been. But today? I had to force myself not to stare. Not to let my eyes linger on the way her jeans hugged her curves and her lips parted when she saw me, like she had something to say but couldn't find the words. Like maybe she felt it, too.

I shake my head. No. Not going there.

"This is a really small town," Andres says after a beat. "I don't think you guys can really avoid each other."

I exhale. "Yeah, well. We'll see."

And yet, no matter what I tell them, no matter what I tell myself...Deep down, that's what I'm banking on.

CHAPTER 7

Mariana

I woke up in pain. Before I even open my eyes, before I move a single inch, I feel it. A dull, throbbing ache deep in my joints, like my bones are too tired to hold me together.

My fingers are stiff; my elbows burn the second I bend them. My body feels like a battlefield, and today, like every morning, I wake up on the losing side.

I begin to massage my hands, gently working my thumbs over my knuckles, wincing as the pain flares up. Mornings are the hardest.

I lie there, staring at the ceiling, willing myself to move. Wishing I could just disappear under the covers. The warmth and safety of my bed are the only things that feel bearable right now, my only refuge from the chaos that is my life.

But this is normal now—pain is just part of my existence, something I wake up with, something I go to sleep with. I tell myself I've accepted it, that I've made peace with the way things are. But deep down, I know that's a lie.

Because how do you ever truly accept that this is forever?

That no matter how much I fight, or how much I push through, this will always be there, waiting for me? I keep telling everyone I'm okay, but damn...how much more can a girl take?

I like to think of myself as a strong person, but even I break sometimes. I wish I could just shut my mind off. Hit a switch. Unplug it like a faulty computer. Wouldn't that be nice?

Hello, God? It's me, Mariana. Any chance we can shut my brain down for a few hours? Just until I don't feel like I'm drowning in my own thoughts? I could really use the break.

I hate this. I hate that my body has the power to keep me prisoner. That something as simple as getting out of bed feels like a battle I have to psych myself up for.

It wasn't always like this. Before, I could roll out of bed without thinking twice—get dressed, start my day, and move through the world without my own body working against me. I used to run on coffee and ambition—late nights, long days, always on the go.

But now, even sitting up feels like a task that drains me before the day has even begun. The things that used to be effortless now take planning, energy, and strength I don't always have.

But now is not the time for my body to be beating me up; I have too much to do. My mom needs me. She needs me at my best. And I don't get to be weak when she needs me to be strong.

I force myself to sit up, blinking at the darkness of my room. The blackout curtains block out every hint of light, and for that, I'm grateful. Whoever invented them? My hero. I hope their side of the pillow is always cool.

I exhale, rubbing my temples, and try not to think about yesterday. But my mind goes there anyway. To him. Seba. My Seb. No. Not my Seb. Not anymore.

It was jarring, seeing him for the first time in years. Like a punch to the ribs, like something long-buried breaking open. It hit me harder than I expected. He looked good. Stronger. More sure of himself than when we were kids. Damn, time has been good to him.

I wonder if he hates me. The thought makes my chest feel tight. I wouldn't blame him if he did, but damn, I hope he doesn't.

~

The hot shower helped, but the ache is still there, lingering in my joints like a dull warning. It always does.

Still, I push through, moving slowly toward the kitchen, where soft sunlight filters through the blinds, casting warm stripes of gold across the counter.

I began making my favorite breakfast—harina de maiz. The scent of cinnamon and sugar fills the air as the ingredients blend together, and instantly, I feel a wave of comfort. It smells like home.

It reminds me of early mornings with my mom and dad. My mom at the stove, my dad making jokes over his coffee, both of them insisting we sit together at the table, no matter how busy the day ahead would be. "Family is everything," she always said.

And she made sure I believed it, too. I'm so glad she did. Because when Papi died, I had something to hold onto. I had memories—so many beautiful ones. Stories I could tell. Moments I could replay in my mind, in my heart. It hurt to lose him, but man, I was lucky to have him.

I sit at the kitchen table, my bowl warm in my hands. The house is quiet. Too quiet. What I would give to hear them laughing together in the living room again, giggling like two kids in love.

I take a spoonful of the harina de maiz and let the warmth spread through me, the familiar taste a tether to something safe. To a different time, a different life.

Isn't it crazy how food can transport you? Food has always been an expression of love in my family.

In sadness, in celebration, in the everyday—my mom made a meal, and we all sat together. We laughed, we ate, and we felt her love pouring into us with every bite.

It's no wonder I found my own love in baking. Maybe that's why I was drawn to Ruth's bakery in the first place. Maybe, without even realizing it, I was searching for a piece of home in The Rolling Pin. I can't believe Ruth closed her shop.

She talked about retiring for years, but I never thought it would actually happen. Not really. I guess I just assumed she'd always be there.

The Rolling Pin, a permanent fixture in Lake City, and Ruth, standing behind the counter with flour on her apron and a knowing smile on her face. But things change. People leave. Even the ones who feel like they never would.

Sometimes, I wonder if she was training me to take over. If every lesson, every critique, every gentle nudge toward perfection was her way of saying: This could be yours someday.

She didn't have kids; there was no one to pass The Rolling Pin down to. I can't imagine her selling it to just anyone. Would I have taken it? I don't know.

Back then, all I wanted was to leave, to see the world, to chase something bigger than Lake City. I thought staying would mean settling. But now...now, I'm not so sure.

And then my phone rings. I glance at the screen, Anna, grateful for the distraction.

"Hey, Anna, what's up?"

"Ugh, we're having a bake sale at the school, and since Ruth retired and closed down her shop, it's been a complete nightmare. I spaced and forgot to place the order at the shop in the next town over, and now I'm screwed. Help. Please. I'll do anything. I'll kiss your feet."

I can't help but laugh. "Please don't do that. Actually, I'll only help you if you promise NOT to do that."

"You got it! No feet kissing. But I do feel bad, especially being so last minute. Is there any way I can repay you?"

I pretend to think for a moment. "Well..."

"Name your price."

"Ajiaco from Tía María will do the trick."

"Done. You're easy."

I smirk. "That's not something I hear all the time."

Anna snorts.

"How many cupcakes do you need, anyway?"

There's a beat of silence.

Then, hesitantly, she says, "So... don't hate me, but we need 200 cupcakes."

I nearly choke. "Two hundred?! By when?"

"...Tomorrow morning."

I squeeze my eyes shut, rubbing my temples. "Ave María, Anna." I should have asked for more than just ajiaco. Two hundred cupcakes? Dios mio.

"I knowwwww. I'm sorry. Butttt, you love me, and you're doing it for the kids!! Go kids!"

"Yeah, yeah. Go kids, all right." I sigh, pushing my bowl away. "Let me go so I can get started on this crap ton of cupcakes."

"Thank you, thank you, thank you, Mari! I owe you—seriously. I'll have Mami throw in a batch of arepas con queso."

I smile. "Now that's an acceptable form of payment. I'll drop them off at your school in the morning. Don't worry, I got you."

"Perfect! Thanks again."

As soon as I hang up, I scan the kitchen.

I open the fridge. The pantry. If I'm going to bake 200 cupcakes, I need to start like yesterday.

I decide on three flavors—funfetti, strawberries and cream, and chocolate s'mores.

I begin gathering the ingredients—flour, eggs, sugar, butter, sprinkles. I grab a bowl of strawberries, their rich red color making my mouth water. I reach for the cocoa powder to make the chocolate s'mores cupcakes.

And then, something unexpected happens. I feel excited. Baking has always had a way of calming me, of making me feel lighter. The way my mom used cooking to show love? That's how I feel about baking.

I feel like a chemist, making sure I measure the perfect amount of each ingredient—too much or too little, and everything falls apart. But it's more than chemistry, it's art.

And Ruth? Ruth was a damn artist; she created the most beautiful cakes and pastries, little bursts of sunshine in every bite. She taught me everything I know about baking. I spent countless hours watching her decorate elaborate cakes, her hands moving with an ease that seemed impossible.

Until one day, she handed me an apron and said, "You've done plenty of sitting around. It's time to get those hands working." And that was that. I learned how to bake, how to create.

The Rolling Pin became my second home. I sometimes wonder if maybe she was preparing me for something more. Maybe she wanted me to take over, but I was too busy wanting to leave. And if I hadn't? Would I have ever met Andrew? My stomach twists.

I shake my head, pushing the thought away, and start baking.

∼

Hours later, I'm finally finished. The last cupcake is frosted, the last container sealed shut.

I take a step back, brushing my hands off on my apron, and survey my work. Rows and rows of perfectly frosted cupcakes sit neatly in their containers, the air still thick with the scents of vanilla, chocolate, and strawberries.

The funfetti cupcakes look like tiny bursts of celebration. The strawberries and cream ones have a delicate swirl of pink frosting, light and airy. And the chocolate s'mores cupcakes? Dark, rich, and topped with toasted marshmallows. They came out exactly how I wanted. Maybe even better.

I hope the kids light up when they see these cupcakes, that they take that first bite and let out that little hum of happiness. That's the best part of baking, seeing people enjoy something I made with my own hands.

I taste-tested everything, of course...strictly for quality control. Not because I couldn't resist. Obviously.

And they taste amazing. I grin, but the moment I take in my surroundings, my smile falters. Oh. My. God. The kitchen is a disaster!

There's flour on the counter, on the floor, and in my hair. A smear of pink frosting streaks across my forearm, and somehow, there's even chocolate on the fridge handle. It looks like a bakery exploded in here.

And I'm not any better; I'm covered in it, too. My shirt has a powdered sugar handprint, my fingers are sticky with melted marshmallow, and my feet ache from standing for hours.

I stretch my arms above my head, rolling out my shoulders, but it does little to ease the soreness. I'm so tired. The sun is long gone now, and all I want is a hot shower, clean pajamas, a glass of wine, and a scary movie. That sounds like heaven.

But first? I need to clean up this disaster of a kitchen. I sigh, grabbing a dish towel and tossing it over my shoulder.

Tomorrow is going to be an early day, but I can't wait.

～

For the first time in months, I woke up before my alarm. I feel like a kid on Christmas morning, excited to get to the school and drop off these goodies. It's nice to have something to look forward to.

I rush inside, several packages of cupcakes teetering in my arms. I can't see over them, and honestly? I'm just praying I make it to Anna without tripping and sending 200 cupcakes flying across the hallway.

I tighten my grip, balancing the weight of the boxes as I carefully navigate through the school. My arms burn, my fingers dig into the cardboard, and I can feel the faintest tremble in my wrists. Just a few more steps. Keep it together, Mariana.

Someone brushes past me, and I nearly lose my footing. I suck in a sharp breath, adjusting my hold at the last second. Crisis averted.

Somewhere up ahead, I hear Anna's voice. Found her. Relief floods through me as I follow the sound, carefully weaving around backpacks, lunch boxes, and tiny humans who seem completely oblivious to the life-or-death cupcake mission happening above their heads.

I finally spot her, standing by a classroom door, deep in conversation with another teacher.

I shift the weight of the boxes, clearing my throat. "Anna —help me before I become a cautionary tale!"

Anna turns, her eyes lighting up when she sees me. "Mari! My hero."

She gestures toward the other teacher. "Analyse, do you remember Mari? The perfect angel blessing us with these incredible cupcakes?"

I laugh. "You know, I could get used to all these compliments. Keep 'em coming."

Analyse grins, and leans in for a hug.

"Of course, I remember Mari. My almost sister-in-law!"

Anna pinches Analyse's arm. "You can't say things like that, Lyse!"

"It's fine, really," I say quickly, forcing a small smile.

Anna distracts herself by peeking into the cupcake boxes.

"Oh my God, these look so freaking good. I want to shove my face in them."

I snort. "Okay, let's not do that."

Anna pouts dramatically before sighing. "Fine, let's get them unpacked and onto the tables before I completely lose my self-control."

A little voice echoes through the hallway, growing closer. "Mama! Mami!"

I turn my head just in time to see Maya barreling toward Analyse.

Analyse catches her effortlessly, kissing her cheek. "Hi, sweet baby girl. Where's Tío?"

Maya points behind her. "Right there, Mami!"

I follow her finger, my eyes landing on him. And just like that, my pulse stutters. Shit. I wasn't expecting to see him today. I look down at myself and grimace.

My hair is in a messy top knot, and I'm wearing leggings and an oversized flannel. Not exactly my best look. If I had known there was a possibility of running into Sebastian Garcia today, I would have at least put on mascara. Not sure why that thought just crossed my mind, and I'm not about to unpack it. Damn, he looks good.

I glance back at Maya, who is now chatting away with Analyse. She has his smile. That same dimple on the left side of her face. My eyes flick back to Sebastian, noticing the two guys standing beside him.

"Who's that with Seb?" I ask.

Anna follows my gaze. "That's Andres and Mateo. They're also firefighters."

I take a second longer than necessary to look at them. "Jesus. Is it like a prerequisite to be ridiculously hot before you can join the academy?"

Anna bursts out laughing. "Right? Like, before they let you in, you have to pass the Hotness Test—"Ooooh, you're a ten. Congratulations, you're now a firefighter!'"

We're both still laughing when Sebastian, Andres, and Mateo walk up to the table. Maya tugs on Seb's hand, bouncing on her feet.

"Tío, look!! SO many cupcakes!" She skids to a stop in front of the table, staring at the rows like she can't decide which one she wants.

"Omg, there are pink ones! And chocolate ones!" She bounces on her toes, clutching Sebastian's hands. "Pleeeease, can I have one, Tío?? Pretty pleeeease?"

Seb rubs the top of her head. "You know your Mami is going to kill me if I give you too many cupcakes. We're still recovering from the six types of ice cream."

Analyse chimes in, arms crossed. "Yeah, princesa, your Tío is still in trouble for giving you all that sugar and handing you back to me."

Maya's face drops.

Seb bends down and whispers conspiratorially. "But if we eat them together, we can say Mateo forced us into it. What do you say? Be my partner in cupcake crime?"

"You know I can hear you, right?" Analyse says flatly.

Seb ignores her and grins at Maya, who giggles. I laugh, and Seb glances up at me—then winks. A small part of me swoons. Okay, a big part. But, I mean, come on. A man who's good with kids? That's always a turn-on.

I started packing up a few cupcakes for Maya. "Which ones do you want, bebecita?"

She stares at them, eyes wide, like she's making the hardest decision of her life. Eventually, she nods decisively. One of each.

My kind of girl. I smile and hand her the small box. "And you, Seb? Can't leave your cupcake crime partner hanging."

Seb grins. "You're right, I can't. I think I'll take the strawberry one."

"Good choice. That's one of my favorites. Do you want me to put it in a box?"

Seb reaches out, gently taking the cupcake from my hand. "Nah, I think I'll eat it now."

I watch as he takes a large bite, remnants of frosting sticking to his lips. I don't think I've ever been so captivated by a man eating a cupcake, but here we are. I quickly look away, pretending to wipe down the table.

Mateo wipes his mouth. "Damn, those were amazing. I need ten more immediately. Oh, and I'm Mateo, by the way, since this jerk didn't introduce us before shoving cupcakes in our mouths."

I chuckle. "Hi Mateo. If you want more cupcakes, throw some cash in that lockbox. We're raising money for the kids."

Andres grins. "I like you."

He gestures at Sebastián. "We've heard a lot about you."

My stomach dips. Wait. What? Before I can say a word, Andres elbows Mateo and shoves him forward.

Seb rolls his eyes. "Sorry about that. It was good seeing you again, Mariana." He grabs Maya's hand and walks away, leaving me feeling a little breathless.

~

After a long day of selling cupcakes, watching kids bounce off the walls from a sugar high, and then spending the rest of the afternoon with my mom, I am completely drained.

The kind of bone-deep exhaustion that makes my limbs heavy and my mind sluggish. But despite that, my thoughts won't shut off.

Anna and I are sitting at my kitchen table, glasses of wine in our hands, playing bingo, a tradition started by our parents that somehow never died.

I absently twirl the stem of my wine glass between my fingers, distracted by the thought that's been eating away at me all day.

Today reminded me of something. Something I haven't felt in a long time. I love baking, I love making people happy with food, I love creating something from scratch and watching people's faces light up when they take that first bite. And when I told my mom my wild idea, the way her eyes lit up... I just knew. I have to do this.

A voice cuts through my thoughts.

"Uh, Mari?"

I blink, snapping my head up to find Anna staring at me. She gestures to my bingo card. "Pretty sure you have bingo and you've just been sitting there staring at nothing."

I don't even hesitate. "What if I spoke to Ruth and asked to take over the bakery?"

Anna's face goes blank. "What?"

I sit up straighter, heat rushing to my face. "She hasn't sold it yet, right? It's just sitting there?"

Anna doesn't respond immediately. Instead, she just stares at me. A curious look on her face, like she's processing the weight of what I just said.

The silence stretches, and suddenly, my brain decides to betray me. Shit. Maybe this is a stupid idea.

What was I even thinking? I never went to culinary school.

I don't have a business degree. What do I even know about running a bakery? I mean, sure, I've spent hours learning from Ruth, but does that actually mean anything? I'm a damn event coordinator. I can plan a hell of an event, but that's not the same thing as owning a business.

I start to backpedal, opening my mouth to say forget it, when suddenly...Anna jumps out of her seat and practically tackles me in a hug.

"So you're staying? Like forever? She asks, eyes wide with excitement.

I hesitate for only a second before nodding, "Yeah. I think I am." The words feel strange on my tongue, like I'm still getting used to them. But as soon as I say them out loud, something in my chest settles.

Her face lights up, and before I can say anything else, she throws her arms around me. "You have no idea how happy that makes me! That's an incredible idea, Mari!" she screams into my ear.

I let out a startled gasp, flailing. "Anna—breathing! I need to breathe!"

She loosens her grip slightly but still doesn't let go. "Right, right. Sorry." She leans back, eyes shining, cheeks flushed. "I just—Mari, this is huge! I'm so excited for you!"

Wait. So... it's not a stupid idea? I bite my lip. "You really think so?"

Anna pulls back just enough to look me straight in the eyes. "Of course. She's basically been prepping you for this since we were kids. There is literally no one better for this than you."

Her confidence in me hits me like a tidal wave. I didn't even realize how much I needed to hear that. I swallow, my heart expanding with something warm and unfamiliar. Hope. Excitement. Maybe even a little bit of belief in myself. I nod, gripping my wine glass tighter.

"Okay," I whisper. I take a deep breath, steadying myself.

First step? Talk to Ruth. If this works out the way I'm hoping... I'll be owning the local bakery. And finally, for the very first time since I was a teenager, the idea of staying in my small town doesn't terrify me—it excites me. It feels right.

CHAPTER 8

Mariana

I wake before the sun, the silence of the house pressing in around me, thick and suffocating. Sleep has been elusive for months, and last night was no different.

Some nights, it's my body that betrays me—aching joints, stiffness that refuses to ease, the deep, dull pain that makes even shifting under the covers feel like a battle.

But most nights? It's my mind. A relentless reel of memories and regrets, of what-ifs that have no answers. Every night, I close my eyes, willing my thoughts to settle, but they don't. They never do.

I slip on a hoodie, the fabric soft and worn, lace up my sneakers, and step outside, inhaling the sharp bite of the crisp morning air. A light fog clings to the street, hovering low, swirling in the dim glow of the street lamps.

The world feels half-asleep, suspended in that quiet space between night and dawn. I don't have a destination in mind—just a restless energy in my limbs, an urge to move, to shake off the heaviness pressing on my chest. So I walk. Letting my feet carry me wherever they want to go.

I slow without realizing it, my steps faltering as my eyes lift to the sign above me. The Rolling Pin. My breath catches. Ruth's bakery.

I knew Anna wasn't lying when she said Ruth retired, but seeing it like this? The once-bright windows are dark, the door shut tight. No golden glow spilling onto the sidewalk, no handwritten specials chalked onto the sign out front.

No scent of warm cinnamon rolls curling through the air. No quiet hum of the oven, no clatter of trays, no muffled laughter from the kitchen. Nothing. A lump forms in my throat.

This place was so much more than a job to me. It was a piece of my childhood, my teenage years, my heart. It's where I learned how to bake, where I first realized that mistakes didn't have to be failures—they could be something beautiful. I can still hear Ruth's voice in my head: "Baking is a science, Mari, but decorating? That's art. If you mess up, make it part of the design."

I close my eyes for a second. I can almost see it—Ruth and me, side by side, aprons dusted in flour, holiday music playing as we decorated cakes, her laughter filling the air.

My hand presses against the door, fingers curling around the knob. Please be open. I turn it gently, half-expecting resistance, but it gives way without hesitation. I step inside.

The air is still, carrying only the faintest trace of flour and sugar—a memory refusing to fade away completely. Dust coats the counters, a fine layer undisturbed for months, drifting lazily in the air, stirred by my presence.

The chairs remain stacked, the display cases stand hollow and bare. It looks...the same. And yet, it couldn't feel more different. The space that once hummed with life, with Ruth—now sits quiet and empty.

I exhale slowly, my heart pulling in two directions. I walk toward the kitchen, my true home inside this place. The second I flick the light switch, something shifts inside me. It still smells like Ruth. Faint vanilla. A whisper of cinnamon.

This place still has so much magic left in it. I know it. I feel it. I need to try. For me. For Ruth. For this town.

I swallow, the first flicker of doubt creeping in. I've been gone for so long. Why would Ruth sell it to me? I don't have a business degree. I don't know what she's looking for. But I want this. Boy, do I want this.

I take one last look around, flick the lights off, and step back into the morning air. I have a conversation to prepare for. One I never thought I'd be having. But one I need to have.

I had been marching straight toward Ruth's house, ready to demand she give me a chance, when I realized... The sun was barely up, and as much as I want to fight for this, I also don't want to start our conversation with her mad at me for waking her up at dawn.

So, I did what any sensible, patient adult would do. I turned right back around and walked home.

Waiting is hell. Minutes feel like hours. I've scrubbed the house from top to bottom. Baked cookies. Rearranged the spice cabinet.

And now, I'm sitting on my couch, notebook in hand, writing a speech to Ruth on why I'm the best person to take over the bakery—a movie playing in the background that I'm definitely not paying attention to.

My knee bounces. My heart races.

Why is time moving so damn slowly? Father Time, you wanna help an anxious girl out right now? If my heart rate keeps climbing like this, I'm going to give myself a heart attack before I even get to Ruth's doorstep.

Sighing loudly, I grab my phone and check the time. 10:05

AM. She should be awake by now... right? She's probably had her coffee. This is fine. It's time. Right?

I take a deep breath. Right.

∼

I march straight toward Ruth's bright yellow door, ready to beg her to give me a chance. It's eccentric, just like her, I love it.

She peeks her head out, gripping her robe tightly, probably prepared to send whoever's knocking at this hour on their way. Then she sees me, and her face shifts—shock, recognition, concern.

"Mariana?? What are you doing here? Is everything okay?"

I open my mouth, nothing comes out. I look at Ruth. Look at my feet. Look at Ruth again.

"Uh, yea— I mean, yes. Everything is great. I just wanted to talk to you about something. Can I come in please? Unless this is a bad time, then I can totally go back home and come back at a time that's better for you. Yep, maybe that's what I'll do. It's early, I didn't mean to bother you. Sorry, Ruth!"

I'm panicking. My feet are already moving away from the door. Ruth sighs, then catches my arm before I can make a full escape.

"Mari, I don't know what's going on, but you're not bothering me at all. Please. I've been up for hours—early bird and all that." She grins, wiggling her eyebrows. "I just made a fresh pot of Café Bustelo, your favorite."

Before I can respond, she wraps me in a warm hug, in an instance it melts years of distance away. For a moment, I'm five years old again, my face pressed against her familiar embrace, the scent of citrus and flowers clinging to her like a second skin.

She pulls back, smiling, and steps aside. "Come in, Mari."

I do, and the second I cross the threshold, it's like stepping straight into the past. Nothing has changed.

The same cozy furniture, the same lace curtains softly filtering the morning light. And by the door, the same candy dish. My candy dish. The one I used to steal from when she babysat me, stuffing sweets into my pockets. I reach for one now, fingers closing around a little strawberry candy, my movements pure muscle memory. Some things never change.

As I follow her into the kitchen, my nerves start to creep back in. I can do this. I can do this. Ruth pours two cups of coffee. "Cream and sugar?"

I nod, fidgeting with my fingers. "Yeah, just one."

She hands me my cup, and then sits across from me at the table. Her sharp eyes scan my face. "Alright, Mari. Talk to me. What's on your mind?"

I take a huge gulp of coffee, buying myself time. "Mmm."

She raises a brow, her eyes roaming over me, taking in my posture. "I don't remember you ever being this nervous around me."

"No, no, I'm totally comfortable! It's not you! I've just had... a weird couple of days. A weird couple of months, really. Well, the past year has been weird." I stand up and start pacing. Ruth's eyes follow me like a cat tracking a laser pointer. Here goes nothing.

"So, yeah," I start, my words tumbling out faster than I can catch them. "You know I've always loved The Rolling Pin ever since I was a kid. I spent half my childhood pressed up against that front counter, watching you work your magic, waiting for you to sneak me a warm pastry when my mom wasn't looking." I let out a breath, forcing myself to slow down, but the nervous energy bubbling inside me won't let up.

"And working there as a teenager was the best. It never even felt like work. It was fun, it was exciting, and it was..." I throw my hands up, searching for the right words. "It was home. That place was home for me."

Ruth watches me, eyes twinkling with patience, but I can't stop now. The dam has burst.

"And I really love to bake, you know that, right?" I fidget with my fingers, my knee bouncing under the table. "Like, I really love to bake. I don't think I ever told you this, but when I was in Seattle, I picked up catering gigs just so I could bake for people again. Nothing crazy, but every time someone took a bite of something I made and smiled—Ruth, I missed that feeling."

I exhale sharply, trying to rein myself in, but it's a lost cause. "Learning from you was a dream. You have so much talent, Ruth. I mean, did you go to culinary school? I don't think I've ever asked that. Or business school? What about a secret bakery society where they teach people how to make perfect frosting swirls? Why have I never asked these things before?"

She chuckles softly, but I barrel on.

"I guess because I never thought I'd be standing here right now." My throat tightens as reality crashes into me. I grip the coffee cup in front of me, staring down at the dark liquid, willing my hands to stop shaking. "But here I am."

I take a deep breath, forcing myself to look up to meet her gaze. "I just want you to know that I think you're incredible, Ruth. And I love The Rolling Pin so much. I swear I'd do right by it. I wouldn't have to change a thing. Okay, well, maybe a couple of things? But not like a lot. Just enough to make it my own, you know? But I'd keep its heart. I'd keep everything that makes it special." I swallow hard, words suddenly catching in my throat.

"It can be my love letter to this town. My way of showing my appreciation for everything it's given me—for you, for my parents, for the people who have always been here for me."

I press my lips together, suddenly panicked that I've said too much. I brace for her reaction. What the hell am I even saying? I exhale sharply. I completely screwed this up. Ruth is staring at me, her mouth slightly open. Probably horrified by the absolute mess of words that just fell out of my mouth. Shit. She's never going to sell me the bakery. I can't even string together a proper sentence. I just ruined this before it even started.

Ruth waves her hands in the air like she's trying to slow down a runaway train. "Mariana. Breathe. Sit down. I have no idea what you just said, and I think we need to start over."

I nod, dropping into my chair like a sack of flour.

"Now," she says patiently. "Before we start this conversation again, I want you to breathe in for three beats, then out for three."

I do as she says. Inhale. Hold. Exhale. I feel lighter.

Ruth places her hands over mine, her touch warm and grounding. "There you go. Now, start over."

I look at her hands—aged, steady, filled with love. She's right. I've never been afraid to talk to her. I lift my gaze, finding new determination. "I want to buy 'The Rolling Pin'."

Ruth squeezes my hands, and I brace for the letdown. Instead, she studies me carefully. "Are you sure, honey? You've always had one foot out the door in this town. I need to know you're really staying—not just for now, but for good."

Her words settle over me, heavy and real, the type of truth I can't ignore. "I'm sure," I say, my voice steady. "I'm staying.".

Ruth watches me for a long moment before her lips curve into a wide grin. "Well, it's about damn time."

I blink. Once. Twice. Did my brain just imagine that? Surely, she actually said, "No damn way," and I just heard it wrong.

"I'm sorry, can you repeat that?"

Ruth chuckles. "I said, Mariana, it's about damn time."

My jaw drops. "I don't think I understand."

She leans forward, eyes twinkling. "Mari, I've been hoping you'd want to take over the bakery someday. I trust only you with my place. I trained you, I taught you everything I know. I know that no one, and I mean no one, will love it like you will. You moving to Seattle was just a blip. Marrying that Andrew fellow—well, we don't have to talk about that. But in my heart, I always knew you'd find your way back home. Back to what was meant to be yours." Her voice is warm, unwavering.

I feel tears prick my eyes.

"You were always meant for this."

I let out a shaky breath. "Thank you, Ruth. Thank you for believing in me. I swear I won't let you down."

She laughs, squeezing my hand. "I'm not worried about that at all."

Then she leans back, smirking. "And Mari? If you want to change a few things, go for it. Make it yours."

I rise to my feet, heart pounding, Ruth standing beside me. She walks me to the door, pulling me into another hug before whispering in my ear: "The place is yours, Mari."

I step outside, walking to my car in a daze. I did it. I own 'The Rolling Pin.' The Rocky soundtrack is playing in my head as I mentally pump my fist in the air.

I freaking did it.

CHAPTER 9

Mariana

The weeks have been flying by as I prepare to re-open The Rolling Pin. I didn't realize how much I needed to get done to get this place up and running again.

Each day blurs into the next, but it's been a welcome distraction. Between the renovations and spending every free moment with my mom in the hospital, I haven't had much time to sit, let alone think.

And, honestly, that's been a relief. The constant movement and constant noise leave no room for doubt. Admittedly, it's been nice being on the go, lost in the hustle and bustle of opening my own place. My. Own. Place. I still can't believe I get to say that. What a dream. How is this even my life? I'm equal parts excited and scared shitless.

I've been having so much fun these last few weeks, I forgot what it felt like. Testing out new recipes has been a dream, and Anna is more than happy to be my designated taste tester.

I want to keep The Rolling Pin mostly the same, amplify what already makes it special, while adding my own roots, my own culture.

I've been playing around with a coquito cupcake recipe, and I think I'm so close to perfecting it. Anna thinks I'm crazy, that the recipe is already great, but great isn't enough. It has to be perfect. I need everything to be perfect.

After hours of cleaning, I finally collapse onto the floor, which is a reminder that I still need tables and chairs, and let exhaustion seep into my bones.

The summer heat has settled in, thick and relentless, and I take a large gulp of ice-cold water. The condensation drips onto my fingers, and the cool contrast against my overheated skin feels too good.

I need to get the air conditioning running in here. Another thing to add to my never-ending to-do list. Every time I cross one thing off, five more things are added.

The bell chimes softly as the door swings open, and a wave of humid air rushes inside. Anna steps in first, and behind her....Oh. Oh, no. Sebastian.

I haven't seen him since the school bake sale. He's in uniform, and damn, he looks good. Broad shoulders, strong forearms, and looking way too damn sexy for me to handle.

My pulse jumps before I can stop it. I need to shut this down. Now. He looks... nice. Like an old friend. A regular old friend. Not someone who used to kiss me with more passion than I've ever felt in my entire life. Jeez, Mari. Get a grip.

"Um, friend, it's looking great in here and all," Anna says, fanning herself, "but it feels like a million degrees."

"I'm aware." I groan, rubbing my temples. "The air conditioner isn't working, and I didn't realize how bad it was until today. Now it's impossible to ignore."

"Ahem."

I look up. Right. Sebastian. I still don't know why he's here.

"Seb, what are you doing here?" My voice comes out too

sharp, my defenses rising fast. I really don't want him to see me like this, sweaty, covered in dust, barely holding it together.

"Ahh, good to see you too, Mariana." He smirks, but there's something behind it, something careful.

"Sorry." I sigh, running a hand through my hair. "I'm just hot... and tired... and there's so much I still need to do."

"Actually," he says tentatively, "that's why I'm here."

I shoot up. "Oh, God. No. Whatever it is, I don't wanna hear it."

Sebastian hesitates, his lips pressing into a thin line. He runs a hand through his hair, and did I mention how good he looks in his uniform? Because, yeah. He looks really good.

"Fine," I huff. "Just say whatever it is before I have a coronary over here."

Seb nods. "The Rolling Pin needs to pass inspection before you're allowed to reopen, and I can tell you right now, the place needs some major safety upgrades."

My stomach plummets. I sit, then stand, then sit again. My vision tunnels, and my chest tightens. You've gotta be kidding me.

I was supposed to be done. I thought I just had to clean, refresh the menu, upgrade the furniture and open the doors. But now...safety upgrades? More expenses? More delays? How much? How long? I can't breathe. The panic rushes in, fast and unforgiving. My head spins as I press my hands to my knees, trying to ground myself.

Anna and Sebastian move at the same time. Anna's hand lands on my shoulder, firm and steady. "Mari, we got you, girl. I know this is a setback, but it's gonna be okay."

Sebastian crouches beside me, his presence solid, anchoring. His hand moves in slow circles against my back, his voice low and steady. "Inhale, exhale, Mariana. Slow, deep breaths."

I'm hyper-aware of everything. His hand. His voice. The

scent of clean soap and smoke clinging to his uniform. The way he feels safe. I do what he says. Inhale. Exhale. My lungs stretch, the panic ebbing away as his touch stays firm, unwavering.

"Good girl," he murmurs.

My stomach flips. I lift my head, meeting his eyes, and shit, I can't look away.

"What am I going to do?" I whisper.

"I'm gonna help you," Sebastian says.

I jerk back slightly, blinking. "Oh no, that's not neces—"

"That's a great idea!" Anna cuts in, grinning.

I shoot her a what the hell look, then glance at Sebastian again. There's something in his expression that makes me pause. Something real.

"I really want to help, Mariana." His voice is softer now, insistent. His gaze locks onto mine, steady and sure.

My throat tightens. I stare at him for a beat, then let out a resigned sigh. "...Okay."

After I agreed to let Seb help with the bakery upgrades, Anna gave me a quick hug and said she had to head out. Seb explained that I apparently need a new fire suppression system —the current system is severely outdated, according to him. Great. Just another thing to add to the never-ending list of expenses.

He also said he knows an HVAC guy who can fix my air conditioner, which is a lifesaver because I cannot decorate cakes in this heat. Frosting would turn into a puddle faster than you can say cupcake, and no one is going to be lining up for something that looks like it barely survived a meltdown, no matter how much they love me or this place.

Seb works three-day shifts at the firehouse, and he helps Analyse with Maya, but he told me he'll be at the shop on his days off. He even said he could ask the guys to pitch in with Maya. I told him he didn't have to do this.

I know he already has a lot on his plate, and the last thing I want is to take time away from him and Maya. But he shut that down fast. Said it wouldn't be a problem, and he wants to help. According to him, Andres and Mateo love spending time with Maya anyway, so they'll be stoked to have more time with her. That made me smile. The way all these guys jumped in to help Analyse, the way they made sure Maya never felt the absence of the man who was supposed to be there for her—it's beautiful.

I don't know all the details about what happened with Maya's dad, but I know enough. Enough to know that he's a complete dickhead for walking out on his baby girl and the woman who carried her. At least they have Seb. And Andres. And Mateo. Seb and Analyse's parents help out when they can, too.

It really does take a village. The thought lingers longer than I expect, settling deep in my chest. Seb never hesitates when it comes to taking care of people. It's just...who he is.

And maybe that's why it doesn't surprise me when, as my brain spirals into panic over the cost of all these upgrades, Seb cuts it off at the root. Don't worry about the labor. He and the guys will do all of it for free. He can get the parts for next to nothing.

When I get home, the house is dark. Quiet. I glance at the clock. 7:00 p.m. It amazes me how much can change in a year.

Just last year, I was in Seattle, married, trying to convince myself I was happy. And now...now I'm a widow, back in my hometown, coming home to an empty house every night.

And on top of it all, my mom is sick. Every part of my life looks different than it did a year ago, and I don't know if I'm mourning what I lost or trying to make peace with what I never really had.

Andrew wasn't a good man. My brain knows that. He did horrific things to me...things I still can't say out loud. He put me through so much emotional and physical trauma, and I'm better now. I know I am; I'm better without him. I survived him.

But damn sometimes, I feel...lonely.

Sometimes, I want to come home and have someone waiting for me. A partner. A home filled with the sounds of laughter, little feet pattering across the floor, but that's not my life. It may never be my life, and I need to accept that.

I move into the kitchen, pour myself a glass of red wine, and throw a bag of popcorn in the microwave. I take a long sip, tilting my head back, fingers pressing into the tension in my neck. Exhaustion seeps into my bones. I pop a few handfuls of popcorn into my mouth, but the appeal fades fast. What I really need is a hot bath.

One of my favorite parts of this house is the deep, clawfoot bathtub. It's so deep that when I sink in, the water covers both my knees and my breasts, wrapping me in heat.

I start the water, as hot as my body can handle, and light candles around the bathroom. The flickering glow casts a soft, golden light over the walls, shadows dancing with each slow breath of air.

Undressing, I twist my hair up and clip it. The second my toes dip into the water, a deep sigh escapes me. It's luxurious.

The heat rushes over my skin, a slow burn that unwinds the tension in my body, inch by inch. I sink in deeper, letting the water cover me, leaning back until my head rests against the cool edge of the tub. Steam curls around me. The citrus scent from the candles mingles with it, clinging to my skin, filling my lungs with something warm, something soft.

I'm struggling to find peace within my chaotic mind, endlessly cycling through my relentless to-do list and my obsessive need for perfection. I feel like a tightly wound spring ready to snap.

Closing my eyes, I attempt to calm myself, my hand gently wrapping around my neck, savoring the warmth of my skin as my fingers glide slowly down to my breasts. I begin to circle the nipple on my left breast with a feather-light touch, lingering there, while my other hand cradles my right breast.

My thoughts drift, and suddenly, images of Seb flood my mind—his sculpted biceps, that irresistible dimple when he smiles, and those deep, captivating brown eyes.

Heat surges through my body at the thought of him, and my hand traces a path down my breasts, past my stomach, to the untouched place that craves attention. I gasp as my hand makes contact with those sensitive nerves, my breath catching in my throat.

My fingers move in tight, circular motions against my sex —pleasure mounting, heart racing—as thoughts of Seb dominate my mind. With the first signs of an impending orgasm, my mouth opens in a long, loud moan, my hand moving faster on its own accord, desperate for release.

I spread my legs wider, slipping a finger inside myself; the intense sensation exactly what I needed to push me over the edge. An explosion of ecstasy courses through my body, and I pant heavily, Seb's name escaping my lips in a fervent moan.

I withdraw my finger, my body twitching with the remnants of my orgasm. Breathing deeply, I am both surprised and bewildered by what just happened.

I shoot up so fast I nearly launch myself out of the bath. Oh, hell no. I did not just do that.

My hand flies to my face, covering my eyes as if that'll somehow erase what I just did. My heart is racing. My skin is warm—too warm.

It didn't mean anything. It was just stress! Sleep deprivation! The heat! I take a deep breath, square my shoulders, and vow to never think about it again.

CHAPTER 10

Sebastian

"So, are you going to tell me how things are going with Mari, or am I doomed to live in suspense forever?"

I look up from where I'm sitting on the floor, playing Legos with Maya. She's built an impressive tower, taller than the last one, and is carefully balancing another piece on top.

Analyse is leaning against the wall, one eyebrow raised and arms crossed, as if she already knows something I don't.

I frown. "I have no idea what you're talking about."

She pushes off the wall and walks toward us, flopping onto the couch beside me with a dramatic sigh. "Don't B.S. me, Seb. You two have history, and you've been seeing her more than you see me these last few weeks."

She's not wrong. I have been seeing a lot of Mariana lately. Between the renovations at The Rolling Pin and all the work she still has left to do, it's been long hours and late nights.

I don't mind. It's a hell of a lot of work, but I meant what I said—I want to help. And if I'm being honest, being around her feels like no time has passed. It's effortless, comfortable.

I simultaneously love it and hate it, because there's one side of me that wants this, to be able to just... exist in the same space without thinking about what happened before. No resentment, no hurt, just a fresh start.

But there's another part, one I don't like to admit exists, that isn't ready to let it all go. No matter how hard I tried, I never completely moved on. I don't know if I ever will.

"Nothing's going on between us," I finally say, picking up a Lego piece and turning it between my fingers. "We're just... brushing everything under the rug. Playing friends. Trying to move on with our lives." I don't know if I meant to say it like that, but the words settle heavy between us.

"All I want is to help her," I add, clearing my throat. "I know how much this means to her. I remember all the time she spent at Ruth's growing up. I don't know what happened when she lived in Seattle, but she seems like she could use a friend right now."

Before Analyse can respond, Maya suddenly jumps to her feet. "I'm gonna go play upstairs!" she announces before running out of the room.

Great. So much for Maya being my buffer. Now, Analyse has me exactly where she wants me.

"Stop looking at me like a cornered animal, big brother." Her voice softens, but there's still that sharp, knowing edge. "I'm just looking out for you."

I exhale through my nose, running a hand through my hair. "You don't have to worry about me. I'm just doing my job and helping a friend along the way."

Analyse tilts her head. "And I get that. You're a good guy, and I love you for it. I just want to make sure you guard your heart. You were a wreck after Mari left. I don't want to see you go through that again."

My jaw tightens. "Thanks for looking out. But I promise, I'm good."

She gives me a long, knowing look, and I hate that she knows me so damn well.

"Don't look at me like that," I mutter, dragging a hand over my face. "I'm good. We're good. Just...friends."

Analyse stands, pressing a hand to my shoulder as she passes. "Whatever you say, Seb." She gives me one last glance before walking away.

I exhale, leaning my elbows onto my knees, staring at the half-built tower Maya left behind.

Just friends. Then why the hell does it feel like I'm lying to both of us?

I walk into The Rolling Pin and spot Mariana cleaning up, her headphones in, completely lost in the music. It's loud enough that I can make out some of the words—Vivir Mi Vida. Figures. Marc Anthony has always been her go-to when she's cleaning or trying to get something done. I think it's because salsa reminds her of her dad.

I remember walking into her house as a kid, the smell of sofrito in the air, and her parents dancing in the middle of the kitchen like they were the only two people in the world.

I used to think that was the kind of love worth having. I used to think we had that. Turns out, I was an idiot. When you're young, you feel everything so intensely. You don't realize that not everything lasts forever.

Mariana moves to the music, dancing a little as she wipes down the counter, softly singing along. She looks...relaxed. Happy, even. It's a rare sight these days. I walk over and tap her shoulder.

She jumps back with a scream so loud that I flinch. "Puñeta, Seba!" She slaps a hand to her chest, eyes wide. "Me vas a matar del susto! You cannot sneak up on me like that!"

I blink. "Mariana, you knew I was coming over. That's not sneaking up on you."

She glares, rolling her eyes. "Whatever, Sebastian. You nearly gave me a heart attack. What if I just dropped dead right now? Fell right to the ground."

I stare at her, waiting for her to laugh. She doesn't.

"Jesus, Mari." I shake my head. "I forgot how dramatic you could be. No one is dropping dead from a heart attack."

She gasps, affronted. "I am not dramatic! Have you ever heard yourself when you lost a video game? Now that was dramatic."

My lips press into a thin line. "I was seventeen. Of course I sounded like an idiot when I lost a game."

She crosses her arms. "Still doesn't explain how you know I wouldn't drop dead from the absolute terror of being snuck up on. What are you, God now?"

I raise an eyebrow. "I don't have to be God to know you weren't about to drop dead."

We hold each other's stare for a beat, and then suddenly, we're both cracking up. Her laughter fills the space between us, soft and full and so damn light.

It's been weeks since I've heard her laugh like that. Maybe even longer. I want to hear it again. I want to make her laugh again. And then, just as quickly as it started, it's gone. She stiffens, something unreadable flashing across her face.

"Uh, I'm gonna go to the back and finish cleaning." Her voice is too casual, too forced.

I open my mouth to say something, but she's already gone, practically sprinting out of the room. I exhale, dragging a hand down my face.

What the hell was that? She was fine, more than fine, a second ago. Talking to me. Laughing. But lately, the second we get too close, she runs. Did I do something wrong?

I sift through the last few weeks, trying to pinpoint the moment things shifted. There has to be something, something I said, something I did. Nothing. Frustration knots in my chest.

Nothing drives me crazier than not knowing what I've done wrong. I don't want to hurt her. I don't want to make her uncomfortable. And the fact that I might have? It fucking kills me.

I don't know what I did. But I'm going to find a way to fix it.

Several hours have passed, and Mariana still hasn't spoken a single word to me. She's been hiding in the back, cleaning, while I worked up front. At first, I figured I'd just let it go, give her space, and come up with a plan to fix whatever the hell I did wrong.

After three hours of silence? Yeah. I'm losing my mind. I try to focus on work, but my patience is running on fumes. Every so often, I hear faint music from the back, much quieter than before, but never her voice. Never a glance in my direction. It's deliberate. And I'm done pretending I can ignore it. By the third hour of this bullshit, I've had enough.

I march toward the back, pushing open the door with more force than necessary. "Did I do something wrong?"

Mariana startles, pausing her music. She looks up at me, eyes wide, confusion flickering across her face. "What are you talking about?"

I cross my arms, leveling her with a look. We're not doing this. "You haven't spoken to me all day. Did I do something to you? Did I say something that made you uncomfortable?"

"I just spoke to you earlier today."

I scoff. "Come on, Mariana. Don't play games. You've been weird with me, and I need to know why. We were fine, and then suddenly, you can't be in a room with me for more than a few minutes."

Her eyes widen. And there it is, a blush creeping up her neck. Interesting.

"You didn't do anything wrong, Seba." Her voice is quieter now, her fingers tightening around the rag she's been holding. "I'm sorry if I've been acting weird. I guess I just don't really know how to act around you. You have to admit, this is... a little awkward."

She shifts, her gaze darting away. The rag in her hands twists, her fingers gripping the fabric tighter than necessary.

"We haven't spoken since high school," she continues. "I know nothing about your life, aside from the fact that you're a firefighter. And you know nothing about mine. I'm not even sure if you want to be friends."

I catch a glimpse of the girl I used to know—the one who never had to think twice before letting me in. The truth is, I don't fully buy her explanation.

There's something else, something she's not saying, but I don't push. Not yet. I want her to open up to me, and if I push too hard, she'll run. And, shit, I'd be lying if I said my stomach didn't flip a little at the idea of us being friends again.

I sigh, rubbing the back of my neck. "Hell yeah, I wanna be your friend. We are friends—doesn't matter how much time has passed."

Mariana laughs softly, and damn if my stomach doesn't flip again.

Before she can say anything else, I grin. "Let's just forget the past, okay? It's wiped from my mind. Clean slate."

"Wiped from your mind, huh?" She arches a brow. "Not sure I like the idea of you erasing me completely, but okay... let's be friends." She smiles at me.

And fuck. It feels like home—the warmth, the familiarity, the way she looks at me, like maybe this doesn't have to be as complicated as I'm making it.

Shit. I'm in trouble.

CHAPTER 11

Mariana

I wake up to the soft chime of my phone, the sound slipping through the quiet of my bedroom, gentle but insistent.

My eyes are still heavy with sleep, my body warm beneath the covers, but I don't even hesitate before rolling over and reaching for it. The glow of the screen illuminates the room in soft blue light, and the second I see his name, a smile tugs at my lips—Seba.

It's been like this every morning since we made the choice to be friends again—since he called me out on my bullshit and told me he wasn't going to let me keep him at arm's length.

At first, I didn't know what to do with it; I didn't know what to do with him being back in my life in a way that wasn't tangled up in old wounds and unfinished feelings. Now, it's become a part of my routine.

I shift onto my side, my fingers swiping across the screen as I open the message, my heart giving that stupid, traitorous flutter it always does when I see his name.

SEBASTIAN

"Rise and shine, Mariana."

I quickly scan the room and realize it's still dark out. Huh, what time is it? I look at my phone to check the time and realize that it's five in the morning. What on earth is Seb doing awake?

MARIANA

"Seba, what are you doing up at this godforsaken hour?"

SEBASTIAN

"Shit. Sorry, Mariana. I didn't mean to wake you. I thought you'd see my text later."

MARIANA

"I guess I forgot to put my phone on silent last night. But, you still haven't answered my question. What are you doing awake?"

SEBASTIAN

"Besides jumping at the opportunity to talk to you? I'm at the station; we had to run some drills."

I reread his last text, my fingers hovering over the screen, my chest tightening in a way that's both overwhelming and impossibly light. A breath of laughter escapes me as I drop my phone against my chest, my smile stretching wide, impossible to contain.

Sometimes, talking to him feels like stepping back in time, like slipping into a version of myself that I thought I'd lost. It's effortless—the way we fall into conversation, the way we tease, the way he makes me feel like no time has passed at all, like we're seventeen again, as if we're still those kids who had no idea what heartbreak really felt like.

Then reality crashes in, heavy and unrelenting; I'm not seventeen anymore—I'm a woman who has lived through things I wouldn't wish on anyone.

A woman whose past is littered with pain, loss, and choices that left scars in places no one can see. A woman who buried her husband and carries the weight of his choices like a stone in her chest.

Sebastian doesn't know any of it, and I'm grateful for that, because when I talk to him, I don't have to be the version of me that's haunted by the past six years. I don't have to see the pity in his eyes or hear the whispered poor Mariana like I'm some tragic story people tell in hushed voices.

With him, I can just be me—the version of myself I thought was lost, the one who existed before the weight of the past buried her.

I wonder, briefly, if he ever suspected. If, deep down, he had an inkling that I wasn't happy, that the life I chose wasn't what I had dreamed it would be. Would he have said I told you so? The answer comes instantly. No. Not him. Sebastian isn't like that; he never has been.

He's a good man, a rare kind of good. The kind that loves without conditions, the kind that doesn't keep score. And maybe that's why, after all these years, after everything that's happened... he still feels like home.

There's a knock at my door, so I run downstairs and swing the door open to find Analyse standing there. I look around to see if Seb or Maya are with her, but she appears to be alone.

"Seb is at the station, and Maya is at a playdate.", She says.

Confused, I say, "Okay... Not that I'm not happy to see you, but what are you doing here?"

Analyse looks me up and down, taking in my pajamas, and says, "Seb says I need friends. So, get dressed; we're going to have a boozy brunch."

~

The late morning sun spills golden light across the patio, warming the wooden tables. The scent of sizzling carne asada and fresh tortillas hangs thick in the air.

El Torito has been my go-to brunch spot for years—before I moved to Seattle, before everything changed.

There's something comforting about being here, about the relaxed chatter of other diners, the promise of bottomless mimosas, and the knowledge that, within minutes, I'll be digging into the best huevos rancheros and chilaquiles I've ever had.

I swirl the stem of my champagne flute between my fingers, watching the bubbles rise, before glancing across the table at Analyse.

She's scrolling through her phone with a lazy kind of ease, her sunglasses perched on top of her head, her hair catching in the sunlight. We were never close growing up. She's two years younger than Seba and me, which, in high school, might as well have been a lifetime.

We never ran in the same circles, and never had the type of friendship that existed outside of the fact that I was dating her brother.

But we did spend a lot of time together—birthday parties, family cookouts, Sunday dinners where I sat at the Garcia family's kitchen table while their mom quizzed me on whether I was eating enough (probably not), and their dad playfully gave Sebastian grief about how he "better treat his girl right." —that version of life feels so far away now, so much has changed, yet, somehow, Analyse is still here.

I take a sip of my mimosa, the tartness of the orange juice cutting through the dryness in my throat. When she showed up at my door this morning, sunglasses on, keys dangling from her fingers, saying simply, "Get dressed, we're going to boozy brunch." I hadn't been surprised—Analyse has always had a way of deciding things for people.

If I'm being honest, I'm glad she's willing to be here with me—willing to still be my friend despite everything that happened between Sebastian and me.

She has every reason to hate me, to be angry, to resent me for breaking the heart of the person she loves most in the world. Instead, she's sitting across from me, sipping her coffee like it's just any other Saturday, like I'm still welcome here, and I don't take that for granted.

Analyse tilts her head, running her finger along the rim of her mimosa glass before taking a slow sip. She sets it down with a soft clink, swirling the golden liquid as she glances at me. "So," she says, her voice light but probing. "How's it going at the bakery?"

I brighten immediately, pushing my mimosa aside and leaning forward. "Really well! Aside from all the work that needs to go into these renovations."

"Right, right." She quirks an eyebrow, lips twitching. "Seb is there every chance he gets."

Guilt tugs at my chest. "Lyse, I'm so sorry if he's there too much. I know he helps you with Maya—I don't want to take him away from her or from you. If it's too much, I can tell him to cut back on hours there. I mean, it's not like I'm paying him or anything."

Analyse lets out a sharp laugh, shaking her head. "Mari, chill. You're fine—he does help with Maya, but that doesn't mean he can't have his own life and do his own thing. Besides, he's still helping out a ton. More than I need, really."

"That sounds so much like him." A grin pulls at my lips. "Being there for everyone and everything."

Analyse takes a slow sip of her coffee, studying me over the rim of her mug before she lowers it. "So, it's been going well between you two?"

I pause. "What do you mean?"

She shrugs, but there's something too knowing in her expression. "I just mean... are you guys friends? Or is there something more going on?"

"Ah." I clear my throat, busying myself by cutting into my chilaquiles even though I suddenly have no appetite. "We're just friends."

"Uh-huh." She says with a smirk, dragging out the sound —equal parts teasing and unconvinced.

"He's been a lifesaver," I continue, forcing my voice to stay casual. "I don't know how I would have gotten through these last few months without his help. I didn't realize how much work the place needed."

"That bad, huh?"

"I wouldn't say bad...but yeah, it definitely needs some TLC. It was sitting there unattended for so long, and it's been a pillar of our community for even longer than that. It was bound to have some wear and tear."

"Totally." Analyse nods, reaching for another bite of huevos rancheros. "I still can't believe you bought the place. I honestly didn't think you'd ever move back here."

"Me neither," I admit, setting my fork down. "I wasn't sure I ever would. But a lot happened in Seattle... I just needed to get away."

Her expression softens as she places a hand on my arm. "What *did* happen while you were there?" Her voice is gentle, hesitant. "I mean, I heard about your husband passing away..."

The air around us stills. My breath catches, the knot in my stomach tightening. Other than Anna, I haven't really spoken about everything that happened with Andrew. The choices I made, the ones he made, the way it all unraveled, the way I unraveled.

Analyse notices the hesitation in my face immediately and rushes to shake her head. "You don't have to talk about it if you don't want to." Her fingers squeeze mine briefly. "I just want you to know that you can talk to me. I know that after you and Seb broke up, we sort of stopped speaking too, and I always hated that. I know you're older than me, but I always considered you not just a friend, but family—a sister."

Emotion prickles in my chest, warming something that I hadn't realized was still cold. "I considered you a friend too, Lyse." I squeeze her hand in return, offering a small, grateful smile. "Seattle was... complicated. I was lonely in a big city, missing my family and friends, that's when Andrew came along. Sometimes, I wonder if I really loved him, or if I was just in love with the idea of not being alone anymore."

I let out a slow breath, shaking my head. "He really wanted to get married. And after a lot of convincing, I said yes. I was so caught up—I thought I was madly in love. But deep down, I knew if I said no, I'd be alone again, and that scared me more than anything. So I said yes, I wish I hadn't— but he met me at my loneliest, and I let myself believe in the illusion. It was all a facade, though." The words sit heavy between us.

Analyse's fingers tighten around mine for a beat before she lets go. "You don't have to say more," she says softly. "You tell me when you're ready."

"Thank you." I exhale, shoulders sagging with relief. "And thank you for bringing me here today."

"Of course, Mari. Not like I showed up at your house and forced you to come with me or anything," She says with a smirk, leaning back and crossing her arms. "Seb was right—I desperately need friends. I love Maya so much; she's my whole life. I want to be everything for her, especially because she doesn't have her father in her life."

Her smile falters just slightly, her fingers toying with the rim of her coffee mug. "But sometimes," she continues, "I need to do a little bit for me too, you know? It's like I give everything I have to everyone else, and I never leave anything for me. It's a bit exhausting."

Her tone is light, almost like she's joking, but the look in her eyes is too honest for that. "Does that make me a bad person?"

I shake my head. "Not even a little. It makes you human. You don't have to feel guilty, Lyse." I shake my head. "Everyone knows how much you love Maya. You're a great mom. And guess what? You can be both a great mom and a mom who needs a break every now and then. It's okay to need a breather, and not just to run errands."

She huffs out a laugh.

"You need to take care of yourself too," I tell her. "Do things that you actually enjoy. I know that Seba helps a lot, but I'm here too. I'm happy to help as much as I can."

"Really?" Analyse raises a brow. "You offering babysitting duties?"

I grin. "Absolutely. Maya and I will have the best girls' nights."

Analyse lets out a dramatic sigh. "I might take you up on that."

"Good." I lift my mimosa. "To new brunch traditions?"

"To new brunch traditions." She clinks her glass against mine, a real, easy smile on her face.

After brunch, I'm stuffed with nachos and guacamole, pleasantly buzzed from one too many mimosas, and absolutely ready to curl up in my bed for a long, guilt-free nap.

The sun is high, the heat thick and sticky against my skin as I stroll down the street, my head light, my steps loose. I'm mid-yawn, already imagining the cool relief of my air-conditioned room, when my phone rings.

I fumble for it, nearly dropping it in my tipsy state before pressing it to my ear. "Hello?" I answer quickly, not checking the caller ID.

A familiar voice greets me, amused and knowing. "Mariana."

I blink against the sun, recognizing him instantly. "Seba? What's up?" I slur, my words just the slightest bit off.

A chuckle rumbles through the line. "I see you and Lyse had a good brunch. How many did it take before you got buzzed? One?"

I scowl, slowing my steps as I wave a hand in the air, despite the fact that he can't see me. "Noooo, for your information, I had three," I announce proudly, lifting three fingers, which, again, no one can see but me.

Sebastian laughs, full-bodied and deep, a laugh that feels like sunshine on a cloudy day. "Three whole drinks? Wow, you're really living life on the edge, Mari."

I gasp, outrage burning through me. "I can live on the edge, Sebastian! I can be wild if I need to."

His laughter only deepens, and I swear I can hear him shaking his head through the phone. "Oh yeah?" he teases, the smile evident in his voice. "You, Mariana Vargas, are the definition of reckless now?"

"You can stop laughing now," I grumble, rolling my eyes at the sidewalk like it's somehow in on the joke.

"Alright, alright." He humors me. "But, to be fair, you've always been a little... risk-averse."

I halt mid-step. "Excuse me?"

"Don't get me wrong," he continues, still entirely too entertained. "It's a good thing! You're careful. You think things through; more people should be like you."

I narrow my eyes at absolutely nothing, fists curling at my sides. "Oh, I'll show you careful."

A slight pause. "What?"

"Where are you?" I demand, suddenly fueled by mimosa-driven determination.

His confusion is palpable. "Right now?"

"No, yesterday," I deadpan. "YES, right now."

There's another pause, then a wary, "Uh... I'm in the parking lot of the station. Just finished my shift."

"Perfect," I declare. "I'm coming over."

"For what?" he asks, suspicion creeping into his tone.

"We're going to do something daring. Something reckless."

Sebastian laughs again, but this time, there's an edge of disbelief to it. "Mariana, you're crazy. You don't have to prove anything."

"Shut up, Seba, and come pick me up."

"You just said you were coming here."

"Yeah, well... I got all excited and now I have to actually follow through, but I'm not about to drive across town when I have a perfectly good friend who *loves* picking me up?"

He groans. "Unbelievable."

"I prefer irresistible."

Another laugh, this one softer, like he's shaking his head at me but still indulging me. "Alright, give me ten."

"Great," I say, then hang up, staring at my phone as the reality of what I just did sinks in. What the hell did I just get myself into?

Exactly ten minutes later, Sebastian pulls up in front of me—right on time, because of course he is. He's always reliable.

My buzz has mostly worn off by now, but there's still a slight lightness in my limbs, a lingering warmth from the mimosas, or maybe from the anticipation curling low in my stomach.

I pull open the passenger door and slide in, the familiar scent of him filling the small space—clean, warm, something undeniably Sebastian. "Hey," I say, glancing at him. I immediately lose all sense of thought. His shirt is snug around his arms, the soft fabric stretching over muscle, and damn, I don't remember his biceps looking this good before.

I'm staring, I know I'm staring, and I still can't stop.

A slow smirk tugs at his lips as he drums his fingers against the steering wheel. "When you're done checking me out, you wanna tell me what we're doing, daredevil?"

Busted. My face flames instantly, and I fumble for a response, clearing my throat. "Seba! You didn't come up with anything in your ten minutes of driving over here?"

He scoffs, shaking his head. "Mariana, you didn't come up with anything in your ten minutes of waiting for me?"

I huff, crossing my arms. "Fair." I glance out the window and then back at him. "Okay, so what do all the cool kids do these days?"

He gives me a look, one brow quirking in amusement. "The cool kids?"

"Yes, the cool kids."

"Mariana," he says flatly, "We're in our thirties. My knees are no longer part of the cool kid club."

I chuckle, nudging his arm. "Seb, we're always going to be part of the cool kid club. It's us."

He looks at me then, really looks at me, and for a moment, something flickers in his eyes—something that makes my heart stutter. Oh no. Reel it in, Mariana.

Before I can spiral too deep, Sebastian's expression shifts, something mischievous creeping into his smirk. "Actually," he says, tapping his fingers against the wheel, "I have an idea."

I narrow my eyes, immediately suspicious. "Oh no. Should I be afraid?"

He glances at me, all playful confidence. "Nah, of course

not." He grins, the corner of his mouth twitching. "You're wild, remember? You got this." He shifts the car into drive, the engine humming beneath us as he takes off toward our mystery destination.

I sink back into my seat, watching the town blur past the window, my pulse picking up the further we go.

Universe help me—Maybe I'm not so wild after all.

~

"Absolutely not!" I shriek, stumbling back from the edge of the cliff, my heart lurching into my throat.

My pulse is a roaring drum in my ears, my breath coming in uneven bursts. Sebastian laughs, hands on his hips, the picture of casual amusement, like he didn't just drag me to the literal edge of death and expect me to willingly throw myself off.

The sky stretches endlessly above us, impossibly blue, the midday sun casting golden light over everything. The breeze up here is crisp, carrying the scent of the lake below, and the sound of the water lapping gently against the rocks. It's beautiful.

But when I look down? All I feel is pure, unfiltered terror. He's such a jerk for bringing me here. He's calling my bluff, and I am about to fold like a cheap lawn chair.

He cannot actually think I'm going to jump off this cliff. Is he out of his mind? Maybe he got too many hits to the head during his fire drills. Maybe some smoke inhalation scrambled his common sense.

"Don't be a chicken, Mariana." His voice is all teasing warmth, but there's something else too—challenge, amusement. The smirk that makes me want to smack him and kiss him at the same time. "You said you wanted to do something spontaneous. Well, here we are."

Sebastian spreads his arms wide, a smug grin tugging at his lips.

I whirl on him, eyes wide. "Spontaneous does not mean attempting death, Sebastian."

He chuckles, stepping up beside me, his arm brushing lightly against mine, sending a shiver through me that has nothing to do with the breeze.

My heart is hammering, and I have no idea if it's from the height or from the fact that he's standing so close. Either way, I'm screwed.

"I don't know, Seba." I gulp, looking up at him, my stomach twisted into anxious knots. "That's a long way down."

He tilts his head, considering me. Then, without hesitation, he hooks his pinky around mine, just like he used to when we were kids, when he'd promise me anything and mean it. And I swear, something inside me shifts.

"Do you trust me?" His voice is softer now, a little rougher, edged with something that makes my skin prickle.

I look up at him, and for the first time, I'm not thinking about the cliff. I'm thinking about him.

The steady weight of his presence. The way he has always, always been there, even when I didn't deserve it. The way he looks at me now, like I could tell him the world is ending and he'd just ask what I needed him to do to fix it. Sebastian has always been my safest place.

"Yes, Seba," I whisper, the words barely escaping my lips, but I mean them. More than he knows.

Something flickers across his face, something raw, something real, but before I can decipher it, he squeezes my pinky and threads his fingers through mine, holding my hand firmly in his. "Then let's jump, Mariana," he murmurs, voice steady. "We'll do it together."

I suck in a sharp breath, nerves twisting through me. "You'll jump with me?"

He doesn't hesitate. "I'd do anything for you."

My stomach flips. I swallow past the sudden tightness in my throat, past the fear trying to convince me to run, and tighten my grip on his hand.

Then...We run—legs pounding against the earth, wind whipping through my hair, adrenaline rushing through me so fast I barely have time to think before—We jump.

For a split second, I'm weightless, suspended between fear and exhilaration. The air rushes past me, cool and sharp, I feel free —free to do something just because I want to, free to prove to myself that fear doesn't control me. I can do this. I am doing this.

The old me might have hesitated, but not anymore. Then the water crashes up to meet me, and I'm swallowed whole.

The water splashes around us, our heads quickly breaking the surface, gasping for air. The cool droplets of water cling to our skin and as we stare at each other, laughter bubbles between us.

Sebastian's arms are holding onto mine now, and we're laughing so hard that I can hardly catch my breath. I can't believe I actually jumped off the cliff. I've never felt anything like that in my life. There are so many emotions running through me right now, I don't know which way is up.

My laughter morphs into tears, and suddenly, I'm sobbing —big, hot tears streaming down my face as emotion overwhelms me.

Sebastian's face shifts to fear; he brushes the hair out of my face and says, "Mariana?? Mari?" His hands are on me instantly, brushing the hair out of my face, searching for any sign of injury. His eyes darted over me—my arms, my legs, my face—his breathing sharp and panicked.

"What happened? Are you hurt?" His voice rises with each

word. "Fuck. I'll take you to the hospital. Fuck. Fuck. Fuck. Talk to me. What happened?"

I place my hands against his and whisper, "I'm not hurt."

A wave of relief washes over his face, "Thank God. Shit, I was so scared. So what's wrong, Cariño?"

His hands are on the sides of my face, and my hands are on his; our faces are so close together that we could kiss if I just leaned in a bit. My heart is racing, tears still streaming down my face.

"This year has been so hard, Seba. I've gone through so much, and now, with my mom being sick. My heart is broken. I've lost so much already; I've lost so much of myself, and now I'm going to lose my mom. I don't know how I'm going to go on without her. Not able to hear her voice, her laugh, or feel the warmth of her hugs. It's all too much."

Sebastian places his forehead against mine, "Mariana, I'm so sorry. I'm here, okay? And not just in that bullshit way people say it because it sounds good at the moment. I mean it. Morning, noon, night—you need me, I'm there. You don't even have to ask. You wanna cry until you can't breathe? I'll hold you through it. You wanna scream at the sky, break something, sit in silence for hours? I'm right there with you. Whatever you need, however you need it. I don't know what happened with your ex. I don't need to know if you're not ready. But I do know this—you never have to go through anything alone again. Not as long as I'm alive. Not as long as you'll have me. I'd stand in the fire for you, Mariana. No hesitation. I'd take every hard moment, every burden, every ounce of pain if it meant you never had to carry it alone. You say the word, and I'm yours. I'll show up every time. I'll stand beside you, behind you, in front of you, wherever you need me. You don't have to be strong with me. You don't have to pretend you're fine. Just let me in. There's not a damn thing in this world I wouldn't do for you. I swear it, amor. I'll be whatever you need. Just let me."

"Why? Why would you do that for me?" I ask.

"Because, I care about you Mariana. Always have, always will."

My mind is racing, a whirlwind of emotions coursing through me. I can't seem to untangle them. His words echo in my head, "I'll be whatever it is you need."

The way he said it, I know he meant every single word, and it cracks something within me open. He will be here for me, no matter what.

The weight of his words is pressing on my chest, making it hard to catch my breath. A lump forms in my throat, neither of us is breaking eye contact.

The sincerity in his words, in his eyes, it's overwhelming. I was married and never once felt this way—this sense of security, this sense of safety.

I want to kiss him so bad. I want to feel the weight of him against me, holding me tightly. But, I can't. He's my friend, and I know that everything that he said to me is because we are friends, and always will be friends.

So instead of kissing him, I wrap my arms around him in a tight embrace, and whisper into his ear, "Thank you, Seba. Thank you so much."

CHAPTER 12

Sebastian

The sun beats down on the basketball court, relentless and unforgiving. The asphalt radiates heat, the type that seeps through your sneakers and sticks to your skin.

Sweat drips down my back, and the air is thick—humid, suffocating. It feels impossible to breathe, but I know that has nothing to do with the weather.

I need this game, I need something to take the edge off, to shut my brain down, to stop thinking about her.

Mateo and I are running a two-on-two against Andres and Cap, and we're getting our asses handed to us. I should've known better than to let Cap be on the other team. He's a damn beast on the court—built for endurance, strategy, and completely wrecking anyone in his way.

Normally, I'd be up for the challenge. Today, I'm playing like complete shit. Every shot I take is off—too much force, not enough aim.

My focus is scattered, my movements sluggish. It's like my body is here, but my mind is somewhere else entirely—and I know exactly where; cliff diving with Mariana wrecked me.

Not just because she actually jumped, though that alone was wild, but because of the way she looked at me afterward.

The way she held onto my hand—like she trusted me more than anything. The way she surfaced from the water, tears mixing with the river, looking at me like she wanted to say something real. Something important. But she didn't, and that silence? That's what's been eating me alive.

I don't know what she was thinking. I don't know if she was crying because she was overwhelmed, or because she was hurting, or because she was feeling something for me that she didn't want to admit.

But I know one thing for sure—Mariana doesn't cry easily. When she does, it wrecks me every damn time.

Lucia is sick. Seriously sick. I know that's weighing on her, suffocating her. It kills me, and I know it's killing her too. Lucia has been in my life since before I could remember.

She's always been this force—warm and strong, fierce in her love. She took care of Anna and me like we were hers, and when Mariana and I started dating, it felt like fate.

Now, all I can do is watch from the sidelines as the one person who has always been Mariana's rock is slipping away. I hate it.

I also can't shake this feeling that there's more—something deeper, something she hasn't said, something about her husband. She's never told me the details, but I know in my gut that something happened before he died. I can feel it, and I swear to God, if that man were alive, I'd be beating the shit out of him right now.

I don't need to know what he did to know he fucked up. I can see it in the way Mariana carries herself—how guarded she is, how much of herself she holds back. I can feel it in the way she hesitates, like she's waiting for the other shoe to drop, like she's still bracing for impact even though the worst has already come and gone.

She needs to feel safe, she needs to know that she can trust me—and I meant what I said, I'll be there. I'll be whatever she needs me to be.

Mateo throws the ball over to me, breaking me free of my thoughts. I catch it, dribbling between my legs, the ball hitting the asphalt with a sharp, steady rhythm.

Cap is guarding me, a solid wall of muscle and experience, and I know there's no way I'm getting around him. I fake a drive, then pivot, making a move to pass to Mateo, but Cap sees it coming. The second I go airborne for the pass, he jumps too, slapping the ball clean out of my hands.

"Damn it," I mutter, already moving to chase it down, but Cap is too fast. He grabs it and sprints toward the basket like he's got rockets strapped to his feet.

Mateo is right on his tail, but Cap fakes left, pulls back, and crosses over so damn smoothly, it's like watching a highlight reel.

"Shit!" Mateo yells, and at the same time, Andres laughs, "Ohhhh!"

Cap doesn't even look at me as he sets up for a clean jump shot. Swish. Game over.

Mateo groans, doubling over with his hands on his knees. "Bro, you're built different."

Cap smirks, wiping his forehead with the bottom of his shirt. "You guys just need to step it up."

I exhale hard, hands on my hips, my breath still coming too fast. I should care that we lost. I should be annoyed, talking shit, demanding a rematch. But I can't bring myself to care, because my head is still with her.

We collapse onto the grass under a tree, gulping down water, trying to cool off. The air smells like sun-warmed earth and freshly cut grass, the distant sounds of kids playing and car engines humming somewhere down the street.

Andres tosses me a water bottle, but I react too late, and it smacks me in the chest before I finally grab it.

Andres eyes me. "Alright, what the hell is up with you today?"

I twist the cap off and take a long drink, trying to buy myself a second before answering. "What are you talking about?"

Andres scoffs. "Oh, here we go. You're really gonna sit there and act clueless?"

Cap watches me carefully now, his expression shifting from relaxed to serious. "Everything good? Something up with Maya or Analyse?"

That gets Mateo's attention too; they all know I'd drop everything for my sister and niece in a heartbeat.

I shake my head. "No, Maya and Lyse are fine." I sigh, running a hand over my face. "It's Mariana."

Mateo immediately grins, like he just won some kind of bet. "Knew it."

I frown. "What?"

He leans back on his elbows, smug as hell. "Told Andres you were in your feelings about Mariana. I just didn't think you'd actually admit it."

Before I can argue, Cap cuts in. "What's wrong with Mariana?"

"Nothing," I say automatically. But even as I say it, I know it's a lie.

Cap tilts his head, studying me. "Then I don't get it."

Andres sighs, shaking his head. "He's in love with her. Again. Still. Who the hell knows. But definitely in love."

I freeze. "What?" I scoff. "I never said that."

"So you're not in love with Mariana?" Cap asks, his voice measured, even.

I hesitate, and that hesitation is all they need.

Mateo snorts. "Yep. That's what I thought."

They all start talking at once, giving me shit, calling me out, refusing to let me keep lying to myself. And fuck, They're right.

I lean back in the grass, staring up at the sky, at the burning sun, at anything but them, because they know me, they know about our history.

They know how I spent years trying to convince myself I was over her, that I'd moved on, that if she ever came back, I'd be fine. Now she's back, and I feel like I'm drowning.

I glance at Andres and Mateo, still running their mouths, then shift my gaze to Cap, who's just watching, thinking.

After a long beat, he says, "Seb, if you have feelings for her, that's okay, you know that, right?"

The others shut up instantly, because when Cap speaks, everyone listens.

I swallow hard.

"You and Mari have history," he continues. "You two grew up together. You fell in love, and then she left—not you, but this city. And yeah, that hurt, that broke you. But that doesn't mean you ever stopped loving her."

I don't say anything.

"If you want to be with her, that's okay," Cap says. "And if you just want to be her friend, that's okay too. Whatever you decide—we support you."

Andres and Mateo both nod.

Suddenly, I feel exhausted—I know that I need to figure this out. I need to decide if I'm willing to risk it all again or if I need to figure out how to finally let her go.

Either way—I need to stop pretending I don't already know the answer.

CHAPTER 13

Mariana

T he hospital smells like antiseptic and sorrow, a scent that clings to my skin, settles in my lungs, and makes it impossible to breathe without feeling like I'm drowning.

I hate coming here. I hate the constant hum of suffering, the quiet sobs of loved ones who have already begun mourning, the sterile white walls that feel so cold, so impersonal, so final. But I come anyway. Because if my mom is here, then this is exactly where I need to be.

The doctors have told me to prepare myself, but there's no preparing for something like this. No way to brace for the inevitable, to soften the crushing weight of reality.

They don't know how much time we have left—days, weeks, months. There are no promises, no guarantees.

Just borrowed moments slipping through my fingers faster than I can hold onto them, and man, I really want to hold onto them. I want to freeze time, to bottle every second, to keep her here forever. I'll never stop needing her.

I step into her room, my sneakers squeaking softly against

the linoleum, announcing my arrival. The TV hums in the background, an old telenovela playing at low volume.

My mother is curled beneath a hospital blanket, smaller than I remember, frail in a way that makes my chest ache.

The hospital gown hangs loose on her frame, her once full cheeks now sunken, her skin dull with exhaustion. When she notices me, her eyes light up, and for a moment, she looks just like my mom again.

"Hola, mija. There's my precious girl." Her voice is thin and fragile.

I force a smile, swallowing against the knot forming in my throat. "Bendición, Mami." I whisper, leaning down to press a kiss to her forehead. "I've missed you."

I take my usual seat beside her bed, my fingers instinctively reaching for hers. Her hand is cold, frail, but she squeezes mine gently like she always does. Like she's still her, even when her body is betraying her.

"How are you, Mija? How's the bakery?" she asks, her thumb brushing lightly over my knuckles.

I take a shaky breath, trying to find some semblance of normalcy in this moment. "It's going well, finally coming together."

She smiles. "That's wonderful, sweetheart. And how are things with Sebastian? He's been helping you, right?"

I let out a small, breathy laugh, already knowing where this is going. "Yeah, he's been helping a lot. We actually went cliff diving last week."

Her eyes widen, and she gasps, bringing a hand to her chest. "Cliff diving? Ave María purísima!"

A real, genuine laugh escapes me for the first time all day. "Sorry, Mami. I was scared out of my mind, but honestly? It was fun."

She shakes her head, a small smile tugging at her lips. "That Sebastian... I'm going to have a long talk with him next

118

time he visits. That boy has always had a way of convincing you to try new things."

I blink, confused. "Wait... when does he visit you?"

My mom tilts her head at me, amusement dancing in her tired eyes. "All the time, mija."

I sit up straighter. "Sebastian comes here?"

She nods, smiling fondly. "Oh yes. He brings me a cafecito con pan de mallorca, and we catch up. I've been trying to coax the bochinche out of him about what's going on between you two, but that boy can keep a secret."

Something in my chest clenches painfully, I had no idea. All this time, I thought I was navigating this grief alone.

But Sebastian? He's been here. He's been showing up, for my mom, for me, even when I didn't know it, even when I didn't ask, even when I never once deserved it.

I shake my head, trying to push past the lump in my throat. "Mom, there's no bochinche," I say, rolling my eyes. "Nothing has happened between us. Just friends, remember?"

My mom hums, unconvinced. "But you want something to happen, yes?"

I groan, leaning back in my chair. "I don't know, Mami."

She narrows her eyes, tilting her head. "Don't lie to me, Mariana. A mother can always tell."

I let out a heavy breath, staring up at the ceiling wishing the answer would be written there. "I went through a lot with Andrew," I admit, my voice quieter now. "And even though I know Sebastian would never do the things he did... I can't help but shut down when I think about what we could become. I can't help but feel..."

My mother's voice is gentle but firm. "Scared?"

I flinch. The word buries itself deep in my chest, hitting like a truth I've been trying to avoid. Scared...I'm terrified.

Deep down, I've always known that everything Andrew

did to hurt me left scars I couldn't fully see—wounds that ran deeper than I ever wanted to admit.

But between his death, my lupus diagnosis, and now my mother's illness, life hasn't exactly given me the space to breathe, let alone heal. I've been surviving, not thriving. Existing, not living.

Now, being back home, being around Sebastian, sitting here with my mother, I'm finally feeling it. The pain, the weight of it. The way it's shaped me into someone I don't quite recognize anymore.

I look at my mom, tears blurring my vision. "Yes," I whisper. "I'm scared, Mami."

Her expression softens, her eyes filled with sorrow—a sorrow I know she wishes she could take from me. "Mamita, I love you, and I'm so sorry for everything you went through. You've carried more than anyone ever should."

She squeezes my hand, her grip weak but still full of the same warmth, the same unwavering love she's always had for me. "That man... ese asqueroso... he wasn't a good man, ripping you away from your friends and family the way that he did. But Sebastian?" She shakes her head. "That boy has loved you since you were kids. He has always looked at you like you hung the stars in the sky. Like you, mi princesa, are the sun his world revolves around."

A sob threatens to break free, but I force it down, my throat burning—Mami doesn't know everything.

She knows Andrew isolated me, that he slowly cut me off from my friends and family, that he made me feel like I had no one but him. She knows how he chipped away at my confidence, how he controlled every aspect of my life until I wasn't sure who I was anymore. But she doesn't know the worst of it.

She doesn't know about the bruises, the apologies that came too late, the way I convinced myself that if I just loved him enough, he would stop.

She doesn't know that there were nights when I was too afraid to move, too afraid to breathe the wrong way, too afraid of what would set him off next.

She already carries enough guilt, enough pain, enough regret for not being able to protect me from the things she does know—if she ever found out the truth, it would break her.

So I let her believe that Andrew's worst crime was keeping me away. That the damage he did was only emotional. That the scars he left behind are invisible. It's easier that way.

Her grip on my hand tightens, and I blink rapidly, forcing back the flood of emotion threatening to consume me.

"You know what your gut is telling you, Mija. You just need to trust yourself."

I bite my lip, looking up, trying desperately to blink away the tears. I want to believe her. I want to trust myself.

But how can I? How can I trust myself when I chose Andrew? When I stayed with him? When I convinced myself for years that it was love? I made the wrong choice once. What if I do it again? What if I take a risk, go heart-first into this with Sebastian... and it all crumbles?

Besides, I broke his heart once. Why would he even want to take that risk with me again? My mother must see the war raging inside me because she squeezes my hand tighter, grounding me.

"You are my daughter," she says fiercely. "You are braver than you think and stronger than you can even imagine. You may be bruised, but you are not broken, mija. You just need to remember who you are."

Her words hit me like an earthquake, shaking something loose inside me, something I've buried for too long. I want to believe her. I need to believe her.

Because if I don't...Then I'm not sure I'll ever find my way back to myself again.

~

I sit beside my mother's bed for hours, talking about everything and nothing all at once. We weave through memories, through laughter, through stories that I've heard a million times but never tire of.

She talks about my papi like he's still in the other room, like he might walk in any second, still young, still full of life. She tells me about the way he used to dance with her in the kitchen, spinning her around like they were the only two people in the world.

How he used to press his hand to her stomach when she was pregnant with me, whispering to me in Spanish, telling me stories before I was even born.

She tells me about myself, too—about the little girl who used to pick mangoes from the neighbor's tree even though she wasn't supposed to. The one who could never keep still during mass, who sang too loudly during Christmas novenas, who had dreams bigger than her body could hold.

She tells me all the things I used to be, all the things she sees in me still, even when I can't see them myself—I cling to every word, because I don't know how many more of these conversations we'll have.

Eventually, exhaustion tugs at her, her words slowing, her voice softening. She blinks at me sleepily, reaching for my hand one last time before sleep claims her, her fingers curling weakly around mine.

"I love you, mi amor," she murmurs, her voice thin but sure. "Never forget who you are."

I swallow the lump in my throat, pressing a kiss to her hand. "I love you too, Mami."

Her breathing evens out, slow and steady, and I stay exactly where I am, watching the rhythmic rise and fall of her chest, counting each breath like a prayer.

The hospital room is quiet, the dim light casting soft shadows across the walls. I lean back in the chair, tipping my head against the headrest, staring up at the ceiling tiles.

I close my eyes, and the first thing I see is him—Seba's smile. The way his eyes softened when he looked at me in the water. The way his voice wrapped around me when he whispered, I'd do anything for you.

I exhale shakily and reach into my purse, pulling out my phone. I don't even think about it—I just open our text thread, scrolling through old messages. I re-read the stupid jokes, the early morning check-ins, the effortless way we fell back into something familiar.

My thumb hovers over his contact- for a long moment, I just stare. I could call him. I could tell him the truth, tell him that I miss him—that I think about him more than I should. That I don't just want to be his friend, or I don't know how to be just his friend.

I could tell him everything. Instead, I press the power button, locking the screen, and set the phone down on the small table beside my mother's bed.

Not yet. I'm not ready. But maybe, just maybe, I want to be.

CHAPTER 14

Sebastian

My phone buzzes on the nightstand, the vibration loud in the quiet of my bedroom. I leap up from my bed, my heart knocking against my ribs as I reach for it.

It's not her name on the screen. Of course, it isn't. It's just a spam text—"50% Off Outdoor & Survival Gear" because I really need that right now. My fingers tighten around my phone before tossing it back onto my nightstand, raking my hand through my hair.

I peer over at my nightstand, staring at my phone, the screen black, waiting. What am I waiting for? For her to text me? For some kind of sign that she's thinking about me the way that I'm thinking about her? Fucking pathetic.

I'm acting like some lovesick kid, waiting for a message that, in my heart, I know isn't coming. I've got better things to do. And yet, my eyes flick back to the screen like maybe something's changed in the last five seconds.

I thought we had a moment that day in the lake. I could've sworn she was feeling everything that I felt. Or maybe I'm just an idiot. Maybe I'm reading into something that means nothing to her. She's left me before; maybe she doesn't feel the same. The thought lands like a punch to the ribs, and I shake it off before it settles too deep.

My house is too damn quiet and too damn big, I hate it.

The silence and open space are a reminder of everything I want but don't have, my thoughts too loud, taunting me. I push off my bed, the restlessness crawling under my skin like a slow burn.

I let out a sharp breath and pace back and forth, rubbing the back of my neck. My entire body feels this wired, restless, chaotic energy coursing through me. Like I need to move.

Like if I just continue to sit here, waiting around, I'll end up doing something stupid. Like running to Mariana's house and telling her everything I feel.

I grab my keys before I can think twice.

I don't realize where I'm headed until I'm already on the road. The streets are quiet, the town winding down for the night, bathed in a dim orange glow from the streetlights.

I roll down the window, letting the crisp air slap me in the face, trying to cool the heat creeping up my neck. Most places are closed, their signs dark, but the diner—our diner—still glows in the distance.

I pull into the lot out of habit. I've been here plenty of times since she left; it's not exactly a place I could avoid living in a town as small as ours.

But every time I come here, I force her out of my head, never letting thoughts of her infiltrate my mind—not about the way she used to sit cross-legged in the booth, stirring her hot chocolate like it was some kind of science experiment, not about how she'd swipe my fries without asking or how she always knew exactly what to say to make me forget everything else.

I sure as hell never sat outside, staring at the place like some idiot caught in the past. Yet, here I am, sitting in the parking lot, gripping the wheel, wondering what the hell I'm doing.

I reach for my phone before I even realize what I'm doing. Her name is there, at the top of my messages. I stare at it, my thumb hovering over the keyboard.

SEBASTIAN

Hey.

The cursor blinks. I type something else.

SEBASTIAN

Been thinking about you.

Delete.

SEBASTIAN

Hope you're doing okay.

Delete.

I exhale sharply and lock the phone, tossing it onto the passenger seat. What the hell am I so afraid of? That she won't answer? Or that she will? That I'll say the wrong thing? That she'll remind me why I never should've let myself hope in the first place? I run a hand down my face, letting my head fall back against the seat. This is stupid, I'm being stupid.

But the truth is, she's in my head. Mariana is woven into me, threaded through my being so deeply that I can't pull her loose, no matter how much I try.

It's not just the memories of her. It's the way my chest tightens when I hear her name. It's the way my mind drifts to her when I least expect it.

She's under my skin in a way that feels impossible to shake.

Like the scent of rain on pavement, lingering long after the storm has passed. Like an old injury, healed on the surface but aching when the weather shifts. Being without Mariana isn't just an absence—it's a loss I feel everywhere.

It's an empty seat beside me on long drives, where she used to sit with her feet tucked under her, singing off-key just to make me laugh. It's reaching for a hand that isn't there, feeling the ghost of her touch in places she used to rest against me. It's hearing a joke and turning to tell her, only to remember that she's not here.

It's passing the old movie theater and remembering how we used to sneak into R-rated films, her gripping my wrist, trying to hold in her laughter so we wouldn't get caught. It's hearing a song from high school and feeling my chest cave in because I can still hear her belting the lyrics, getting half the words wrong, not caring at all.

It's waking up in the middle of the night, heart pounding, convinced for a split second that she's still mine. That if I just reach across the sheets, I'll find her there. But my hand only meets empty space, and reality crashes down so hard it steals the breath from my lungs.

It's not just missing her, it's more than that. It's carrying the share of her absence everywhere I go. She's everywhere because she was my everything.

No matter where I go, I see her—I feel her. I can't escape it because, for so long, she *was* my whole world. I tell myself I got used to life without her. I tell myself that I've moved on.

But the truth is I don't think I ever learned how, and that terrifies me.

Just as I'm about to start my car, my phone vibrates. My pulse kicks up, my breath catching. I snatch it up, half dreading, half hoping. But it's not her. It's Mateo. I debate letting it go to voicemail, but the alternative is sitting here, drowning in my own thoughts.

I swipe to answer. "What?"

Mateo laughs. "Damn, good to hear your voice too, man. You good?"

I rub my temple. "Fine."

"You sure?" Mateo drawls, amusement lacing his voice, the hint of a smirk clear without even having to look at his face.

I don't answer.

"Let me guess." Mateo chuckles. "It's about your hot ex who came back into town, and everyone's thirsting over her?"

Something sharp and possessive coils in my chest. I scoff, gripping the wheel tighter. "Shut the hell up."

Mateo laughs. "Ah. So *it is* about Mari."

My jaw locks. Mateo must hear the silence, because his grin practically drips through the phone. "Dude. Are you seriously still in this pretending you don't care phase? Because I'm gonna keep it real with you; some other guy out there won't hesitate the way you do."

A muscle in my jaw ticks. "Yeah?" I say, voice low. "Well, some other guy better not fucking look at her like that."

Mateo barks out a laugh. "See? Now we're getting somewhere."

I roll my eyes. "Did you just call just to be a pain in my ass, or did you need something?"

Mateo is quiet for a second. "I'm just saying... If you still care about her, maybe stop pretending you don't."

I swallow hard. "It's not that simple."

"Yeah, it never is." A beat of silence. "But maybe it doesn't have to be as complicated as you make it."

I don't have an answer to that.

Mateo sighs. "Alright, I'll leave you alone. Just... don't let fear make the decision for you, man."

The call ends, and I sit there, gripping the phone, my knuckles white. I let out a long breath, staring at my reflection in the rearview mirror.

I know what I want, I just don't know if I can survive losing her again—but maybe Mateo is right.

I grab my phone again, open our messages, and—the screen goes black. Battery dead.

I huff out a laugh, shaking my head. Maybe that's a sign. For now, I throw the phone onto the seat, put the car in drive, and head home.

CHAPTER 15

Mariana

The scent of fresh pan sobao and honey clings to the air, even with the faint bitterness of sawdust mixing in.

The bakery isn't finished just yet—half the shelves still needed to be installed, the walls still needed a second coat of paint, and the display cases weren't stocked with the pastries that lived in my head before they ever made it into the oven.

This was supposed to be a simple renovation. Fix the fire suppression system and the broken tiles. Replace the flickering overhead lights. Make the space functional.

But somewhere along the way, I stopped thinking about what was easy and started thinking about what was me. Ruth told me to make the place my own, and I finally decided that she was right.

Now, warm terracotta tiles line the floor, reminding me of the homes in Ponce, where the afternoons stretched lazy and golden, where my abuela's laughter carried through the open windows.

Hand-painted tiles framed the front counter, the deep blues and rich yellows a nod to the streets of my mother and father's home, where color wasn't just a decoration—it was life.

I wanted this place to feel like home. Not just any home, my home. A space where the scent of quesitos, mallorcas, and pastelillos de guayaba greeted people at the door.

Where café con leche wasn't just coffee, it was a ritual, comfort. A reminder of long afternoons in my abuela's kitchen when we visited each summer, watching her pour just the right amount of sugar into my cup while she hummed old boleros.

This wasn't just a bakery. It was Ponce, it was family. This bakery is the piece of me I didn't know I was trying to hold onto until now. I've faced so much loss since leaving this town —more than I ever expected. And somehow, Seba became part of it too.

He stood at the back of the room, measuring a strip of wood against the wall, his brow furrowed in concentration. His presence here was something I should've gotten used to by now—but I hadn't.

He was too much. Too close, too steady, too damn persistent. I pulled my attention back to the countertop in front of me, kneading dough with more force than necessary.

Maybe if I focused on my work, I wouldn't focus on him. Except, that was impossible. Seba was always here, and even if he wasn't, I think my mind would still wander to him.

A moment later, he walked over, stopping at the other side of the counter. The space between us felt too small, or maybe it was just the memories rushing in, reminding me how effortless it used to be, how right it once felt to stand this close. But that was the past. Now, we are just friends.

"You know you don't have to do all this, right?" I said, glancing at him as he drilled a shelf bracket into place.

"You need the help."

I huffed. "I can figure it out myself."

"Yeah? That's why you almost broke the espresso machine last week?"

I locked my gaze in place. "That was an accident."

"Uhuh."

I could hear the grin in his voice, and it set something hot and restless in my chest. I groaned, throwing a piece of dough at him. He caught it easily, laughing, and it made my stomach flip.

It wasn't fair. He wasn't supposed to still make me feel this way. Not after all these years. Not after I was the one who chose to leave, meanwhile breaking his heart.

I reached for the flour, but at the same time, so did he. Our fingers brushed. I froze. So did he.

The air stretched thin between us like a thread pulled too tight, ready to snap at any moment. I should move. Seba's fingers shifted, barely, but enough to make it clear that he wasn't pulling away. Neither was I. But why? Why wasn't I pulling away?

His eyes flicked to mine, something unreadable swimming beneath the surface. Something dangerous. Something that terrifies me.

"Mariana," he murmured, my name thick in his throat.

A shiver rolled down my spine. I knew this moment. I remembered how it felt to stand on the edge of something irreversible, and this felt exactly like that. Like we would make a move that would change things forever, a move we wouldn't be able to turn back on.

Then something sharp and cold cut through the moment. Panic. A feeling lodged so deep in my bones that I didn't even realize it was still there. A feeling that I've spent this past year trying to run away from, pretending it didn't exist.

My heart slammed against my ribs. I had kissed the wrong person before. I had been touched by hands that didn't care if I wanted it or not.

Seba's touch had never been like that. It never would be, and logically, I knew that. I knew that Seba would never do the things Andrew did to me, the physical and mental pain he had caused. I knew this, yet my body didn't know how to separate the past from the present. My stomach twisted, and suddenly, I couldn't do this. I just couldn't.

Seba's breath brushed against my skin. His fingers lifted, just barely, like he might close the distance. I didn't move.

He leaned in close, our breath tangling with one another's, but right before I felt the sweet sensation of his lips touching mine, before the final thread between us snapped—I turned my head, his lips landing at the corner of my mouth instead, barely brushing my skin.

A hitched breath escaped me. The tension between us crackled like a live wire. For a moment, I thought he'd move away. But, he didn't.

Instead, he let his forehead rest against mine, his breath shallow, like he was barely holding himself together. I could feel it, the restraint, the heat, the weight of everything we weren't saying, and it destroyed me.

For a long moment, neither of us spoke. Seba exhaled sharply, stepping back, dragging a hand through his hair. Not frustrated, no, Seba had always had patience with me—just trying to steady himself.

When his eyes met mine, his expression shifted. I knew he saw it. My hesitation. My fear. He knew me. Suddenly, he wasn't looking at me like a man waiting for a kiss, but as someone who knew me, knew everything about me, and knew that something was wrong.

"Mariana..." His voice was softer now, like he was trying not to startle me.

I swallowed hard, forcing my arms around myself, creating a shield. "Don't," I whispered.

Seba's brows furrowed. "Don't what, Mariana?"

"Just don't." I'm silently begging him, please don't push, don't ask, don't see too much. I shook my head. "I can't. I just can't."

Seba was silent for a moment, studying me. His jaw clenched, like he wanted to push but was fighting himself not to.

Finally, he nodded. "Okay."

He stepped back, his eyes lingered, watching me too closely, like he was filing this moment away to pick apart later, and I hated that. I hated that I wasn't ready to let him in. Not yet.

I didn't turn until he was gone. When the door shut behind him, I let out a slow, shaky breath. My hands trembled as I braced them against the counter, my pulse hammering too fast, too hard.

Seba wasn't like him. Seba had never been like him. He will never be like him.

Yet, my body still reacted like it didn't know the difference. I closed my eyes, pressing my fingers against my temples, breathing through the tightness in my chest.

I should have told him. I should have explained why I stopped. But I wasn't ready. Saying it out loud would make it real—too real.

The more people who knew, the less I could pretend it wasn't still haunting me and until I was ready to face it, this thing between us, whatever it was, could never be real.

I stared at my reflection in the small bakery window, the dim light catching on my features. I wasn't the girl I had been when I left this town—the girl who smiled easily, who moved through life with a lightness I barely remember now.

She was hopeful, full of dreams that felt just within reach. Maybe some part of that girl still lived inside me, buried beneath years of someone I never chose to be. But I wasn't sure I knew how to find my way back to her.

CHAPTER 16

Sebastian

I should leave. I should walk out of here, drive home, take a cold shower, and do anything to shake off the feeling of her, the ghost of her almost kiss still burning on my lips.

But instead, I'm standing in the parking lot of her bakery, hands braced on the roof of my car, breathing like I just got the wind knocked out of me. I guess maybe I did.

For a second, I thought she was going to kiss me. For a moment, I thought she was finally going to let her have this, have me, have us again.

I wanted her so damn bad, but at the last moment, she turned away. She turned me away. The way she physically recoiled, the way her whole body tensed like she wasn't just afraid but terrified... It felt like a punch to the ribs.

This wasn't just hesitation; it was something else. Something that I don't quite understand yet. I can feel it in my bones. I just don't know if it's something she'd ever let me understand.

I force myself to move, climbing into the driver's seat, but I don't turn the key right away. My hands grip the wheel, my knuckles bone white. I should be angry, frustrated, embarrassed even. But I'm not.

I'm wrecked. The way she pulled away like I'd hurt her, the way she wrapped her arms around herself as if she were holding herself together with every fiber of her being.

There was something in the way her voice shook when she said, "I can't." It felt like more than her rejecting me; it felt like she was protecting herself. But from what? From me? I've never hurt her. I never would.

I press my forehead against the steering wheel, squeezing my eyes shut. I don't know what happened to her after she left. We didn't remain in touch and for the sake of my heart and sanity, I didn't keep tabs on her.

I know she moved away. I know she got married, and I know that she lost him. That is about all I know of her time away from here, away from me.

I wish I knew what their marriage was like, what kind of man he was to her. I don't know what she went through, what she carries, or what makes her shake at the idea of kissing me or being with me. It guts me.

I understand if she's still in mourning, she lost her husband. But it felt like more than that. It felt like she was genuinely scared. I can't help but think back to when we were young; she used to grab my hand first and pull me in when I hesitated.

And now, she's so scared of being close to me that she can't even look at me without her whole body shutting down. It fucking kills me.

I inhale deeply, trying to clear the weight sitting on my chest. The more I think about it, the worse it gets. The tight way she held herself, the way she couldn't meet my eyes, the way she reacted like I was something to fear.

This isn't just about us or about starting over. I can feel it.

She's been hurt, not just emotionally, but in a deeper way. I don't know how to ask her about it.

I don't want her to feel pressured, but I want to understand. I *need* to understand. Not because I want to fix it or fix her, but because I need her to know that she doesn't have to carry it all alone.

She doesn't have to keep running, protecting herself from something that isn't me. I'm here for her; I will always be here for her.

I finally start the truck, pulling onto the quiet streets of our town. Everything feels too still, too heavy. It feels like the universe hasn't caught up to the fact that something has just shifted between us.

I roll down the window, trying to clear my head, but it doesn't help. All I can think about is her. The way she said my name, hesitant, trembling, like she was afraid of how it sounded in her own mouth. All I can feel is the space where her lips almost touched mine, and even though she's not in this car with me, she's everywhere.

I park in front of my place. I should go inside. I should go to sleep, wake up, and move the hell on. But I don't want to, and I couldn't even if I tried.

Because I know the truth now. I've known it since the moment I saw her again in Ink & Paper, and it shook up my world. It's the thing I've been trying to shove down, to ignore, to pretend it isn't there.

The realization that I'm still in love with her hits me with full force; I'm not sure I ever stopped. It slams into me like a wave crashing so hard it drags me under, stealing every ounce of air from my lungs. I sit there, blinking at the empty darkness before me, but all I see is her.

I don't know what to do now. I don't know how to show her that with me, she is and always will be safe.

What I do know is that I can't walk away from this. I can't

continue to fight what I've been feeling. Not when I just got her back. Not when she's right here, just out of reach.

I pull out my phone, staring at her name in my contacts. I don't text her, don't call her.

I just sit there, the weight of the night pressing against my chest, and let myself feel it. Because this? This isn't over. Not even close. And when she's ready, when she feels safe enough to let me in—I'll be waiting.

CHAPTER 17

Mariana

The dough beneath my hands was too warm. Too sticky. Too much of a damn mess. I gritted my teeth, kneading harder, trying to work it into something salvageable, but it wasn't cooperating.

Neither was my body. The stiffness in my fingers had started earlier. A dull, familiar ache spread through my joints, making every movement feel heavier than it should. I ignored it. I had work to do, things to fix, recipes to perfect.

The pain wasn't the worst part. No, it was the fatigue. That creeping, marrow-deep exhaustion that wasn't just tiredness. It was a shutdown. A refusal. My body's way of reminding me I wasn't in control of it anymore. I hated it.

I hated that even after everything, even after I'd worked so hard to rebuild myself, my own body was still working against me. Simple things—kneading dough, rolling out pastry, lifting a bag of flour—tasks that used to be second nature now drained me completely.

The things I used to do without a second thought, the things that once felt tedious, now felt impossible. Every movement stole a little more of my energy, like my body was hoarding it, rationing it out like I wasn't capable of deciding for myself.

The way it chipped away at me wasn't just physical—it was mental. How do you come to terms with feeling trapped in your own body? How do you not resent the fact that the things that once took zero effort now demand everything from you? The exhaustion isn't just something you feel—it becomes part of you, shaping your days, your choices, your future.

I leaned my weight into the dough, pressing down harder, fighting against the growing tremor in my hands. I wasn't weak. I wasn't fragile. I could handle this. I could handle anything. I always did.

The bakery was quiet, just the hum of the ovens and the occasional creak of the old pipes. I should have gone home an hour ago, but I wasn't ready to face the silence there. I wasn't ready to sit alone with my thoughts.

Sebastian. I could still feel the almost kiss hanging between us, the way his breath brushed against my skin, the way my whole body had locked up like I'd been yanked in time.

I hadn't meant to flinch, but I had, and he noticed. I hated that the memory made my chest feel tight, like my ribs were pressing in too hard. It wasn't his fault. It wasn't about him. But I knew Seba. He'd be thinking about it. Overanalyzing each moment. Picking every second apart.

The front door chimed, and I jolted, my hands still buried in the dough. For a second, I assumed it was Analyse, only she would ignore the "Closed" sign like it didn't apply to her.

But when I turned, it wasn't her...it was him. Seba stood in the doorway, I exhaled, keeping my hands moving. Or, I guess, *two* people. "You're supposed to be home."

"So are you." Seba's voice was calm, but I knew him well enough to hear the undercurrent beneath it. The quiet concern.

I didn't look up. "I'm working."

He was silent for a bit. Then, the sound of footsteps, slow, deliberate. I could feel him watching me, studying me, waiting for me to crack first.

I kept kneading. The dough was warm, but my fingers were stiff and uncooperative. I could feel the staring, the way my knuckles resisted every moment, but I gritted my teeth and kept going.

Then, Seba reached out and stilled my hands. Not rough or demanding, just gentle, sure, impossible to ignore. "Mariana." His voice was quieter this time. "You're in pain."

I tensed, the words cutting straight through me. I didn't like that he could tell. I didn't like that he saw something I hadn't even said out loud. I pulled my hands from his grip and wiped them on my apron. "I'm fine."

Seba exhaled, slow and even. "You always say that when you're not."

My jaw locked. "And what, you think you know better than me?"

His expression didn't change. "I think you're stubborn."

I huffed, turning back to the dough, "That's not news."

"Mariana."

The way he said my name was low and steady, not giving me an inch of space to run from it. It made something shift in my chest. I swallowed. Kept kneading.

"Did you eat today?" he asked,

I didn't answer, not out of stubbornness, but because I couldn't remember.

Seba sighed, stepping around the counter and closing the space between us. "You do this, you know. Work yourself into exhaustion and then pretend like it's fine. Ignore your body until it forces you to stop." His eyes flicked to my hands, then back to my face. He saw too much. He always had. But I wasn't fragile. I wasn't someone who needed to be saved.

"I don't need you to take care of me," I muttered.

Seba's jaw ticked. "I never said you did."

The words hung between us, thick and heavy. I should tell him to leave. I should turn away, but for some reason, I just can't. I won't. Instead, I sighed, pressing the heels of my palms into the counter. "I was diagnosed with lupus after Andrew died."

The words were quiet, but they hit the air like a crack of thunder. Seba stilled. I didn't look at him. I didn't want to see whatever was written across his face.

"I started feeling off months before," I said, keeping my voice even. "Fatigue and joint pain, but I ignored it. I thought it was stress taking its toll on my body." I exhaled sharply. "Then I collapsed one day while at work, and landed myself in the hospital, and gave everyone a scare. That's when they figured it out."

I finally turn to meet his eyes. They were steady, unreadable. Waiting. "So yeah." I crossed my arms. "I have lupus. No, there's no cure."

My arms tighten across my chest, the words leaving me automatically, practiced—I've said them a hundred times before.

"I just have to live with it. I take it day by day."

Seba didn't say anything right away. He just watched me, and it made me feel like I wanted to crawl out of my skin.

Please, please, please, don't pity me. Don't change what you think about me. When I couldn't take any more of the silence, I snapped, "What? The word came out sharper than I intended, edged with frustration, but I didn't care. I just need him to *say* something.

His head tilted slightly. "I was just wondering how long you were going to carry that by yourself."

I blinked. My throat went tight, "I'm not-"

"You are." His voice wasn't accusing. He was just being him, honest, factual. My pulse thrummed, too fast, too loud.

"I don't need a caretaker," I whispered.

Seba exhaled, shaking his head. "That's not what I'm trying to be."

"Then what are you trying to be then, Seba? Enlighten me, please."

His eyes held mine. Unwavering. "Mariana, don't you get it? I want to be everything for you. I want to be the person who cares for you. The one who takes care of you, not because you need me, but because I need you. I want to be the one who holds your secrets, your safe place, the man you can count on. There isn't a single damn thing I don't want to be for you. If you just let me. If you just open up and admit that what we had didn't end the night you left. That we've been frozen in time, waiting for each other. Let me be everything for you, Mariana. Please. I beg you. Let me be yours."

And that undoes me. Tears begin streaming down the sides of my face. "Seba, there's more that I need to tell you."

Seba watches me, his hands resting on the counter, his body still, like he knows if he moves too fast, I might bolt. What he doesn't realize is that I can't bolt. I'm rooted here. With him. "You don't have to tell me," he says quietly.

My throat closes. I don't know how to say what I need to say—what he needs to know if this is ever going to become anything. I don't know if he'll look at me differently once he does. God, I hope not. But I know that I have to tell him.

I've spent so long pretending it wasn't real, ignoring the memories when they surface, convincing myself that if I just keep moving, it can't catch me. But it's here now. Waiting. Seba doesn't speak. He just waits. Patient. Gentle. Unmoving. The most patient, gentle, loving man.

I exhale, slow and shaky, pressing my palms against the counter. "My ex-husband..." I don't realize how hard it is to say it out loud until I do. The words sit in the air like lead. Too heavy. Too real. "He used to hurt me."

143

Seba goes still. Not just physically, but something in him sharpens, locks into place. But he doesn't speak. He doesn't do anything that might stop me from finally saying the words I have never said out loud.

"At first, it started out small," I whisper. "He'd want me home by a certain time. Want me to keep my location on, just so he could 'feel safe.'" I let out a brittle laugh. God, how many times did I believe that lie?

Seba doesn't move, but I feel his pulse thudding through the air between us.

"After I married him, it got worse. He began to isolate me from everyone, claiming that it was to keep our marriage sacred. That the outside world wouldn't understand a love like ours, that they'd be jealous, that they'd try to break us up." I swallow hard, my nails digging into my palms. "He had people follow me."

Seba's breath hitches.

"He would tell me where I'd been, who I'd spoken to. And if he didn't like my answer..." My voice catches.

Seba stiffens.

I force the rest of the words out. "He constantly called me names, told me no one would ever want me. That I was disgusting, a pig. A waste of space."

Seba's hands curl into fists.

I should stop now. I should stop because if I keep going, if I say the rest of what I have to say, there's no taking them back. But I can't stop, because he has to know. "Then, he began to hit me."

Seba's entire body locks up. Like he's been frozen solid. Not a twitch, not a breath, not a single sound. The anger rolls off him like waves crashing against the rock.

He doesn't shout, doesn't swear, doesn't throw anything. He just stands there, still, silent—like he knows that if he moves, if he speaks, he will break something.

"And I stayed," I whisper.

Seba squeezes his eyes shut.

"I stayed for years. Even when it got bad." I stare at the countertop, shame creeping up my throat. "I thought it was my fault," I admit. "I thought if I just stayed small enough, quiet enough, obedient enough...it would eventually stop."

Seba shakes his head. A slow, subtle movement. Like he can't bear to hear it, but he forces himself to listen anyway.

"But it never stopped," I murmured. My fingers curl against the counter. "It only got worse, so much worse. To the point where I didn't know how I was going to survive." I swallowed hard, my voice barely above a whisper. "And then...he died."

Seba's eyes snap to mine.

"He went out drinking that night," I say, voice hoarse. "I was so relieved to have some space from him—but also terrified because I knew what it meant. Drinking always made it worse, and in the morning, he'd play it off like he didn't remember, like he wasn't himself when we both knew that wasn't true."

I swallow hard, "But that night, he overdid it. Drank too much. And, of course, he didn't call an Uber—he never would. He was too proud of that. So he got behind the wheel, rammed his car into a pole, and died on impact." Seba exhales, slow and measured.

I take a trembling breath. "Thank goodness he didn't hurt anyone else."

Seba doesn't speak. He doesn't interrupt. He doesn't tell me that I should've left or that I should've known better. I have spent so long pretending that I was fine, that I could handle everything, that I was strong enough. And yet, the moment I was finally free of him? My body stopped pretending.

I let out a hollow laugh, one that doesn't quite feel like my own. "Isn't that ironic?"

Seba's brow furrows.

"All those years I spent with him, convincing myself it was fine," I whisper. "That I could handle everything, That I could take it, that eventually he'd stop." I exhale sharply. "And the second I was free? My body gave up on me."

Seba's jaw tightens. But he doesn't argue or dismiss it. Because he knows this is my truth.

"Mariana," His voice is softer now. Like he's afraid of breaking me. My stomach twists. I don't want pity. I don't want to be looked at like something fragile.

"I'm not broken," I bite out.

Seba moves before I can stop him. His hands come up, framing my face, thumbs brushing against my cheekbones.

"I know," he murmurs.

That's when I break. He doesn't pull me in, he doesn't press, but he's there, waiting. He's letting me decide, and so I do—I close the space between us, lifting onto my toes, pressing my lips to his.

The second I do, everything crashes, the grief, the fear. The weight of everything I have held in for so long. Seba exhales against my mouth, his hands sliding into my hair, holding me steady as I shatter.

The kiss is slow, deep, aching. Like a promise, like a new beginning. He moves with me. Not demanding or forceful. Just there, holding, reassuring, unraveling every tightly wound thread inside me.

I don't know how to do this. How to love without fear. But with Seba? It doesn't feel like fear at all. It feels like coming home.

Seba presses his forehead to mine, his breath warm, steady. "You're safe," he murmurs.

CHAPTER 18

Sebastian

After that kiss in the bakery, we barely made it to my house. The drive is a blur filled with stolen glances, breathless laughter, the heat of her hand in mine, squeezing, holding, like she's afraid to let go. Like if she does, this moment might disappear.

I steal glimpses of her in the passing streetlights—flushed cheeks, swollen lips, eyes dark with something unreadable. Wanting. Waiting.

Every second stretches between us, thick with anticipation, with everything we've held back for so damn long. By the time I pull into the driveway, my grip on the steering wheel is too tight, my pulse too loud, my body too aware that she's right there.

We barely make it inside before we're on each other again. It's not careful or slow. It's years of tension snapping all at once, years of wanting, years of holding back crashing into this single, undeniable moment.

Mariana's hands are in my hair, gripping, pulling, dragging me deeper. Her mouth is urgent, searching. And I fucking let her. Because I know this isn't just about wanting me, but about finally letting herself have something good. Something safe. Something that she wants, not something she's afraid of.

I press her against the wall, my hands skimming down her sides, gripping her waist. She gasps into my mouth, her fingers fisting the fabric of my shirt, like she can't get close enough.

My hands slide beneath her thighs, lifting her with ease— like they remember every inch of her, like touching her is something I was never meant to forget.

She wraps herself around me, locking her legs at my waist, fitting against me like she's always belonged there. I begin to rub against her core. Her breath is ragged, her lips hot, reckless, demanding. Fuck, I never want this moment to end.

But then, she stills. Just for a second, but enough that I feel it, enough that I know. I slow instantly, my grip on her loosening, softening.

Her breath shudders against my lips, and I pull back just enough to see her. Her eyes are wild, dark, stormy. But beneath it all is fear. Not of me—Never of me, but of herself, of this, of what it means to finally want something again.

I cup her face, thumb brushing along her cheekbone. "Mariana," I murmur, voice low, steady. "We don't have to rush. We'll go at whatever pace feels right for you. I'm here, and I'm not going anywhere."

Her fingers tighten against my chest. She shakes her head, swallowing hard. "I don't want to stop." Her voice is so quiet. But so damn sure. She's not running. She's choosing this. She's choosing me.

I kiss her again, but this time, it's different. It's slower, deeper, memorizing every second of this. My hands move carefully over her, like she's something rare, not because she's fragile, but because she hasn't been treated like she should be. And I'll be damned if I don't make her feel it now.

With shaking hands, I lift her shirt above her head,

revealing her delicate curves and the soft skin of her neck. My fingers graze her collarbone and she shudders at my touch.

Her eyes meet mine, dark pools of desire, and I can feel the heat emanating from her body. As she begins unbuttoning my jeans, my own breaths quicken and my heart pounds, aching for her.

Our bodies intertwine, limbs tangled and hearts racing. I lay her gently onto my bed, her skin warm against mine, and I can't help but marvel at the beauty lying beneath me. She arches her back, pressing her body against mine, and I can feel her need for me. I'm aching for her touch, my body trembling with anticipation.

Our lips crash together, re-exploring each other's mouth. My hands caress her sides as I slowly peel away her remaining clothes, revealing more of her flawless skin. Fuck, she's perfect. She tugs at my shirt and I help her remove it, our lips barely parting. Soon, we're both bare, skin against skin, drinking in the sight of each other.

I trail kisses down her neck, savoring her soft sighs. My lips find her breasts, teasing and tasting as she arches into me. Her fingers tangle in my hair, urging me on.

I kiss lower, across her stomach, her hips. She gasps as my mouth reaches her center, her thighs trembling. I explore her folds with my tongue, savoring her sweetness as she writhes beneath me. Her fingers grip the sheets as I circle and flick, alternating pressure and speed.

I can feel the tension building in her body as her breaths come faster. She moans my name, spurring me on. I slide two fingers inside her, curling them as I continue to taste her. Her hips buck against my face as I find that perfect spot. She's close now, her whole body quivering.

I increase my pace, drinking in her gasps and cries of pleasure. Suddenly, she stiffens, back arching off the bed. A long, low moan escaped her lips as waves of ecstasy crashed over her.

I hold her hips, not letting up until the last tremors subside. She collapses back onto the bed, chest heaving.

I kiss my way back up her body, savoring the saltiness of her skin. Her eyes flutter open as I reach her face, a dreamy smile playing on her lips. She pulls me down for a deep, languid kiss, tasting herself on my tongue.

Her hands roam my back, nails lightly scratching, sending shivers down my spine. I groan into her mouth as she wraps her legs around my waist, pulling me closer.

The heat between us is electric, every point of contact igniting sparks across my skin. She rolls us over suddenly, straddling my hips. Her hair falls in a curtain around us as she leans down to kiss me again. I run my hands up her thighs, relishing the softness of her skin. She grinds against me teasingly, drawing a low moan from my throat.

Slowly, tortuously, she pulls me up to her, our bodies sliding against each other as she captures my lips in a searing kiss. I can feel the aftershocks of her pleasure still rippling through her body. Her hands roam my back, nails lightly scratching, sending shivers down my spine.

Slowly, deliberately, she rocks her hips against mine. I groan at the sensation, my hands gripping her thighs. She continues her languid movements, building the friction between us. Her breasts sway enticingly and I can't resist reaching up to cup them, thumbs brushing over her sensitive peaks. She gasps, arching into my touch.

She rocks her hips slowly, sliding along my length. I can feel how ready she is, her wetness coating me.

Her eyes lock with mine, pupils blown wide with lust. I grip her hips, urging her on. With agonizing slowness, she lifts herself up and then sinks down onto me. We both gasp at the sensation as she takes me in fully. She's so tight, so hot around me. I fight to keep my eyes open, not wanting to miss a moment of her beauty.

She begins to move at a slow, deliberate pace. Her breasts swaying with each roll of her hips. I reach up to cup them, thumbs circling her nipples. She moans, head falling back as she arches into my touch. Her nipples harden under my fingertips as I caress and knead her soft flesh.

She leans into my hands, quickening her pace slightly. I can feel every inch of her as she rises and falls, her inner walls gripping me tightly. The friction is incredible, sending waves of pleasure through my body with each movement.

I thrust up to meet her, matching her rhythm. Our bodies move together in perfect synchronicity like we were made for each other. Like she was made for me.

She braces her hands on my chest, nails digging in slightly as she grinds down harder. I groan at the sensation, my hands moving to grip her hips. Her skin glistens with a fine sheen of sweat, giving her an ethereal glow in the dim light. I'm mesmerized by the sight of her above me—head thrown back in ecstasy, lips parted as breathy moans escape.

Her movements become more urgent as passion overtakes us both. I sit up, wrapping my arms around her to pull her flush against me. Our lips meet in a searing kiss, tongues tangling as we breathe each other's air.

She grinds down harder, taking me impossibly deeper. I groan into her mouth, overwhelmed by the sensation. My hands roam her back, tracing the curve of her spine. Her fingers tangle in my hair, tugging gently as she breaks the kiss to trail her lips along my jaw.

Heat builds between us, coiling tighter with each roll of her hips. I can feel her trembling in my arms, so close to the edge. I slide a hand between our bodies, fingers finding that sensitive bundle of nerves. She cries out at my touch, her rhythm faltering.

"Let go," I murmured against her neck. "I've got you."

My words seem to shatter the last of her restraint. She

arches against me, crying out as waves of pleasure crash over her. I hold her close, drinking in every gasp and shudder. Her inner muscles clench around me rhythmically, pulling me deeper. It pushes me to my own peak and I follow her over the edge with a deep groan.

For long moments, we stay locked together, our ragged breathing the only sound in the dim room. Slowly, the tension drains from her body and she collapses against my chest. I stroke her back gently, savoring the silky feel of her skin.

The sweet fragrance of cherries in her hair blends with the lingering musk of our passion, a heady mix of warmth, skin, and something undeniably us.

The air is thick with warmth, heavy with the scent of her skin and the remnants of everything we just shared. Mariana is curled against me, her body soft but not fully at ease. I feel it in the way she shifts every few seconds, in the way her fingers twitch, in the almost imperceptible wince when she moves her arm. She's sore and in pain. I know she won't say a word about it because she never does. So I do what she won't ask for. I take care of her.

I press a kiss to her temple, then carefully slip out of bed. She makes a sleepy, half-protesting sound, her fingers barely gripping my arm as if to pull me back. "I'll be right back," I murmur. "Close your eyes."

She doesn't. Of course, she doesn't. She's stubborn as hell. Instead, she watches me as I disappear into the bathroom, her gaze unreadable, lingering. I run warm water over a towel, wringing it out until it's just the right amount of heat. Not scalding, but warm enough to soothe.

When I return, she's still watching me. I sit beside her, gently pressing the warm towel to her skin. She inhales sharply, her breath catching at the sudden heat.

I drag it slowly over her, wiping the remnants of us away. She watches me the entire time. Not stopping me, not speaking. Just letting me do this for her. Her fingers twitch against the sheets, like she's not used to being cared for like this. I press the towel to her hip, brushing my thumb along the inside of her thigh, soothing, not teasing.

"Okay?" I murmur.

She swallows. Nods. Her voice is barely there when she whispers, "Yeah."

But I don't miss the way her body finally relaxes. I set the towel aside and reached for the bottle of oil I had grabbed earlier. Lavender and eucalyptus, calming, warming.

I pour some into my palms, rubbing them together, heating the liquid before I touch her. Her eyes flutter closed as I start with her hands, kneading gently and working out the tension in her fingers and her knuckles. I don't rush. I don't speak. I just learn her this way, with my hands.

With every slow, deliberate press of my thumbs into the joints I know ache, into the places she won't admit are hurting. She melts under the touch, her breath evening out, her fingers twitching slightly but no longer with tension.

I work my way to her wrists, applying just enough pressure to ease the stiffness, feeling the way she exhales, the way she sinks deeper into the pillows. By the time I reach her elbows, she lets out a soft, broken exhale. A sound that hits me harder than anything else.

I shift lower, lifting one of her legs into my lap. She tenses. Not from fear or hesitation, but from somewhere deeper. She's never had anyone do this for her. She's used to handling everything alone. She's used to pretending it doesn't hurt.

I move slowly, rubbing the oil into her calves, over her knees, up to her thighs, feeling the stiffness, the swelling beneath my hands. She exhales sharply, a mix of pain and relief.

This is more than just touch. This is healing. This is

undoing years of neglect, of her pushing through the pain alone. This is her letting me in.

"Mariana," I murmur.

She swallows hard.

I cup her face, holding her steady, "You're safe," I whisper. I pull her against me, her body curling into mine, her breath steady but fragile. Her fingers rest against my chest, tracing lazy circles over my skin.

"You didn't have to do this," she whispers.

I press a slow kiss on her hair. "Yeah, I did."

She's silent for a moment. Then, barely above a whisper, she says, "Thank you."

I close my eyes, exhaling. "Always."

CHAPTER 19

Mariana

The firehouse came into view as Sebastian pulled into the lot, the smell of grilled meat and charcoal thick in the air. Laughter and music spilled from the backyard, where familiar voices mixed with the occasional clang of a spatula against the grill.

Through the windshield, I spotted Analyse standing with a drink in hand, chatting with Mateo, while Maya ran in circles around them, a blur of pink sneakers and wild curls. My stomach flipped. We were really doing this.

Seba must have felt it because his fingers suddenly slid over mine, warm and steady, anchoring me. "You ready to shock the hell out of them, Mi Tesoro?" he asked, amusement lacing his voice.

I turned to look at him, at that smug, boyish grin that made me want to roll my eyes and kiss him at the same time. "Oh, they're not ready."

He grinned, but before I could even reach for the door handle, his grip on my hand tightened slightly. "Don't open your door," he said, already unbuckling.

I frowned. "Why-"

He was out of the car before I could finish the question, jogging around to my side.

By the time he pulled open the door, a satisfied smirk on his face, I was equal parts amused and exasperated.

"Seriously?" I asked, biting back a smile.

He shrugged, offering me his hand. "What? Sue me for having manners, princesa."

I rolled my eyes but took his hand anyway. And just like that, we were stepping into the firehouse chaos—together.

"OH MY GOSH!" Maya shrieked before we even made it fully into the yard, stopping mid-run, hands on her hips, "Are you Tío Seb's girlfriend?!"

The entire backyard went silent. Analyse turned, eyes wide, followed by a slow, wicked grin. Mateo and Andres, big, loud and completely incapable of minding their own damn business, whipped their heads toward us.

Sebastian groaned. "Maya!"

She gasped dramatically, "Oh! Are you getting Married?! Tío Seb and Mari sitting in the tree, k-i-ss-i-n-g."

Laughter erupted. Someone whistled. Someone else cheered.

Sebastian sighed, rubbing his face, but I was too busy laughing to care. Analyse arched a brow, arms crossed. "So, Do I get to say 'I told you so' now, or...?"

Sebastian shot her a look, then turned back to Maya, who was standing in front of them now. Sebastian scooped Maya up, spinning her in the air and making her squeal with laughter. "Maya, you little troublemaker, are you trying to put me on the spot?"

She giggled, wrapping her arms around his neck. "Just answer the question, Tío Seb!!"

He sighed dramatically, giving me a playful look before turning back to her. "Alright, alright. If I say yes, do I get extra bbq?"

Maya gasped. "YES! You do like her! I knew it!"

The backyard erupted into cheers and laughter as Sebastian groaned, setting her down. "Now you've done it, bebecita; they're never going to let me live this down."

As the BBQ went on, I found myself caught in the flow of it all. Sitting with Analyse as she teased Seba mercilessly. Laughing as the guys tried to out-grill each other, each claiming their steak seasoning was superior. Holding Maya on my hip as she told me all about her favorite bedtime stories. As the sun dipped lower, casting a golden light over the yard, Seba pulled me aside, away from the noise.

"You okay?" he asked, his hand settling on my waist.

I nodded, watching as Maya chased Mateo around with a styrofoam sword. I guess she's a warrior princess. "Yeah. I am."

His thumb brushed against my hip, slow and steady. "Good. Because I don't plan on letting you go this time."

My heart clenched. I look up at him, at the way the fading sunlight softened the sharp edges of his face, and I let myself believe that maybe everything really would be okay. He kissed me then, slow and deep. A promise made through his touch, a promise I was finally letting myself believe.

The sun had set, and the crackling fire cast a warm glow over the fire pit, the flickering light dancing across our faces. The night air was crisp, but the flames and the scent of roast marshmallows made everything feel cozy.

Most of the crowd had gone, leaving just me, Analyse, Seb, Mateo, Andres, and their Captain, Nathan, relaxing around the fire, passing around the last of the s'mores.

Maya, still buzzing from way too much sugar, suddenly ran over, gasping, "Tío Seb!" barreling toward him at full speed. "I just remembered! You have to give Mari a prize!"

Sebastian, who had been mid-bite into a s'more, barely managed a swallow before arching an eyebrow at her. "Was I supposed to give Mariana a prize?"

Maya planted her hands on her hips, the offended look on her face priceless. "Uh yea, Tio." She lets out an exasperated sigh, crossing her arms tight over her chest, clearly disappointed in his lack of common sense. "You're supposed to give her a prize because she's your girlfriend now."

Andres chimes in, humor in his tone, "Yeah, she's gonna need a prize for dealing with you."

A chuckle ripped through the group, and I couldn't help the stop that spread across my face as Maya turned her attention to me, "Did he give you a prize yet, Mari?"

I bit my lip, glancing at Seb, who was watching me with that damn smirk that made my stomach flip. "Not yet," I said, playing along, tilting my head, my expression feigning concern. "Should I be worried?"

Maya gasps, horrified, and says solemnly, "Oh yes, you should be. This is serious, Mari!" She whirls back toward Sebastian, jabbing her tiny finger in his direction. "Tio, I'm going to tell abuela. You have to give her a prize right away!"

Sebastian scrubbed a hand over his jaw, clearly amused. "And what kind of prize do you think she deserves."

Maya taps a marshmallow-covered finger to her chin, deep in thought. "Hmm..." she says. Then, her face lights up. "A princess crown! Because Mari is a princess!" she declares.

Andres nearly chokes on his beer, while Mateo bursts out laughing. Sebastian shot them both a look before turning back to Maya with a solemn nod. "You're absolutely right, cariñito. Mariana definitely deserves a crown."

I raised an eyebrow, smirking. "Oh? And where exactly are you going to find one?"

Sebastian leaned in, dropping his voice low enough for

only me to hear. "I can think of a few ways to make you feel like a queen later."

Heat rushed to my cheeks instantly. I elbowed him lightly, half-glaring, half-blushing. "Behave."

He winked. "Not a chance."

Meanwhile, Maya had already moved on, twirling around the fire pit, still giddy with excitement. Analyse shook her head, laughing. "Alright, alright, you two, enough corrupting my daughter."

She faces Maya, so much love in her eyes, "Mamita, we have to get going, okay? It is wayyy past your bedtime."

Maya groans. "Ahh mami, but I'm not even tired!" Stifling a yawn.

Analyse laughs, "Sure you're not, mi amorcito. Come on, let's get going." She lifts Maya into her arms, waves goodbye to everyone, and begins to walk toward her car.

Sebastian pulls me in closer as the fire crackles between us, warm and cozy, but it was his touch that I felt the most. I let out a slow breath, sinking into him, into this. For once, I'm not bracing for the other shoe to drop.

CHAPTER 20
Mariana

The fluorescent lights hummed softly above us, the steady beep-beep-beep of the heart monitor filling the quiet room. The hospital smelled like illness and stale coffee, the scent clinging to my clothes, making my stomach turn.

But none of that matters, not when mami lay still in the hospital bed, her frame small and frail against the crisp white sheets.

Sebastian's fingers tighten around mine, grounding me as I hesitated just inside the doorway. "You okay?" he murmured, voice low.

I swallowed hard. Was I okay? No. Not really. But I nodded anyway.

Her eyes fluttered open at the sound of our voices, tired but still sharp with recognition. For a second, I could almost believe she wasn't sick, that she wasn't slipping further away from me every day.

Her lips curved into a weak smile when she saw me, but when her gaze drifted to Sebastian standing beside me, her smile faltered, then widened. "Mija..." Her voice was thin but warm. "You came with Sebastian?"

I let out a breath I hadn't realized I was holding. "Si, mami. He came here with me."

Sebastian stepped forward, his usual confidence tempered with quiet respect. "Hi, Señora Vargas," he said, his voice softer than I'd ever heard it.

Mami scoffed, shifting slightly against the pillows. "Señora Vargas? Ay, Sebastian, after all these years, you're still calling me that? Dios mio, I changed your diapers, muchacho. You're like a son to me."

A small, surprised laugh left me, and even Sebastian cracked a grin.

"Fair point," he admitted. "Bendicion, mami."

Her gaze flickers between the two of us, something thoughtful settling in her expression. "So, out with it, since you both are here, does that mean you're together?

I hesitated, but Sebastian didn't even bat an eye. He turned his head, catching my gaze, and then looked back at her. "Yeah. We are."

Mami exhaled slowly, her eyes softening. "Bueno."

Just that, not I told you so, not it took you long enough— Just bueno, typical mami. It felt like everything was settling into place exactly as it was meant to.

Tears burned the back of my throat, but I forced myself to blink them away as I reached for her hand, careful with how delicate her skin had become. Reality setting in on how little time we have left together leaves me mourning all of the time I let pass us by.

"We never should have let so much time pass," I whispered.

She squeezed my fingers weakly. "Sometimes, mi amor, love is just waiting for us to be ready."

I bit my lip, glancing at Sebastian, whose expression was

unreadable, his hand still wrapped around mine, and I knew that he was thinking the same thing I was. We had lost so much time, spent years apart, living separate lives.

But now? I knew one thing for certain. I never wanted to live apart from him again. A comfortable silence settled between us, the warmth of Sebastian's palm against mine.

Then, Sebastian shifted beside me and cleared his throat. "Mariana," he murmured, squeezing my hand before letting go. "Would you mind grabbing us some coffee?"

I blinked, tilting my head, "You drink hospital coffee now?"

His lips quirked up, but his eyes remained serious. "I just want to talk to your mom about something."

Something flickered in my chest—curiosity, hesitation. But when I glanced at my mom, she was already watching him, her expression unreadable. Whatever this was, it wasn't something I was meant to hear.

I swallowed, nodding. "Okay."

I leaned down, pressing a soft kiss to Mami's cheek before slipping past Sebastian, my fingers grazing his arm as I moved toward the door. The door clicked shut behind me, leaving Sebastian and Mami alone.

CHAPTER 21

Sebastian

The firehouse was quiet, the rare lull between calls where the guys either caught up on sleep or found new ways to waste time. The familiar hum of the overhead lights and the distant sound of a radio playing from the locker room filled the space, but my focus was on the half-empty water bottle I rolled between my palms, my mind somewhere else entirely. I was leaning against the counter in the kitchen when I heard footsteps approaching.

"Alright, Garcia," Mateo drawled, dropping into the seat across from me with a lazy smirk. "You've been suspiciously quiet today. That's not like you. Spill."

Andres strolled in behind him, arms crossed over his chest, grinning like he already knew the answer. "I think we all know why."

I sighed, already regretting telling these idiots anything. "I have no idea what you're talking about."

Mateo snorted. "Oh, come on. Don't play dumb. You're practically wagging your tail like a damn golden retriever every time someone mentions Mariana's name."

Andres nudged me with his elbow. "So? How's it going?

You guys official-official now? Or are you just still figuring shit out?"

I rolled my eyes, but the smile I tried to fight off still crept up. "Yeah, we're together. It's really good."

Mateo raised an eyebrow. "Good? Just good? Because you look like a guy who just won the lottery, and I highly doubt it's because of the overtime pay."

I let out a breath, shaking my head. "Fine. It's better than good. It's everything, man."

And that was the truth. I hadn't felt this settled, this right, in years. Being with Mariana again wasn't just some nostalgic trip down memory lane, it was something real. Something that made the world feel less heavy.

"Damn," Andres muttered, shaking his head. "Look at him. Completely gone."

"Tragic, really," Mateo added, sighing dramatically. "I never thought I'd see the day when Sebastian Garcia became the poster boy for hopeless romantics."

I shot him a look. "I will throw this water at you."

Mateo smirked. Andres laughed, clapping a hand on my shoulder. "Nah, man, it's good. You deserve this. She's always been it for you, huh?"

I swallowed, my chest tightening at the weight of that truth. "Yeah. She has always been."

Before either of them could grill me further, Nathan walked in, eyeing the three of us with his usual calm, assessing gaze. "What's going on here?"

"Oh, you know," Mateo said, grinning. "Just watching Garcia turn into a goddamn Hallmark movie."

Nathan's brows lifted slightly. "Mariana, huh?"

I nodded. "Yeah."

He was silent for a beat, then exhaled slowly. "I'm happy for you, man. Really."

I smiled. "Thanks, Cap."

"But..." Nathan continued, his voice even and careful. "Just be smart about it."

I frowned. "What do you mean?"

Nathan crossed his arms, leaning against the wall. "I mean, she left before. You ever wonder if she might do it again?"

My jaw tightened. "She was eighteen. She wanted to experience college in a new city. That's not the same as just...leaving. She came back. She bought the damn bakery. She's building a life here."

Nathan nodded, but his gaze didn't waver. "She didn't have to break up with you to do that."

The air in the kitchen shifted, the easy banter from earlier snuffed out like a flame. Mateo cleared his throat, clearly wanting no part in this conversation.

Andres, ever the peacemaker, clapped me on the back. "Nathan's just looking out for you, man. We all are."

Nathan held up a hand. "I'm not saying she doesn't love you. I'm just saying don't let the past repeat itself. You've always been the all-in type, Garcia. Just make sure she's all-in, too."

I exhale sharply, running a hand through my hair. "I trust her."

Nathan nodded. "I trust your judgment, man. We all care about you and just want to make sure you're being careful. Not getting too caught up too quickly."

The tension in my chest didn't ease, but I forced myself to nod. "Yeah. I hear you."

Nathan clapped me on the shoulder once before heading for the door. "Good. Now, quit hogging the kitchen. Some of us actually need to eat."

Mateo and Andres exchanged a glance, both wisely deciding not to say anything else as they followed him out, leaving me alone in the kitchen with way too many thoughts running around my head.

~

Laying in my bed at the firehouse, my thumb hovers over her name in my call log. I hit dial, bringing the phone up to my ear. She picked up after the second ring.

"Hey, Seba." Her voice was warm and soft, and just like that, the tension that I'd been carrying eased. I exhaled, a small smile tugging at my lips. "Hey, hermosa. What are you doing Friday night?"

A pause. Then, a quiet, amused laugh. "Why? You asking me on a date?"

I stretched out on the cot, staring up at the ceiling. "You know it, baby."

She hummed, and I could picture the smirk on her lips. "And what exactly do you have planned?"

I grinned. "I can't tell you all my secrets, Mi tesoro."

She huffed out a laugh. "Mysterious. I like it."

I closed my eyes, letting myself sink into the warmth of her voice. "So, is that a yes?"

A beat of silence, then—"Yeah, Seba. That's a yes."

CHAPTER 22

Mariana

The past few weeks have been a blur, like slipping into a life I thought I'd lost. Being with Sebastian again feels effortless, like muscle memory, like something that was always meant to be.

We've been spending time together—long walks through town, late-night drives with no destination, mornings in my bakery.

We've visited my mom, too, sitting by her bedside, sharing quiet moments where she just watches us with that knowing look in her eyes.

Analyse and Maya have become a regular presence in my days—the easy way Analyse teases Sebastian, reminding me of how much history I've missed out on.

I've been getting to know the guys at the firehouse more, too—spending time around them, seeing the way they laugh, the way they look out for each other, the way they care about him. About us.

And now, as I sit beside Sebastian in his truck, the road stretching ahead of us, it all feels surreal. Like the past is no longer something looming behind us, but something we are finally rewriting.

The trees lining the winding road blurred past the window, and in the quiet hum of the truck's engine, I could feel my heartbeat in my throat. Sebastian's fingers drummed lightly against the steering wheel, his other hand resting on the gearshift.

Every so often, his eyes lingered on me, his fingers tapping against the steering wheel in time with whatever thoughts he wasn't saying out loud.

"You're being suspiciously quiet," I said, my voice lighter than I felt.

He smirked, keeping his eyes on the road. "I just don't want to spoil the surprise."

I huffed out a laugh, but it wasn't forced. He always did that. He always had a way of making things feel easier than they were. "A surprise, huh? You really went all out for this date, didn't you? You know we've already dated before, right?"

He shot me a sideways glance, a look that used to make my knees weak back when we were teenagers. "Not like this, we haven't."

I bit my lip, trying not to smile too wide. This was dangerous. Being with him, letting myself relax into this moment. It felt too easy.

When he pulled into the clearing, my stomach tightened. The lake stretched out before us, the moonlight glinting off the water just like it had when we were younger.

I stared at the dock, the gentle glow of lanterns casting warm light over the wooden planks, the soft setup of blankets and pillows, the small boat tied up like it had been all those years ago. A lump formed in my throat.

"Seba...is this...?"

He grinned, unbuckling his seatbelt, "Our spot? Yeah. I thought it was time we came back."

I swallowed hard, my fingers gripping the edge of my seat. "I can't believe you remembered."

He stepped out and walked around the truck, opening my door before I could move. "Mariana," he murmured, offering his hand. "When it comes to you, I remember everything."

I stared at him for a second too long before taking his hand, his warmth steadying me as I stepped down onto the grass. The dock creaked under our weight as we walked toward the setup he had arranged.

I glanced at the boat, at the way the water lapped gently against the shore, and I let out a breathy laugh. "You're actually serious."

He pulled a beer from the cooler, popped the cap, and handed it to me. "When am I not?"

I shook my head, amused. "You're ridiculous."

He grinned. "And yet, you're still here."

I rolled my eyes but clinked my bottle against his anyway. "I sure am. To old memories."

He held my gaze, something deeper flickering behind his eyes. "To new ones."

My breath caught, and for a second, I forgot how to exhale. We sat on the dock, picking at the food he had packed, the conversation flowing easily. It always was with him, effortless, no matter how much time had passed.

But there was something different about it now. There was a weight behind every laugh, every glance. The past was still there, lingering between us, but it didn't feel suffocating. It felt like something we could rewrite.

After a while, he stood, extending a hand to me. "Come on."

I raised an eyebrow. "Come on where?"

"We're taking the boat out."

I hesitated. "Our boat?" The words felt strange on my tongue, heavy with memories.

Sebastian held my gaze, nodding once. "Yeah. Our boat."

He must have sensed my unease because his voice softened. "Trust me."

And that was the thing with Sebastian, I always did. I let him lead me to the boat, stepping in carefully as he untied it from the dock. He rowed us out, the lantern light from the dock fading behind us, the lake stretching wide and endless around us.

The silence between us wasn't awkward. It was charged—heavy with the weight of all the years we had spent apart, of everything left unsaid, of words neither of us had dared to speak out loud yet.

I wrapped my arms around my knees, the night air cool against my skin. "I used to dream about this place," I admitted quietly.

He rested an elbow on the edge of the boat, watching me. "Yeah?"

I nodded, staring at the reflection of the moon rippling in the water. "For years, I'd dream about being back here. But in my dreams, I was always alone."

He exhaled slowly, his voice steady. "You're not alone now."

I looked at him then, my chest tightening at the way he said it. A promise. A fact.

The boat rocked gently, and Sebastian shifted closer, his knee brushing against mine. His hand found my chin, tilting it slightly, forcing me to meet his gaze.

"I've missed this," he murmured.

I swallowed hard. "Me too."

He ran his thumb over my jaw, slow and careful. "You have no idea what you do to me, Mariana."

I leaned in, closing the space between us. Sebastian met me halfway, his lips warm and sure, his hands anchoring me against him. There was nothing hesitant about this kiss. No uncertainty. Just heat and familiarity, the way we always fit together.

I curled my fingers into his shirt, deepening it, feeling the soft sigh he let out as I pressed against him. The water rocked beneath us, the quiet ripples against the boat the only sound, besides our breath.

"You look so fucking sexy in that dress." He says against my lips. "I don't want tonight to end."

I let out a soft laugh, breathless. "Me either."

Sebastian's eyes darkened as he pulled me closer, his hands sliding down to my waist. The moonlight danced across the water, casting ethereal shadows on his face. I traced my fingers along his jaw, feeling the slight stubble beneath my touch.

"We don't have to end it," I whispered, my heart racing.

He leaned in, capturing my lips once more. The kiss deepened, years of longing poured into every touch. The boat rocked gently beneath us, the water lapping softly against its sides.

Sebastian's hands roamed my body, slipping under my dress and leaving trails of heat in their wake. I arched into him, my fingers tangling in his hair.

The cool night contrasted with the warmth of our bodies, sending shivers down my spine. I tugged at the hem of his shirt, pulling it over his head. Moonlight gleamed on his skin, highlighting the familiar planes of his chest. I ran my hands over him, relishing every curve and dip.

He unzipped my dress with reverent slowness, peeling it away as if unwrapping a gift. His eyes roamed over me, dark with desire and something deeper. "God, you're beautiful," he murmured.

I pulled him close, skin against skin, relishing the warmth of his body against mine. Our lips met again, urgent and hungry. Sebastian's hands roamed my curves, drawing soft gasps from my throat.

The cool night air raised goosebumps on my exposed skin, a delicious contrast to the heat building between us. With careful movements in the gently rocking boat, Sebastian laid me back onto the blankets. He hovered over me, his eyes searching mine. "I dream about this all the time," he whispered.

I reached up to trace his cheekbone. "Me too," I breathed.

He lowered himself, pressing his body against mine. I wrapped my legs around his waist, pulling him closer. Sebastian groaned softly, burying his face in my neck.

His lips and tongue traced a path down my throat as his hands explored lower. I arched against him, lost in sensation. The boat swayed beneath us, the water lulling us into a rhythm. The night was still and silent, except for the sounds of our breath and lips meeting.

Sebastian's kisses trailed down my body, leaving a trail of heat in their wake. I tangled my fingers in his hair, urging him on. His hands roamed over my skin, learning every inch as if for the first time.

Suddenly, he stilled and pulled back slightly. His hands patted around his pockets, a crease forming between his brows. "I don't have...?" he exhaled, looking at me, hesitant.

I knew what he was asking, "I want to feel just you. I'm on the pill." I say.

His expression changes, "Yeah? You want me bare, baby?"

I nod eagerly.

In one fluid motion, he positioned himself between my legs. His eyes locked onto mine as he slowly entered me. We moved together in perfect harmony, the boat rocking gently beneath us. Our bodies slick with sweat and our breaths mingled in the cool night air.

I clung to him tightly, lost in the sensations coursing

through me. As we reached our peak together, time seemed to stand still. Our bodies shook with pleasure as we called out each other's names into the stillness of the night.

Afterward, we lay tangled in each other's arms as we watched the stars above us twinkle in approval. He looked up at me then, "I never stopped loving you, Mariana. Not for a single day."

My heart clenched at his words. I cupped his face in my hands, pulling him up for a deep, searing kiss. "I love you too," I breathed against his lips. "I always have."

His arms tightened around me, and for a while, I let myself get lost in his warmth, in the steady rise and fall of his breath, in the way his fingers traced slow, lazy patterns against my skin.

But then, before I could stop myself, the words tumbled out. "I don't get it."

Sebastian shifted slightly, looking up at me, his brows drawing together. "Don't get what?"

I exhaled, staring up at his face, "How you do it."

His fingers brushed along my side. "Do what, hermosa?"

I swallowed. "How you love me like this. In the morning, I wake up a mess. Some days, I can't even look at myself in the mirror without picking apart every single thing that's wrong with me. By the afternoon, I swear I will convince myself I don't need anyone, that I can handle everything alone."

My voice wavers, and I hate it. "Sometimes I get mean, frustrated with my body, frustrated with everything. Sometimes, I push people away. I'm stubborn when I shouldn't be, complicated when it would be so much easier not to be—and you're still here."

Sebastian exhaled through his nose, shaking his head, "Loving you is the easiest thing I've ever done, Mariana." His voice was calm, sure, completely, utterly certain. "It's not a choice. It's not something I have to think about. It just is."

I squeezed my eyes shut, my chest too tight, my ribs aching

under the weight of all the things I wanted to believe. "Even when I'm impossible?" I whispered.

His hand slid up my jaw, tilting my face toward his, his thumb brushing along my cheekbone. His gaze burned into mine, so full of love I might drown in it. "Especially then. Eres mi reina, Mariana. Mi corazon. Mi hogar."

CHAPTER 23

Mariana

T he night started with a bottle of wine, an ungodly amount of fries, and a little bit of chaos. Anna had texted me earlier in the day: "You owe me a night of drinking and chisme. I don't make the rules."

I'd laughed at my phone before replying, "Fine. Bring wine. No rules."

And now here we were, two glasses deep, sprawled on my couch, a mess of takeout containers spread out on the coffee table. The living room was warm and cozy, the scent of vanilla candles mixing with the salty aroma of fries and the rich tang of red wine.

Anna tucked her legs under her, holding her glass. "Okay, but real talk," she said, eyes sharp, ready for all the bochinche she could get. "How the hell did we get here? Because a few months ago, you swore up and down that you guys were 'so in the past,' and now you're taking boat rides under the moonlight?"

I groaned, sinking back against the couch. "It's not that dramatic."

Anna made a high-pitched noise, "Are you serious? Sebastian freaking Garcia? The love of your life? The boy you would have married if you didn't move? Who, by the way, has been hopelessly in love with you since forever—probably before that, to be honest." She waved her wine glass, nearly sloshing it on the couch. "That's the definition of dramatic."

I sighed, tilting my head back. "It's different now."

Anna narrowed her eyes. "Different how?"

I hesitated. The words sat at the back of my throat, tangled between fear and truth. "Because I'm different now."

She didn't argue or push. She just gave me the space to be; she knew me well enough to understand that the weight of those words was real, that I didn't need prodding—just presence.

I took another sip of wine, rolling the glass between my hands. "I spent so long thinking I had to do everything alone. Even when I was with Andrew, I never felt like it was a true partnership. And after Andrew, I thought that I was better off alone, that if I let someone in and leaned on them, it would mean I was weak." I let out a soft laugh. "But Sebastian never makes me feel weak. He makes me feel like..."

Anna leaned in, waiting.

I swallowed. "Like it's safe to want something again."

Her face softened. "Damn. That was beautiful."

I rolled my eyes. "Shut up."

She grinned, but before she could respond, there was a knock at the door. Anna shot me a look. "You expecting someone?"

I frowned. "No."

I got up, padded toward the front of the door, and when I swung it open, Analyse stood on the other side, holding two bottles of wine in the air, one in each hand.

"Hope you don't mind me crashing. But Sebastian told me you guys were here, Maya's spending the weekend with my parents, and I'm in need of a girls' night."

I blinked. "No, of course not! The more, the merrier.

Anna perked up from the couch. "Ay dios mio! Nowwww it's a party!"

Analyse laughed as she walked in, kicking off her shoes like she'd been there a hundred times before. She held up one of the bottles. "I figured you wouldn't be drinking the good stuff, so I brought something decent."

Anna gasped. "Rude!"

I snorted, taking the bottle from her. "She's not wrong."

We refilled our glasses, and just like that, the night shifted into something easy, something effortless. There was something about being surrounded by women who knew you inside and out, who could call you out on your bullshit while also hyping you up to ridiculous levels.

At one point, Anna stood, one hand on her hip, waving her glass. "Okay, important question."

Analyse smirked. "This is going to be stupid, isn't it?"

Anna ignored her. "Mariana. How good is Sebastian in bed? Because if you tell me he's anything less than mind-blowing, I will be personally offended."

I nearly choked on my wine. "Anna!"

She gasped, pointing. "Oh my god! That reaction says it all."

Analyse groaned loudly, slapping a hand over her ears. "Nope. Absolutely not. That's my brother. I don't need this mental image. I'm leaving."

Anna smirked. "No, you're not. Sit down."

Analyse dramatically pressed her hands to her temples. "Mariana, please, spare me. I already have to witness the eye contact. Don't make me hear about it too."

Anna cackled. "The eye contact?"

"It's disgusting," Analyse said flatly. "They look at each other like they're starring in a telenovela. I feel like I should turn away half the time."

I groan, covering my face. "I hate both of you."

Analyse just grinned, clinking her glass against mine. "No, you don't. Can we talk about something else?"

Anna waggled her eyebrows. "Fine. Let's talk about how you're basically married now."

"I AM NOT-"

"Oh, you totally are," Analyse cut in, smirking, "You two are disgustingly in love. It's cute."

Anna sighed dramatically, swirling her wine. "Just like old times."

I huffed, crossing my arms. "We're taking it slow."

Anna snorted, "Taking it slow? You're all over each other in public."

Analyse nodded. "I'm pretty sure Maya already thinks that you're her Tia, meaning you're my sister!"

I let out a loud groan. "You two are impossible."

Anna grinned. "You love us."

I sighed, taking another sip of wine. "Unfortunately."

The conversation shifted after that, melting into old stories and new confessions, a ton of laughter. By the time the wine bottle was empty, and we were all sprawled across the couch, giggling at nothing, I realized that this night was exactly what I needed.

Anna propped herself up on one elbow, eyes gleaming. "Okay, but enough about us—what about you, Analyse?"

Analyse made a face. "What about me?"

"Oh, I don't know," I said. "Any new confessions you'd like to share?"

Her expression stayed carefully neutral, but the slight flicker of her gaze didn't go unnoticed. "Nope."

Anna narrowed her eyes. "Not even a tiny little crush?"

Analyse smirked, reaching for the empty bottle as if contemplating whether she could squeeze another drop out of it. "Wait, did I miss the memo? Why are we even talking about me? I thought tonight was the *Mariana's Love Life* special."

"Oh, that means yes," Anna said triumphantly.

"I hate you both," Analyse muttered, but the way she bit back a smile only made me more certain.

I stretched my legs out, feigning casual. "You and Mateo have been spending a lot of time together…"

Analyse groaned, flopping back onto the couch. "Oh my God. Not this."

Anna's eyes widened with delight. "Mateo?" She waggled her eyebrows. "Now *that* would be interesting."

Analyse exhaled sharply, grabbing a couch pillow and shoving it over her face. "I hate you both *so* much."

Anna patted her knee. "That's fair. But we love you."

Silence settled over us for a beat, and eventually, Analyse stretched, yawning as she nudged Anna's leg with her foot. "Alright, we should probably call it. Some of us have responsible things to do tomorrow."

Anna groaned, rolling onto her stomach. "Ugh. Reality."

Analyse rubbed a hand over her face. "Yep. And it's coming for us in about six hours."

I sighed, sinking deeper into the couch. "Okay, but tell me this wasn't exactly what we needed."

Anna hummed in response, her wine glass balanced on her stomach, eyes half-closed.

It had been a damn good night—wine, laughter, my girls, and just the right touch of chaos.

CHAPTER 24

Mariana

The smell of fresh paint still clung to the air, mixing with the scent of vanilla and sugar from a test batch of pastries I'd baked earlier. The Rolling Pin was nearly ready. I stood in the center of the bakery, hands on my hips, surveying everything I had poured my heart and soul into over the last several months.

The new glass cases gleamed, the walls were painted a soft alabaster, and the little wooden sign above the register proudly bore the name of the shop, with a small Puerto Rican flag in the corner. Everything was perfect, exactly how I wanted it to be.

I should have been feeling excited, but for some reason, something gnawed at me. The room felt off. It felt too quiet, too empty. I exhaled, shaking the feeling off, and grabbed a cloth to wipe down the countertops for what had to be the tenth time tonight.

I'd already deep-cleaned the place, but the nervous energy buzzing under my skin wouldn't allow me to sit still. So here I was, cleaning and re-cleaning, knowing full well I'd pay for it later.

The exhaustion would hit me in a few hours—my joints aching, my body heavy—but stopping felt impossible. Between the stress and the anticipation, rest wasn't an option.

I should be celebrating; the grand opening is just days away. After months of renovations, planning, and second-guessing my every decision, The Rolling Pin was about to become mine in every way. I wanted this so badly.

When I went to Ruth and asked for this place, I hadn't thought that she'd actually give it to me. But damn, I would have been heartbroken if she hadn't. I should be ecstatic right now.

This was my fresh start. This was supposed to be my proof that I could do something on my own. So why did it feel like something was slipping through my fingers?

I turned to the display case and began adjusting the decorative tray, lining them up, stepping back to examine my work, and then lining them up again.

Everything needed to be perfect, even though no one would notice if they were a little off. As I was inspecting the trays for what had to be the fifth time, my phone vibrated on the counter.

I didn't have to look. I already knew who it was. Sebastian. I hesitated before picking it up to read his texts.

SEBASTIAN

Still at the bakery?

Want me to come by? I'll bring you coffee.

Warmth bloomed in my chest, unbidden. I love how he always knew exactly when to check in, how he always knew when I needed something—even when I wasn't sure myself.

My fingers hovered over the keyboard. I should say yes. I should let him show up with coffee, wrap his arms around me, and tell me I was doing an amazing job, because I know that's exactly what he'd do if he were here.

But instead, I hesitated. Instead of answering and saying, "Yes! Please come over, I need you.", I set my phone down and turned away.

A tiny, nagging voice in my head whispered, What if I'm relying on him too much? When had I last gone a day without talking to him? When had I last made a decision without instinctively thinking about what he'd say?

I walked to the front window, resting my palms against the cool glass as I looked onto the quiet street. The town had long since settled in for the night, the warm glow of lamplight spilling onto the sidewalks.

Sebastian had been there for me through everything. The bakery renovations. The nights I was too tired to cook for myself. The mornings my joints ached from my lupus flare-ups and he'd massage warmth back into my hands, easing the stiffness.

He made me laugh when I forgot how. He never made me feel weak, even on the days when my body felt like the enemy. I know without a doubt that he'd drop everything in a heartbeat for me if I needed him; his texts to me tonight prove that. All the while still being an amazing Tío to Maya, helping Analyse every free moment he had, and working at the firehouse.

Sebastian had unknowingly made himself part of the foundation that I was rebuilding, and shit, that scared me. What if I needed him too much?

I ran a hand through my hair, gripping the strands at my nape as I walked toward the back storage area. The Rolling Pin was supposed to be mine. My fresh start.

I've spent so much time this past year trying to rebuild myself after my marriage, after what that put me through, after Andrew's death, after my diagnosis, after trying to piece together the woman I had once been. What was I doing? Am I doing it again? Am I letting myself lean on Sebastian too much instead of proving I could do this alone?

Sebastian had been so much of my support. From sanding down the old counters with me to staying up late when I was too anxious to sleep, and I let him. Because it was easy to let him in. Easy to need him, but easy wasn't safe; I knew that all too well.

What would happen if I started depending on him too much? What would happen if I lost him? Or, if I lost myself to him? I spent so many years letting Andrew completely take over my life. I spent so many years not being in control, being forced to depend on someone else.

I grabbed a large container of flour from the corner shelf, setting it on the work table with a soft thud. The bulk storage bins needed to be refilled before opening day, and it was something mindless to keep me busy, something that wouldn't require overthinking.

I twisted the lid, carefully scooping flour from the massive bag into the counter. The motion was repetitive. Scoop, pour, level. Over and Over again. My hands moved on instinct, but my mind was somewhere else.

Flashes of my past flickered in my thoughts—the months after Andrew died, after I was finally free from him. The first time I had gone grocery shopping alone, without the fear of being followed, without the tight knot of dread twisting in my stomach as I hurried through the aisles, knowing that if I took too long, he'd accuse me of cheating. The way my hands had shaken at checkout, expecting my phone to buzz with a demand, a threat.

The night I had slept in a bed that was only mine, without the weight of someone else beside me, without the fear of waking up to a hand tightening around my neck.

I had spent so much time trying to be strong on my own. I wasn't alone anymore, and that terrified me. I set the scoop

183

down, flexing my fingers slightly as a dull ache began to form in my knuckles. My joints feel tight and stiff. A warning sign. I had overdone it; I had worked too late. Again.

The desire to call Sebastian flashed through my mind instantly. He'd rush over, massage my hands, and tell me to stop being so damn stubborn and let him take care of me.

The thought lodged itself in my chest, sharp and suffocating. The fact that my first instinct was to rely on him made my stomach twist.

I forced myself to focus on the task at hand—restocking the shelves, checking the inventory list, and making sure everything was perfect for the grand opening.

I could do this on my own. I need to do this on my own.

The hours stretched long. By the time I looked at my phone again, it was after midnight, and Sebastian hadn't texted again. I glanced at my phone. Sebastian's messages still sat there waiting. Guilt and unease twisted in my stomach. I picked it up, thumbs hovering over the keyboard.

MARIANA

> Sorry, I got caught up in stuff. You know how it is. I'm heading home soon.

I hesitated before adding:

MARIANA

> Thanks for checking in, though. I appreciate it. Hope you had a good night.

I stared at the words before sending them, feeling a lump form in my throat. I hit send, then locked my phone before I could second-guess myself.

Sebastian didn't deserve my distance, I know this, but I

needed to remind myself that I could do things alone. I am capable. I can make decisions and be strong, and I don't have to lean on anyone. I'm not just rebuilding this bakery. I'm rebuilding myself.

I grabbed my purse, threw it over my shoulder, and flicked off the lights. The bakery fell into darkness, except for the soft glow of the streetlamp filtering through the windows. I locked the doors, the soft click echoing in the silence.

For a moment, I stood there, staring at the quiet space. I had dreamed of this. I had wanted this. So why can't I let go of these feelings inside?

CHAPTER 25

Sebastian

N ight two of a 48-hour shift, and I could feel it in every muscle, every slow blink that lasted a second too long. Two days of routines, some brutal, had left my body aching and my mind clouded with fatigue.

The firehouse was quieter now, the usual hum of conversation replaced by the occasional scuff of boots against the tile and the distant murmur of a late-night news broadcast.

We still have a few hours until shift change, but I wasn't sure I'd actually sleep before heading home. Not with my thoughts tangled up in her. The coffee in my cup had gone cold. I should have gotten up to make a fresh one, but instead, I just sat there at the firehouse's kitchen table, twirling my phone between my fingers and staring at the last message from Mariana.

MARIANA

Sorry, I got caught up in stuff. You know how it is. I'm heading home soon.

Thanks for checking in, though. I appreciate it. Hope you had a good night.

It was a normal message. Simple. Casual. Too casual. Very unlike my Mariana. I tapped my thumb against the screen before locking my phone and tossing it onto the table with a quiet thud.

"You waiting for her to text you back?" Mateo's voice cut through the quiet, and I looked up to find him smirking at me from the other side of the table.

Andres dropped into the chair beside me, shoving a forkful of leftover pastelillos into his mouth before pointing at my phone. "Damn, man, you've got it bad."

I rolled my eyes and leaned back in my seat. "Shut up."

Mateo glanced at Andres before shaking his head. "Did we say anything wrong?"

Andres swallowed his bite and grinned. "Nah, just facts."

I sighed, stretching my arms above my head. "I'm just tired."

"Sure," Mateo mused, leaning forward with his elbows on the table. "Tired from checking your phone every three minutes?

Andres raised an eyebrow. "Dude, you've been weird all night. What's going on?"

I ran a hand down my face and sighed. I was being weird, wasn't I? I could feel it. This tightness in my chest, like I was waiting for something.

Mateo leaned back in his chair, stretching his arms behind his head. "Man, I gotta ask...How's it really going with you two?

I frowned. "What do you mean?"

Andres snorted. "You know exactly what I mean. You're glued to your phone, you've been zoning out since dinner, and now you're just sitting there staring at her messages."

I pressed my lips together, debating how to answer. Because the truth was, I didn't know what to say. Everything had been going great.

We were together again, something I thought I'd never get back. We were happy. We had been so in sync. So why did it feel like I was losing her?

"Yeah," I said finally, but it didn't come out as confident as I wanted. "We're good."

Mateo raised an eyebrow. "Yeah?"

Before I could answer, Nathan walked into the room, grabbed a mug from the counter, and poured himself some coffee. "You sure?"

I shot him a look. "Why is that everyone's favorite question tonight?"

Nathan shrugged. "Because you look stressed." He took a sip of his coffee, then nodded toward my phone. "How many times are you gonna check your messages?"

I sighed, gripping the mug in front of me. "She's been busy with the bakery. That's all."

Nathan studied me for a second, then leaned against the counter. "And she's letting you in on it, right?"

The words hit me square in the chest. Because the answer was...no. Not as much as she had been before. Lately, Mariana had been pulling back, little by little. Cancelling plans to stay late at the bakery. Replying later and later to texts. Answering with shorter messages. I hadn't even noticed how much it was bothering me until now—until I sat here, letting more of my messages to her go unanswered.

Mateo must've seen something shift in my face because he sighed. "Look, man, I'm not saying there's a problem. I just know you. I know how you are with the people that you love."

Andres nodded. "You are always all in. And that's great. But...is she doing the same?"

I didn't have an answer for that.

Nathan's voice was quieter this time. "Just be careful. That's all I'm saying."

I just picked up my phone, staring at Mariana's last message. Something had shifted, but what the hell happened?

~

The night was cool, the faint scent of smoke lingering in the air from an earlier controlled burn. I let the door swing shut behind me and leaned against the railing, my fingers tapping against my phone screen.

I pulled up Mariana's message again. Still simple. Still normal. But the more I stared at it, the more I realized...She didn't say goodnight. She didn't say "see you tomorrow". She didn't say anything that made it feel like she was thinking about me at all.

I knew all too well what it felt like when Mariana started pulling away. I've been here before. Shit. I ran a hand through my hair, gripping the back of my neck as a gnawing unease settled into my stomach. Had I done something wrong? I don't think I had. But then why wouldn't she just talk to me? Was this just Mariana being Mariana?

I knew she had a tendency to close herself off when she was stressed, but I thought we were past that. I thought she knew she could lean on me. Because I love her. And loving her means wanting to be in the trenches with her, helping her through the bad days, through the flare-ups, through the nights when her past came creeping in.

It means knowing when something is wrong—even when she won't say it. It means feeling the shift before she even realizes she's pulling away. She doesn't have to do it alone; she doesn't have to keep fighting it by herself. But, does she know that?

Does she know that when she walks into a room, my world tilts back into place? Does she know that when she leaves, something in me goes quiet—like I'm waiting for her to return before I can breathe right again? Does she know that I feel her before I see her? That there is no version of my life where she isn't in it? That there never has been?

If she saw herself the way I see her, she'd never doubt a damn thing again. If she knew what it was like to love her, to be loved by her, she wouldn't pull away. She wouldn't question. She wouldn't make me sit here, staring at my phone, wondering if she's already slipping through my fingers again.

I exhaled sharply, looking down at my phone, at the last message sitting there, and before I could think too hard about it, I typed out a new one.

SEBASTIAN

Okay, hermosa, I hope you got home okay.

I stared at the message for a long moment before pressing send. I wasn't going to push. I wasn't going to overthink. Maybe I was just imagining things; maybe everything was fine. Deep down, I couldn't shake the feeling that something had shifted. And for the life of me, I couldn't figure out why.

CHAPTER 26

Mariana

The room was dark, the only sound was the slow hum of the ceiling fan above me. I lay there, unmoving, eyes open but unfocused, staring at the faint outline of the dress against the far wall.

My body felt like it belonged to someone else—heavy, aching, uncooperative. The first sliver of sunlight crept through the blinds, cutting across the sheets. It was morning. I should get up. I should be at the bakery. I should call Sebastian. I know I'm not going to do any of those things. I can't.

A dull, throbbing ache sat deep in my joints, radiating outward like an unwelcome guest settling in. My lupus flares always start like this—slow, creeping, until suddenly, even the simplest of movements felt like war against my own body.

I squeezed my eyes shut, tears pricking at the corners, willing it to go away, but my body didn't care about my willpower. My hands, curled loosely against the sheets, felt stiff and swollen. My knees pulsed, protesting before I even attempted to shift them. A sharp, frustrated breath escaped me.

"Please, not today," I gritted out, my voice rough, almost desperate. I don't have time for this today. I hate this.

For a brief moment, instinct urged me to grab my phone from my nightstand and text Sebastian. He'd come over without hesitation. He would hold me close, tucking a blanket around my shoulders, desperately trying to shield me from the weight of the pain.

His voice would be a quiet murmur—something soft and reassuring. He'd bring me water, remind me to take my meds, and rub gentle circles on my back when the ache became too much.

He would make me food, even if I say that I'm not hungry, making sure I ate even just a little. He would take care of me, not just in the ways I let him, but in the ways I didn't know I needed.

And that's exactly why I couldn't call him. I can't rely on someone else to take care of me; I need to take care of myself. I need to handle this on my own. My chest tightened, but I ignored it. I needed to get up. I needed to move.

"Come on, Mariana," I muttered, forcing a breath through my nose. "Be the boss bitch that you are and get your ass up." I clenched my jaw, steeling myself.

I gritted my teeth and forced myself upright, my body immediately resisting. A sharp pain shot through my legs, and I had to brace myself against the mattress. My breath left me in a slow exhale, controlled, measured. "You can do this," I whispered. "You've done it before."

Swinging my legs over the side of the bed, I planted my feet on the floor, willing my body to cooperate. The stiffness made my movements clumsy, like I was walking on borrowed limbs, but I ignored it. If I gave this pain attention, it would win. And I refuse to let it win. I refuse to let this take over my life.

I stood, gripping the dresser for balance. My fingers curled against the cool wood, knuckles aching. The mirror above it reflected back a version of myself I didn't quite recognize—exhausted, my warm complexion dull and sapped of its usual vibrance, eyes heavy with fatigue.

I reached for my brush with a trembling hand, dragging it carefully through my hair. Strands came loose, slipping between my fingers, catching in the bristles.

My breath hitched, and I blinked hard, but the tears I had fought earlier finally broke free, slipping down my cheeks in silent surrender.

Maybe I should stay home today. No. The bakery needed me.

There was always something to do—final touches, recipe testing, orders to confirm. I'm so close to the finish line. Sitting in bed all day wasn't an option.

I just needed a little time, a little movement to loosen up. I shuffled toward the bathroom, and I pressed my hands beneath the warm stream, hissing at the immediate sting before the heat began to soothe.

This was fine. I was fine, and I would handle this alone.

The knock on my front door came an hour later, just as I was finishing my second cup of tea. I froze. My phone had been on silent all morning, and I hadn't checked it, I hadn't wanted to.

I knew there were messages from Sebastian, maybe even a missed call or two, but I couldn't bring myself to open them. Another knock, louder this time.

I sighed, dragging myself toward the door, each step slow and deliberate. Please don't be Sebastian. I know that the moment I see his face, my willpower will break.

I pulled it open. Anna.

She didn't even hesitate. The second she saw me, she

pushed past, stepping into my apartment like she owned the place, a plastic bag hanging from her wrist.

"Okay, now that I see that you're alive" she said, voice sharp, eyes narrowed. "Tienes exactamente tres segundos para decirme por qué carajos no has estado contestando el teléfono."

Okay, she's pissed. I exhaled, already too tired for this conversation. "Anna-"

"No, no, no," she cut me off, kicking the door shut behind her. "You don't get to disappear on me, Mari; you know better."

"I wasn't disappearing," I muttered, moving back toward the kitchen.

Anna followed, because, of course, she did. "Oh, really? Because I called you, like five times, texted you eight, and even tried calling the bakery. No answer. You know that's my definition of disappearing, right?"

I grabbed my mug, sipping my tea slowly. "I just needed a quiet morning."

Anna's sharp eyes scanned me, her mouth pressing into a line. "You're having a flare-up, aren't you?"

I hesitated a second too long. Her sigh was immediate. She tossed the bag onto the counter and folded her arms. "Contestame, Mariana."

"It's not a big deal," I said quickly, waving a hand. "It's not even that bad today."

Anna raised an eyebrow. "Mariana Camila Vargas, no me mientas. Not that bad? So bad that you ignored your phone all morning?"

I bit the inside of my cheek. "It's fine. I'm fine."

Anna wasn't buying it. She stepped closer, tilting her head slightly, eyes narrowing. "Where the hell is Sebastian? I'm surprised he isn't here taking care of you. Did he go to get some food or something?"

The air in the room shifted. I shook my head, not meeting her gaze. "No, he's not out getting food. He's not here because I didn't call him."

Silence. Then—"Why not?"

I busied myself with my mug, stirring nothing. "Because I don't need to."

Anna's voice was softer now. "Mari..."

I sighed, setting my mug down with a soft clink. "I just... I don't want to rely on him for everything. I can handle this on my own, I've been doing it since I was diagnosed." I hesitated, my fingers tracing the rim of the mug. "I don't want to feel like I'm becoming a burden."

"Yeah, and how's that working out for you?" she shot back, voice edged with frustration.

I scowled. "I don't need a lecture."

"No," she said, crossing her arms. "You need someone to tell you that you're being stupid."

I narrowed my eyes. "Excuse me?"

Anna huffed. "Mariana, come on. You're doing that thing again. The "push everyone away, suffer in silence, I can do it all by myself" bullshit. You're not fine. You shouldn't have to be fine all the time. That's why people love you. That's why Sebastian loves you."

My stomach clenched.

She sighed, rubbing her forehead. "I'm not saying you're weak. I'm saying you're allowed to need people."

I swallowed, staring at the mug between my hands. The truth sat heavy on my tongue, thick and unspoken. I was scared. Scared of letting myself lean on someone again. Scared of needing Sebastian too much. Scared of what would happen if I lost him.

Anna's voice softened. "Mari, I know what happened before made you feel like you have to do everything on your own. I get it, but this isn't that. He isn't him ."

I shook my head. "You don't get it."

"Then help me understand." Anna pleaded, leaning forward, her eyes searching mine with quiet desperation.

My chest ached, a different kind of pain now, something deeper. I opened my mouth, then closed it. I couldn't say it. I couldn't admit that if I lost Sebastian, it would break me.

Anna sighed, watching me carefully before grabbing the plastic bag she'd brought. "Well, too bad, because I brought you the Ajiaco from my mom, and I'm not leaving until you eat it."

A small laugh bubbled up before I could stop it.

Anna grinned. "There she is."

She pulled two bowls and spoons from my cabinet, poured the soup into them and handed me one. "I won't push. But don't shut me out, okay?"

I nodded, but deep down, the fear still sat there.

CHAPTER 27

Mariana

After Anna left, I sat curled up on the couch for a long time, knees drawn to my chest, staring at the wall, willing myself to move. My body felt too heavy, too drained to do anything but exist.

The thought of spending the whole night like this—alone, stiff, exhausted, fighting against my own body and my own damn mind felt unbearable. So I called Sebastian.

I hadn't wanted to. I'd spent the entire day trying to convince myself I was fine, that the ache in my joints and the exhaustion sinking into my bones were just minor inconveniences. Manageable. But the second I was alone, reality hit me like a weight pressing into my chest. I wasn't fine, and the worst part? I didn't want to be alone, and that scared me more than the pain.

So I called him. I barely had to say the words. He heard it in my voice.

"I'm coming." That was it. No hesitation.

By the time I made it to the front door, headlights were cutting through the darkness. Sebastian didn't say anything when he saw me. He just held out his hand and waited. I took it.

He helped me into his car, his hand warm and steady against my back, his presence grounding. The drive to his house was quiet—no pressure, no expectations, just the soft hum of the radio and the occasional glance from him, checking on me.

Sebastian kept the heat on low, knowing the cold made my joints worse. His fingers tapped idly against the steering wheel, matching the rhythm of the music playing through the speakers.

I glanced at him from the corner of my eye. Even in the dim glow of the dashboard, I could see the tension in his jaw, the way his brows furrowed like he was thinking too hard. He didn't ask me what was wrong. He didn't need to.

Instead, he reached over at a red light, wordlessly adjusting the blanket he'd brought for me onto my lap. That was Sebastian. Always paying attention, always knowing exactly what I needed before I did.

When we got there, he made me drink water and wrapped me in a warm blanket, his touch gentle, his presence unwavering. He held me close, his fingers threading through my hair in soothing strokes. I fell asleep listening to the steady rhythm of his breathing.

Warmth. That was the first thing I noticed when I woke up. Not just from the blankets wrapped around me, but from the air itself—soft, lived-in. It felt safe here.

The space beside me was empty, but his presence was still everywhere. His scent lingered on the pillows, woodsy and familiar. I let my fingers drift across the sheets, still warm from where he'd been.

On the nightstand, a bottle of water and my pain meds sat neatly beside my phone—plugged in and fully charged. He must have done that before he left the room.

The faint rustle of movement drifted in from the kitchen. The low hum of a song—some old reggaetón tune he probably didn't even realize he was singing along to.

I exhaled slowly, shifting under the covers. The worst of the flare-ups had passed, thankfully. I should be relieved. My body didn't ache nearly as much as last night.

My fingers still felt stiff, but not as bad. But there was something creeping in now. Something that had nothing to do with lupus.

I was getting used to this. That realization settled into my chest, heavy and sharp, because this wasn't supposed to be easy. Loving someone, needing someone, wasn't supposed to feel safe.

And yet, with Sebastian, it did. I swallowed hard and forced myself to sit up. My body protested the movement, but I ignored it. I needed to shake this off.

I swung my legs over the edge of the bed, planting my feet on the floor. If I just got up, if I just focused on anything else, this feeling would pass.

But before I could take a single step, Sebastian appeared in the doorway, barefoot, hair still damp from his shower, wearing nothing but sweatpants hanging low and a knowing smirk.

"Morning, princesa."

I rolled my eyes, trying to ignore the flutter in my stomach at how good he looked so damn effortlessly. Damn, this man is fine.

I sank into a chair, wrapping my hands around the coffee mug he placed in front of me. "Tell me you didn't burn the house down making breakfast," I teased.

"Excuse you," he said, feigning offense. "I happen to make an incredible breakfast."

"Uhuh."

He let out an exasperated gasp. "Rude. I cook all the time, you know."

I snorted. "You grilled burgers last weekend."

"And they were fantastic," he shot back. "But this morning, I outdid myself. You deserve a good morning, Mariana."

Something in my chest pinched. It was the way he said it. So simple, so certain, like I deserved this without question.

I took a sip of the coffee, letting the warmth settle inside me. Sebastian reached out, brushing his fingers along my wrist, his touch light and deliberate.

"You're stiff," he murmured, his brows furrowing slightly.

I hated how easily he could tell. "I'm fine," I said quickly.

He didn't argue. He just took my hands in his, his thumbs tracing slowly, careful circles over my knuckles. The way he touched me—gentle, focused, and completely attuned to me —made my throat go tight. I didn't stop him, but I should have. Because every time he did this, it became harder to remember how to be alone.

I pulled my hands back, flexing them. "See? Good as new."

Sebastian sat back, watching me carefully. "You sure?"

I forced a small, easy smile. "Positive."

He didn't look convinced, but he didn't push. Instead, he stood up, stretching. "Pancakes are getting cold."

I let out a small laugh, standing too. "You're really proud of these, huh?"

"Damn right, I am."

But as we walked to the kitchen, something lodged itself in my chest. An unwanted thought, an unwanted fear. I wanted to be here. I wanted this. I really did.

But deep inside, there was still this small part of me that was scared. Scared of where I've been. Scared of what I've gone through. Scared of what this could be. And most of all, scared how it would kill me if I lost this.

Breakfast was good. Annoyingly good. And he knew it, grinning every time I took a bite. The easy warmth between us felt dangerous. So I focused on his voice instead. He was telling me about a prank they pulled at the firehouse last week.

"So, Andres was in the middle of a shower, right? And I -"

I nearly choked on my coffee. "No."

"Oh yeah," he said, smirking. "We filled up a bucket of ice water, got the rookies to distract him, and then—bam!" He clapped his hands. "Right over the top of the stall."

I burst out laughing. The image was too ridiculous. Sebastian grinned, eyes crinkling at the corners. It was one of those rare moments where everything felt untouched by the weight of my own mind. That was, until it didn't.

The fear sat in my stomach like a stone. I pushed my food around my plate, my appetite suddenly gone. Sebastian must have noticed because he reached across the table, touching my wrist lightly.

"You okay?"

Lie. Just lie. "Yeah," I said, smiling quickly. "Just thinking about the bakery, there's still so much to do."

He nodded, satisfied with that answer. But I hated myself for giving it. Because the truth? I'm a damn mess, and I don't know how to fix it. I look at Sebastian, and all I can think about is how much I love him—how deeply, hopelessly in love I am. Boy, am I screwed.

Sebastian left for work later that morning. I kissed him before he walked out the door, but something felt different. I told myself it felt the same as always, but it didn't.

Not because he had changed, but because I had. I knew this feeling. I'd felt it before. The slow, creeping hesitation. The quiet unraveling of something I should have been holding onto. The last time I felt this way, it was senior year.

Sebastian kissed me at graduation and held me like he thought love alone could make me stay. And for a second, I let myself believe it. But I still left. I had to.

I told myself that I needed to experience life outside of this small town, that this place, this love, wasn't enough. The truth was, I was scared back then too. Scared of what it meant to love someone like him—completely, deeply, all at once. Scared of what it meant to build my future around a person instead of my own dreams, So I left.

I left and did the same shit I was running away from. All my decisions became about Andrew. What a fucking mistake that had been.

I turned my world upside down for a man that didn't love me. Not really. He loved control, power, the way he could shape me into whatever version of me best suited him, and I let him. I fucking let him. Why the hell did I do that?

So what was I doing now? Running again? Pushing Sebastian away because I was scared of what it meant to stay? Or was I just trying to save us both from the inevitable heartbreak?

Because I knew how this story ended. Love wasn't enough to keep me from leaving before, and love sure as hell hadn't saved me from Andrew. So what made me think it would save me now?

I leaned against the counter, staring at the half-empty coffee cup I hadn't even realized I was gripping. Sebastian was gone, and the house felt too quiet without him. A small part of me was relieved.

I was alone, I could finally breathe, finally think, finally try and get myself together. But another part of me, a much larger part, felt hollow. Because I'd been here before. Closing myself off. Creating space before someone else could take it from me.

I should stop. I should let myself have this. I should let myself enjoy true happiness, but the truth settled deep in my chest, thick and suffocating.

Everyone leaves. Everyone hurts you. Leave before you are left. No matter how badly I didn't want to, I needed to pull away. I needed to protect myself and my heart.

CHAPTER 28

Mariana

The room was too quiet. That was the first thing I noticed as I stepped inside. The usual hum of machines was still there, the steady beeping of the monitors keeping rhythm in the background. But the sound that used to make me feel safe, the sound of my mother's voice filling the space, talking, teasing, scolding, laughing, was softer now, thinner. I hated that.

She looked up when I walked in, her lips curving into a slow, knowing smile. "Ah," she murmured, her voice raspier than usual. "Mi amor."

I swallowed against the tightness in my throat and lifted the bouquet of lilies in my hand. "They didn't have flor de maga," I said, stepping toward her bed. "But these aren't bad, right?"

She hummed in approval. "These are beautiful. Thank you, mi amorcito."

"I know flor de magas reminds you of home."

"They do. But now these... these will remind me of you."

I smiled, setting the flowers in the vase by her bedside. "I'll go somewhere else next time and make sure I find the flor de magas."

She let out a soft laugh. "My sweet, stubborn girl."

It was easier to focus on arranging the flowers than to look at her too closely. She was tired, more than last time. Her skin was paler, her frame even smaller beneath the blankets.

I wasn't stupid; I knew what was coming. I just wasn't ready for it. I sat in the chair beside her bed, pressing my hands between my knees to keep them from shaking.

She reached for my wrist, her grip weak but warm. She always did that. Held onto me, even when she was the one barely holding it together. She held me. Used what little strength she had for me.

"You look like your mind is running a mile a minute," she observed.

I let out a slow breath. "Just thinking."

Her eyes twinkled with something familiar. Something amused. "About my Sebastián?"

I groaned. "Why do you call him that?"

She chuckled, but her fingers squeezed mine lightly. "Because I've known that boy since before he could walk. He's always been one of mine."

Something about that sentence made my chest ache. Because she was right. Sebastian had always been hers. And in some ways, he had always been mine too.

Since we were kids. Anna, Sebastian, and I were known as the three musketeers. Running around, causing chaos, creating our own adventures in our little town.

Anna and I would force Sebastian to learn dance routines and perform them in front of our parents. We were all best friends. Anna was like my sister.

But Sebastian and I? We had always felt... connected. Two parts of a whole.

"He's treating you well, right?" she asked, watching me closely.

I nodded. "Of course he is."

"And you're happy?"

That made my throat tighten. Because the answer was a resounding yes. I am. So. Damn. Happy.

But happiness has never been the problem. Sebastian had always known how to make me happy. She must've seen the hesitation in my face because she exhaled, shifting slightly in the bed.

"Mariana..."

I didn't like the way she said my name. Like she already knew. Like she saw the doubt creeping into my chest before I even spoke it out loud.

"You don't have to protect yourself from love, mi vida," she said, her voice softer now.

I let out a short, bitter laugh. "That's not what I'm doing."

She just gave me a look. The sort of look only a mother could give. The type of look that said she saw through every lie I was telling myself. She always knew.

"You think I don't know you?" she murmured, a quiet laugh slipping out as she shook her head. "You've been protecting yourself from love since you were a little girl. Always so independent. Always needing to do everything on your own."

I looked away. "That's not a bad thing."

"No," she agreed. "But letting someone love you isn't a weakness either."

My stomach twisted. She was right. I knew she was right. But knowing something and believing it were two different things.

"It's not just about losing them, Mami," I whispered.

Her gaze stayed steady, patient. "Then tell me what it is about."

I let out a shaky breath. "Andrew..." I forced his name out. "He hurt me, Mami."

She stilled. Her fingers tightened around mine. "What?

"You always told me to call you, Mami. But I didn't. Because I knew if you heard my voice, you'd hear the truth.The truth I couldn't admit to myself. That I wasn't okay. That my marriage wasn't okay. That I wasn't safe."

A tear slipped down my cheek. "Andrew. He...he wasn't who you thought he was."

Her expression shifted—shock, confusion, then something darker.

I exhaled sharply. "It wasn't just words, Mami. It was control. It was..." I sucked in a breath, my voice barely a whisper. "It was bruises. Shoving. Grabbing my wrist so hard I thought he'd snap it. Screaming in my face so close I could feel his spit on my skin. And every time I thought about leaving, every time I even tried..."

A sob cracked through me. "He made me believe I had nowhere to go."

She made a soft, pained noise—a sound that broke something inside me. "Mariana," she whispered, eyes glassy. "Why didn't you tell me?"

"Because I knew." My voice shook, "I knew that if I called you, if I heard your voice, I'd break. I knew you'd tell me to come home. And I knew...that if I let myself hope and then failed to leave...it would be worse."

Her breathing was uneven now, grief and guilt lining every inch of her face.

"Mami, he convinced me I was nothing. That I was only worth something because he loved me. And I let him. I let him take everything away from me."

Her grip on my hand tightened—weak, but full of fury.

Her dark eyes flashed, and for the first time in months, she looked like herself. Like Lucia Vargas, the woman who could level a grown man with just one look.

She reached up, cupping my cheek, "No."

The ferocity in her voice startled me.

"Ese cabrón didn't take anything from you, Mariana." She pushed herself up straighter, her voice gaining strength, the rage fueling her. "That man?" She let out a sharp, bitter laugh. "Ese hombre no era hombre. Él era basura. He was nothing. A coward, a weak, pathetic excuse for a man who had to tear you down because he knew—HE KNEW he could never stand next to you as an equal."

My throat tightened, tears pooling in my eyes. She wasn't done.

"And you?" She pointed at me, her chest rising and falling as her breath shook with emotion. "Tu, mi amor? You survived. You endured. You made it out. No me digas ni por un segundo that he took anything from you—because look at you. You are here. You are standing, breathing, fighting, even when you think you can't. He tried to break you, and he failed."

She gripped my chin, forcing me to meet her gaze. Her eyes blazed with something raw. Something fierce. "You are my daughter. Tu eres boricua. You come from a long line of women who do not bow. We do not break. He tried to destroy you, and look at you—you are still here."

My lip quivered, a sob pushing at my chest. She exhaled, softer now, cupping my face like she used to when I was little. "You are not what he did to you, Mariana. You are not his words. You are not his hands. You are yours. Always you."

I broke. A ragged sob tore through me, shaking me down to my bones. My face crumpled, tears spilling freely now, no longer held back, no longer swallowed down like I had learned to do for years. "I don't know how to let someone love me the right way, Mami. I don't know how to need someone without being afraid. Without waiting for the hurt."

She reached up, her hands trembling but steady, and wiped the tears from my face like she had when I was little. "Mariana, mi amor... You already know how." Her voice was fierce, but so damn gentle, like she was willing me to believe it. "The way you love me. The way you love Anna. The way you loved your father. Dios mío, the way you still love that man even now. You already know what love is. And Sebastian?" She shook her head, gripping my chin, making me look at her. "He is not Andrew. He never was. He never will be."

I sucked in a shaky breath, my throat aching.

She gave me a knowing, tearful smile. "And you? You were never broken, mi vida. Just scared. You don't have to be scared anymore."

"Te quiero, Mami."

"Te quiero, mi amor."

I turned and walked out, feeling the weight of her words settling into my bones.

The cemetery was quiet, except for the whisper of the wind rustling through the trees. I pulled my jacket tighter around myself as I stepped onto the worn path, my sneakers crunching softly against the gravel. It had been too long since I'd last come here.

Maybe because I hated the way it made everything feel too damn real, or maybe because standing in front of this gravestone always left me feeling like I was still that broken girl from all those years ago.

A senior in high school, standing at his funeral, clutching

my mother's hand, trying so hard to be strong. I wasn't strong, though. Not then, and definitely not now.

I swallowed hard as I approached his headstone, my breath catching the second my fingers brushed against the cool, engraved surface.

Luis Vargas
Beloved Husband. Cherished Father.

I traced the letter with trembling fingers, my throat tightening. The words were too small. Too simple. A single stone, a few carved words, could never sum up the great man that he was. The best husband. The best father. He loved us so fiercely.

My knees gave out before I even realized I was falling. I sat there, knees pressed into the damp earth, the cold creeping in through the denim of my jeans.

"Papi, I miss you so much." My voice cracked.

"There hasn't been a single day that's gone by where you aren't in my thoughts. Where the sound of a song or the smell of cafecito doesn't rush back a memory of you." My lips trembled as I sucked in a shaky breath.

"Every day since you've been gone, I've wished for just one more day with you. Just one more conversation. One more time hearing you say you love me. One more time feeling one of your bear hugs—the one where you'd lift me off my feet, squeezing all the air out of me just to hear me laugh. Hell, I'd even take one more time of you grounding me, if it meant you were here."

I let out a weak, broken chuckle. "What I wouldn't do to hear your voice right now."

The wind picked up slightly, or maybe it was just my imagination, but I closed my eyes, pretending that, just for a second, I could hear him. Pretending that he was still here.

I wrapped my arms around myself, rocking slightly. "Everything feels so messed up right now, Papi. I feel so lost. So confused. I was never ready to lose you; I was just a kid. And now I have to be ready to lose Mami too." My voice broke on the last word, my breath catching in my throat.

I sniffed hard, brushing the sleeve of my jacket against my face. I hated crying. "There's just been so much hurt. So much loss. I can hardly bear it. My heart aches, Papi. A world without either of you just feels so damn lonely." A single sob escaped my lips before I could stop it. I pressed my hand against my chest, trying to breathe through it, trying to force down the weight of grief pressing into me.

But it wasn't just grief. It was fear. I had spent my entire life trying to be strong, trying to be independent. Trying to prove that I could survive everything and anything.

But, my god. I didn't want to keep surviving loss. I wanted to stop losing people. I wanted to stop feeling like love was just another countdown to my heartbreak.

My fingers curled into fists against my thighs as I shook my head. "There's so much that you both will never get to see. You didn't even get to see me graduate." My voice was barely above a whisper now, too raw, too fragile. I pressed my forehead against my knees, letting the silence settle between me and the grave.

I wiped at my eyes, sniffling hard. "I don't know what to do, Papi. I really don't."

And for a second, I closed my eyes and imagined what he would have said if he were sitting beside me. That I was being too stubborn. That life didn't wait for people to figure their shit out. That love was meant to be held onto, even when it was terrifying.

I exhaled shakily, tilting my head toward the sky. The stars flickered against the inky black, endless and vast. I couldn't keep people forever. But maybe, I could stop running from them while they were still here.

I reached forward, brushing my fingers lightly over the engraved letters one last time. "I love you, Papi. Always."

CHAPTER 29

Sebastian

I tapped my fingers against the side of my beer bottle, only half-listening as Analyse went on about something Maya had done earlier that day.

I caught pieces of it—"drew a masterpiece on the wall," "called her teacher abuela by accident," "insisted on wearing pajamas to school because Tío Seb lets me."

Normally, I'd be laughing, probably giving Analyse shit about how Maya clearly inherited her stubbornness. But tonight? Tonight, my mind was elsewhere. Or rather, on someone else.

"You've been staring at your phone for five minutes straight." Analyse's voice cut through my thoughts, her eyes narrowing. "Did you and Mari have a fight or something?"

I blinked, looking down at my phone like it had just appeared in my hand. "No."

"Then why do you look like someone just gave you bad news?"

I sighed, setting my beer down on the porch railing. "She's been weird...distant."

Analyse frowned. "How distant?"

I hesitated before flipping my phone screen toward her, showing her the most recent message from Mariana.

MARIANA

Can't talk right now, I'm exhausted. I'll call you later.

That had been hours ago. No call, no follow-up, and maybe I'm an overbearing asshole. Maybe this was fine; maybe I was overthinking it. She's busy; she has the bakery to deal with, and then everything that is going on with her mom. I get it. She doesn't have to text or see me every moment of the day. But it didn't feel fine. I know her. This doesn't feel like our normal.

Analyse glanced at me, then at the phone, then back at me again. "Sebastian, this is a normal message."

"It doesn't feel normal."

She arched her brow. "Because she didn't immediately drop everything to FaceTime you?"

I clenched my jaw. "That's not-"

Analyse sighed, setting my phone down between us. "Look, I get it. You're in that can't eat, can't sleep, think about her every moment kind of love phase."

I scowled. "That's not a phase."

She smirked. "Exactly. Which means you gotta stop spiraling just because she's busy, big bro. You knew she'd be stretched thin opening the bakery."

"I know."

"Then what's really bothering you?"

I rubbed my hand over my face, letting out a slow breath. I knew what it was. I knew exactly why this was eating me up inside. "Last time I felt this?" My voice came out quieter than I intended. "She left."

The teasing disappeared from Analys's face. She nodded slowly, sitting back. "So that's what this is about."

I swallowed hard. "She's doing it again—pulling back. I can feel it, Lyse."

I hated saying it out loud. I hated admitting that fear still lived inside me, that there was some part of me still waiting for history to repeat itself.

Analyse was quiet for a long moment before she sighed. "Okay, but have you actually asked her about it?"

I hesitated. Because no, I hadn't. What the hell was I supposed to say? Hey, are you planning on running out on me again, or am I just paranoid?

"She's got a lot on her plate," Analyse said gently. "And yeah, I get why you're worried. But this isn't ten years ago. You're not two dumbass teenagers. She's not that same girl."

I nodded, but I wasn't sure that mattered. Maybe she wasn't that girl anymore, but I was still the guy who watched her leave, who had my heart torn in two, who wasn't good enough to make her stay, and I didn't know if I could do it again.

Later that night, I parked down the street from Mariana's place, gripping the steering wheel. I wasn't sure what I was doing here, only that I couldn't shake the feeling that something was off.

What the hell is wrong with me right now? This isn't me. I've never been so insecure in my life, never felt so scared of losing someone.

This isn't how I wanted to handle whatever it is that's going on between us. If she needed space, I had to give it to her. Even if every instinct told me to knock on her door, to make sure she was okay.

I sighed and pulled out my phone, typing a quick message instead.

SEBASTIAN

Hey baby, are you awake?

A few minutes passed. Then -

MARIANA

Yeah. Just tired.

I hesitated. Then -

SEBASTIAN

How's your mom today? Do you want some company?

A long pause. Long enough for doubt to creep in.

I stared at my phone, waiting for the typing bubble that never appeared. Mariana was leaving me on read. Fuck.

The pit in my stomach grew. My grip tightened around the phone, jaw clenching. This wasn't just being busy. This was distance. And I felt it like a punch to the gut.

I exhaled sharply, shoving my phone onto the passenger seat. Waiting around wouldn't change anything. I need to just respect Mariana's needs. I pulled the car into drive and left, the pit in my stomach growing with every mile.

CHAPTER 30

Mariana

T he house was dark when I stepped inside, the faint glow of the streetlights seeping through the blinds. I didn't bother turning on the overhead light.

The silence was thick, settling around me like a second skin as I dropped my bag by the door and toed off my shoes. I should feel better, lighter. I had gone to see my mom. I had gone to see my dad. I had whispered the things I hadn't been able to say out loud in a long time. But instead of comfort, all I felt was exhaustion.

I exhaled slowly, my fingers trailing over the counter as I walked into the kitchen. The weight in my chest was suffocating, pressing down like an ache I couldn't quite shake. I reached for the bottle of wine sitting unopened near the sink, my hands moving on autopilot as I pulled a glass from the cabinet.

I should call Sebastian; he texted me earlier. Checking in, asking about my mom, but I ignored it. Not because I didn't want to talk to him. But because I did. God, I really did. But talking to him meant letting him see this side of me. That part that was breaking. The part that wasn't strong enough to hold everything together.

I poured the wine, watching as the deep red liquid sloshed into the glass. I took a sip, letting the warmth settle into my stomach, but it didn't do anything to drown out the thoughts.

I glanced at my phone, the screen dimly lit with his last message asking if I wanted some company. I sent a quick reply.

MARIANA

Not tonight.

I stared at the words. Distant. A knot formed in my stomach. He would answer soon. He always did. And when he did, he'd be patient, kind—more than what I probably deserved.

I took another sip of wine, gripping the stem of the glass a little tighter. I walked over to my bedroom, trailing my fingers along the dresser as I passed it.

My eyes landed on the framed photo sitting there—one of my parents, arms wrapped around each other, smiling like they had the whole world ahead of them.

Papi would have loved that Sebastian and I were back together. He would have told me that life was too short to let fear keep me from something good, and that I was a fool if I didn't hold on.

But guess what? Papi was gone, and soon, Mami would be too.

And if losing them was this unbearable, if grieving them made my chest feel like it was caving in, then how the hell was I supposed to let Sebastian into that same space? How the hell was I supposed to survive another loss?

I swallowed hard and looked away from the picture, blinking back the sting in my eyes. I climbed into bed, pulling the blankets over me, willing myself to just sleep. But all I could think about was the weight of my phone on the nightstand. The short text I sent to Sebastian, pushing him away.

The space in my bed that suddenly felt too empty. Why didn't I just let him come over? Why is it so hard to just let him be here for me? Why am I so broken?

CHAPTER 31

Mariana

T he scent of quesitos, pasteles de guayaba, and warm
tembleque filled the air, wrapping the bakery in the
comforting embrace of home.

Notes of coconut, cinnamon, and vanilla lingered with
every inhale, mingling with the buttery sweetness of freshly
baked mallorcas and pan sobao.

It smelled like my childhood, like early mornings in my
abuela's kitchen, like everything I thought I had lost but
somehow found again. I stood in the center of The Rolling
Pin, letting it all sink in.

Behind the counter, a framed recipe for flan de vainilla,
written in my mother's looping script, hung like a quiet
blessing over the kitchen. A small woven basket beside it held
cinnamon sticks and star anise, the same way my abuela used
to store them, their scents mingling in a way that made my
heart ache with longing and comfort all at once.

I had poured everything into this place. Every part of me
was embedded deep into the walls. The late nights spent painting, the early mornings perfecting each detail—choosing the

perfect lights, the right color scheme, the little personal touches only I would notice.

This wasn't just a bakery. It was a piece of me. And tonight, it was finally open again.

Laughter and conversation filled the space, the warmth of familiar faces making the air hum with joy. Sebastian stood near the counter, arms crossed, watching me with that look— the one that made my stomach flip. The one that made me feel like I was the only person in the room.

Anna and Analyse hovered near the dessert case, arguing over which pastry to try first, while Nathan stood off to the side, sipping a cup of coquito, trying to act like he wasn't enjoying it as much as he actually was.

Mateo and Andres had, of course, already migrated to the coffee station, one insisting that traditional café con leche was superior, while the other made a dramatic case for black espresso with just a pinch of azúcar.

I exhaled slowly, my chest tight with emotion. I had done this. I had brought them all here, and then I saw Ruth. She stood near the entrance, hands clasped together, her sharp brown eyes sweeping across the bakery with a quiet kind of pride. My stomach twisted. I wiped my palms against my apron before crossing the room.

"Ruth," I said, heart pounding.

Her expression softened immediately. "Mariana," she greeted, her voice thick with warmth.

I swallowed hard. "Well? What do you think?"

Ruth let out a soft chuckle, glancing around again. "I knew you'd made me proud," she said simply.

The words hit me like a gust of wind. "You really think so?"

She nodded. "This place was always meant to be yours. I just had to wait for you to see it, too."

My throat tightened.

"I kept telling everyone I'd sell when the right owner came along," she continued, shaking her head. "But the truth is, I wasn't ever going to sell it. Not unless it was to you."

A shaky breath left my lips.

"You belong here, Mariana," Ruth said, voice gentle but firm. "And this bakery? It belongs to you."

Tears burned the backs of my eyes before I could stop them. I reached forward and hugged Ruth tightly, inhaling the faint scent of lavender and honey that always lingered on her clothes. "Thank you," I whispered.

She just patted my back. "You don't need to thank me, niña. Just keep making those quesitos the way your mama taught you."

A soft, wet laugh slipped from my lips. "I promise."

As soon as I turned around, Sebastian was there, pressing a glass of champagne into my hand. His voice was low, meant only for me. "I am so damn proud of you, Mi Tesoro."

I looked up at him, at the warmth in his brown eyes, and my heart stuttered.

"You really did it," he continued. "You made this place yours."

The emotion in his voice made my throat tighten all over again. Before I could say anything, Mateo clapped his hands together loudly.

"Alright, alright, everyone!" he called out. "Before we all slip into a sugar coma, let's take a second to celebrate the woman of the hour."

Andres grinned, already raising his glass. "To Mariana!"

"To The Rolling Pin!" Anna added.

"And to making sure she never stops feeding us!" Analyse chimed in, making everyone laugh.

Sebastian lifted his own glass. His gaze never left mine. "To you, Mari," he said, voice steady. "And to everything you're building."

Glassed clinked. Laughter bubbled around me. I barely had time to breathe before he closed the space between us. His lips met mine, soft, lingering, yet full of unspoken promises.

My heart stuttered, then soared. The noise around us faded, the world narrowing to the taste of champagne on his lips, the heat of his hand resting at my waist.

When he pulled back, his forehead touched mine, his voice a whisper. "This is only the beginning, Mariana."

And with him beside me, I knew he was right. Then my phone rang.

The sound cut through the moment like a blade, sharp and immediate, slicing into my chest before I even looked at the screen. The hospital. No. Not today, please. Not now.

My fingers shook as I reached for it. I could feel the eyes on me—Sebastian's, Anna's, Ruth's—but their voices blurred, everything muffled as the world shrank to the flow of the screen in my hands.

I knew. Even before I answered, I knew.

Because I had felt this before—the hollow dread when my dad's doctors called, the crushing silence before they told me he was gone. The same sick certainty the night Andrew never came home. Loss had a feeling...a weight. And it was settling over me now.

Swiping the call open, I brought the phone to my ear, my breath already shuddering. "Hello?"

"Ms. Vargas?" The nurse's voice was gentle. Apologetic. Final. The heart-wrenching voice people use when they know the words they're about to say will shatter you. "I'm so sorry."

No.

"Your mother passed away a few minutes ago."

No, no, no, no, no—My knees buckled.

The world tilted, blurred, imploded. My breath caught in my throat, jagged and sharp. There was a roaring in my ears, a violent crashing, like ocean waves pulling me under, dragging me into the dark. I tried to speak, but nothing came out.

The walls of the bakery blurred, the light too bright, too cruel. My mother...My mother was gone. I pressed a hand to my stomach, my body folding in onto itself, my chest caving as a sob ripped from my throat.

Someone was calling my name.

A hand touched my arm, warm and steady, but I jerked away violently, a broken sound escaping my lips. I couldn't breathe. My chest wouldn't expand, my lungs refusing to work. I had to get out.

I stumbled toward the door, nearly crashing into one of the tables. My vision was fractured, nothing making sense, the room bending and swaying under the weight of the words still hanging in the air.

Dead. She's dead. She's gone.

The words slammed into me, over and over, battering my ribs, breaking me open from the inside out. My mother was dead. A sob tore from me—ugly, raw, primal.

I barely made it outside before my legs gave out, and then I was on my knees. The pavement scraped against my skin, but I didn't feel it. I didn't feel anything except the pain cracking through my chest like an earthquake.

I rocked forward, my hands clenched into fists, pressing into the concrete as if that could hold me together. It couldn't. Nothing could. My mother was dead.

"Mariana!"

The voice cut through the storm, distant and worried, and then there were hands on me, strong, and familiar. Sebastian.

I tried to push him away, but he didn't let me. His arms came around me, solid, unwavering, pulling me into his chest.

And I broke. A ragged, gut-wrenching sob tore from my throat, my entire body shaking violently against him.

The grief ripped through me, clawing at my ribs, my skin, my soul. Sebastian's arms tightened, his hand pressing against the back of my head, holding me together when I was coming undone.

"I've got you," he murmured, his voice thick, wrecked. "I've got you, Mariana."

I buried my face into his chest, the scent of cedar-wood and warmth and home filling my senses, but it wasn't enough. Nothing was enough.

The Rolling Pin was still behind me, full of light, full of life—but she wasn't here to see it. She would never see it. She would never see me. A fresh wave of grief slammed into me, brutal and merciless.

Sebastian held me tighter, his own breath uneven as he whispered, "I'm so sorry, baby. I'm so, so sorry."

I couldn't speak. I couldn't do anything except sob into his arms, letting the pain tear me apart.

Grief is a strange thing.

It doesn't arrive all at once. It doesn't hit in one clean wave. It seeps in, little by little, until it's everywhere. At first, I felt numb. A cold, empty void stretching inside me, swallowing everything in its path.

I went through the motions. Answered phone calls I barely remembered. Nodded through conversations I didn't hear. Let Anna and Analyse take over planning the funeral because I couldn't bring myself to do it.

The Rolling Pin still smelled like coconut and vanilla, but it was all wrong now. I hated it. I hated that life just kept going when it felt like mine was over.

That customers still came in, their voices too bright, too alive. That the world didn't pause, didn't acknowledge that something inside me had been ripped out. That I was walking around with a hole in my chest that nothing could fill.

The exhaustion started creeping in a few days later. The deep, aching kind. The type of exhaustion that settled in my bones and refused to leave. It wasn't just the grief—it was my body turning against me, flaring in protest of everything I'd been forcing it to endure.

My joints stiffened, the dull throbbing in my hands and knees intensifying with every sleepless night, every moment spent curled up on my couch instead of moving, eating, *existing*. But even when the pain became impossible to ignore, it still wasn't the worst of it.

Because, for once, my chronic illness wasn't the cause of my suffering. The grief was worse. It was heavier. It was all-consuming.

Sebastian kept calling. Kept texting. At first, I ignored them all. Then, when I finally picked up, I gave clipped answers.

"I'm fine."

"I just need some space."

"I have a lot to do."

I could hear the worry in his voice, the way he hesitated every time I cut the conversation short. The way he didn't know how to fix this.

He came by twice. The first time, I let the phone ring until it stopped. Ignored the knock at my door. Ignored the ache in my chest when I heard his voice on the other side, soft and careful, as if saying my name too loudly might make me break.

The second time, he got inside. I don't know if Anna let him in or if he still had the same spare key from when he helped with the bakery's renovations.

But when I turned the corner from the kitchen, there he

was. Standing in my living room, his hands stuffed into his jacket pockets, his brown eyes tight with something between worry and panic. I froze. He looked at me like he was afraid I was already gone.

"Hey," he said, his voice too gentle. Too careful.

I swallowed hard, arms crossing over my chest. "Sebastian, I—"

"You don't have to say anything." He took a hesitant step forward, then stopped. "I just...I don't want you to be alone."

My throat burned. I wanted to tell him I wasn't alone— that I had Anna, and Analyse, and Ruth, and everyone else who had surrounded me these past few days.

But none of them were *him*, and that scared me. Because if I let him in, it would hurt more when I lost him, too.

So I shook my head. "I just...need time, Seb."

His jaw tightened. "You've been shutting me out."

I swallowed. "I'm fine."

His eyes flashed with something close to frustration. "No, you're not."

My fingers curled into fists at my sides. "What do you want me to say? That I'm falling apart? That I feel like I can't breathe most days? That I wake up and, for a second, forget she's gone, and then it hits me all over again?"

His shoulders fell slightly, but he didn't look away. "You don't have to say anything," he murmured. "I just want to be here."

I shook my head again, feeling something inside me crack open, something raw and sharp and ugly. "That's the problem, Sebastian," I whispered. "You can't be here. Because one day, you won't be. And I can't..." My voice broke. I squeezed my eyes shut. "I can't do this again."

A long beat of silence stretched between us. Then, softly, painfully, he exhaled. "I'm not him, Mariana."

I flinched. But he wasn't angry. His voice wasn't cruel or

demanding. It was quiet. Devastated. I looked up, and what I saw in his expression nearly undid me.

Sebastian was afraid. Afraid that I would do what I always did. That I would run. That I would push him away until there was nothing left for him to hold on to. And the thing is, I couldn't even promise him that I wouldn't.

Instead of answering, instead of letting him in, I looked away. "Please, Seb, just go. I need space." I whispered.

For a long moment, he didn't move. Then, with a slow nod, he took a step back. "Okay," he murmured. "Okay, Mariana."

And then, he walked away.

I stood there, staring at the empty space where he had been, the silence in my apartment so loud it felt deafening. I should have called him back. I should have stopped him.

But instead, I sank onto my couch, pulled my knees to my chest, and let the grief swallow me whole.

CHAPTER 32

Mariana

Dirt and roses. That's what I would remember.

The way the earth smelled raw and damp, heavy with the scent of rain that hadn't yet fallen. The soil looked too dark, too rich, like it belonged in a garden, not in a grave. Like something was meant to grow from it, not be buried beneath it.

The cloying perfume of wilting white roses clung to the air, thick enough to choke on. Their petals were soft, too soft, fragile in a way that made my stomach turn. They weren't supposed to be here, not like this, not wrapped in shaking fingers, not held over an open grave.

I tightened my grip on the single rose in my palm, the thorns biting into my skin. It felt like a betrayal, an offering to the ground instead of a person.

The casket creaked as it was lowered into the grave, the sound splitting the air, slicing through the cold afternoon like a blade. I flinched.

Somewhere in the crowd, a muffled sob broke free. A voice cracked on a whispered prayer, footsteps shifted on the damp grass. I heard everything and nothing at once.

The priest kept speaking, his words blending into the low hum of grief that hovered over the cemetery. I didn't register what he was saying. Because this was it.

This was the moment they took her from me forever. I had told myself I wouldn't cry. I had spent the morning numbing myself, pressing my nails into my palms, focusing on the weight of my mother's favorite lavender shawl draped over my shoulders.

Anything to keep myself upright, in control, breathing. But standing there, watching them take her from me for the last time, something inside me snapped.

I wanted to scream.

I wanted to claw my way into the earth and pull her back.

I wanted to shake the people standing around me, tell them to do something, to stop this, to make it right.

But no one could. No one even tried. Because this was how it was supposed to go, wasn't it? People died. They got buried, and the living just... moved on.

My chest seized violently, my body curling inward like something had caved in on itself. I had the horrible, irrational thought that maybe if I threw myself into the grave, if I screamed loud enough, cried hard enough, begged with every broken part of me, maybe the outcome would change. Maybe this was a mistake. Maybe she would wake up.

Instead, I stood frozen; my fingers dug into the rose until my palm burned, blood slicking against the stem. I barely felt it. I couldn't move, couldn't breathe.

All I could do was watch as my mother was swallowed by the earth, and no matter how much I wanted to stop it, to change it, to bring her back—I couldn't. She was gone, and I was still here.

Sebastian was beside me. A solid presence in a world that suddenly felt paper-thin, fragile in a way that made me feel like if I moved too fast, too suddenly, everything would shatter around me. I didn't look at him, but I knew he was there.

I could feel him shift closer, just slightly. A breath of warmth in the cold, numbing air. A tether to the present, to the world that was still moving forward while I stood frozen in grief. He wasn't touching me, but he was close enough that I knew he would if I let him.

He was close enough that if I leaned, just a little, just for a second, I knew that he would catch me. But I wouldn't. I couldn't, because if I let him hold me, if I let myself collapse into him, the grief would break open like a dam, rushing out in a way I knew I wouldn't be able to control, and if I fell apart now, in front of everyone, in front of him...I wasn't sure I'd ever put myself back together again.

A low, broken sound tore from my throat before I could stop it. It wasn't a sob, not fully, but it was enough to make Sebastian tense beside me. I felt it, the way his body stiffened, the way his breathing hitched just slightly, like he knew I was unraveling.

I felt the moment he almost reached for me, and the way his fingers curled at his side, like he was stopping himself from pulling me in. Like he knew, even without me saying it, that I wouldn't let him. But he wanted to, and for one agonizing second, I considered it.

I considered turning toward him, letting my forehead press against his chest, letting his arms wrap around me so I wouldn't have to hold myself upright anymore.

But the moment passed, and instead of leaning into him, I stepped forward. Just enough to make it clear I didn't want to be touched, and just enough to make the space between us a choice.

The cold air rushed into the gap between our bodies, a physical reminder of the warmth I had just refused. Sebastian's hand dropped away, his fingers curling into a loose fist at his side. I still didn't look at him, but I felt the moment his breath left him in a slow, controlled exhale. I knew that exhale; I've heard it before, in moments where he was trying to stay steady, trying not to push me.

He was trying to hold himself back when all he wanted to do was be there for me, but I wasn't ready for that, I wasn't ready for him. So I stood there, staring at the open grave, letting the distance between us settle like another weight in my chest.

The casket settled at the bottom of the grave. The priest's voice droned on, meaningless words about eternal peace, about how she was in a better place. I hated him for saying it.

I hated that the sky was gray, but it wasn't raining. I hated that people were crying, that they had the luxury of grieving openly, while I felt like I was choking on my own breath. I hated that I was still here, standing above ground, while my mother was beneath it.

Someone handed me a handful of dirt. My fingers curled around it, the soil damp and cool against my skin. I stared at it, my vision blurring.

"Ashes to ashes, dust to dust."

No.

No.

I forced myself to move forward, to open my palm.

The dirt slipped through my fingers, falling in slow, uneven clumps onto the casket below. The thud was too loud in my ears. Too final. I took a step back.

And another.

And another...Until Sebastian's hand caught my arm.

It was light, just a gentle brush of warmth against my sleeve. Not pulling. Not forcing. Just reminding me he was there.

I didn't look at him. I just swallowed back the scream that threatened to rise in my throat, pulled away, and turned my back to the grave. Because if I looked at it for one more second, I would break, and I wasn't ready to break.

Not yet.

CHAPTER 33

Mariana

T he Rolling Pin felt wrong. It was too bright, too warm, too alive. The overhead lights glowed softly against the terracotta tiles, reflecting off the hand-painted designs that framed the front counter. It was beautiful, it was full, and I wanted everyone to leave.

People filled the bakery, their voices hushed but constant, layering over each other in a low, steady hum, a noise I could feel more than hear, vibrating beneath my skin like static.

They whispered condolences over cups of coffee and picked at small plates of food they weren't hungry for. They stole glances at me, their expressions shifting between pity and something softer, something unbearable.

"Your mother was an incredible woman."

"She was so proud of you, Mariana."

"She's watching over you now."

I wanted to scream. I so badly wanted to tell them to stop talking, stop pretending, stop trying to fill the silence with empty words that didn't bring her back.

Because she wasn't watching over me. She was fucking gone.

She was buried under six feet of cold, damp earth, wearing the delicate gold necklace she never took off—the one with my initials and my father's, M & L, so we would always be close to her heart. That's where she was, not here, and definitely not watching.

No matter how much I wanted to, I couldn't reach her, and that thought twisted in my stomach like something sharp, cutting deeper with every breath. So I kept moving.

I refilled coffee cups, cleared empty plates, and wiped down tables that didn't need wiping. I had to keep my hands busy, and keep my feet moving, because if I stopped, even for a second, I'd break. I wasn't ready for that.

So I moved.

And moved.

And moved.

Sebastian stood near the counter, watching me, his gaze was heavy, full of something I couldn't name. Not pity, not sympathy, no...It was something else, something more careful, more knowing, and I felt it every time I turned my back.

I tried to ignore it, until suddenly, he was right beside me. He was close enough that I could feel the warmth of his body, even in the crowded bakery.

"You haven't eaten," he murmured.

I blinked, startled by how close he was, and how quiet his voice had gotten. I turned slightly, meeting his gaze for the first time all day. "What?"

His brow creased slightly, like he knew I had heard him but wasn't ready to acknowledge it. "You haven't eaten anything all day," he repeated. Steady. Unshaken. He held out a plate, a small pastellilo, flaky and golden, and still warm.

I swallowed hard, my throat tight; this was one of my favorites. My mother used to make them every Sunday night. The memory landed like a weight in my chest. I shook my head, too fast, too sharp. "I'm not hungry."

Sebastian didn't move. His jaw tightened slightly. "Mariana..."

His voice was too soft and too careful. He already knew I was unraveling and was trying not to spook me. I didn't want that; I didn't want him treating me like I was delicate, like I was something breakable.

I squared my shoulders, exhaling hard through my nose. "Sebastian, I said I'm not hungry."

A long silence stretched between us. For a second, he didn't move. Then, slowly, carefully, he set the plate down beside me, and walked away. He didn't argue. He didn't try again. He just... left.

Something about that felt worse.

CHAPTER 34

Mariana

The bakery reopened three weeks after the funeral. It had been twenty-three days since my mother died.

Twenty-three days of waking up and feeling like I was slipping further and further away from myself. Twenty-three days of pretending, of forcing myself out of bed.

Now here I am, standing behind the bakery counter and plastering on a careful, distant smile for customers who didn't know how to look at me anymore.

I'm keeping my hands moving, kneading dough, measuring sugar, wiping down counters that weren't dirty, doing anything to avoid the weight of the grief pressing against my ribs.

I told myself that I just needed time. Every morning, I repeated it like a mantra, like a prayer, like something I could will into being if I said it enough.

"Just give it time, Mariana."

"Time will soften the edges."

"Time will help."

But every morning, I woke up feeling like I was sinking deeper. It was as if the world had tilted slightly off its axis, just enough to throw everything off balance. I was walking through a space that had once belonged to me, but no longer fit.

And worst of all, I could feel myself slipping away. Sebastian knew it too. He called and texted every day, and always made sure to check in.

At first, I answered, always keeping my voice light and neutral, giving him short, clipped responses.

"Yeah, I'm fine."

"The bakery's been busy."

"No, I don't need anything."

Then, I started letting the calls go to voicemail. At first, I told myself I'd call him back later. When I wasn't so tired. When my head wasn't pounding. When the weight in my chest wasn't so suffocating. But later never came.

Then I started leaving his texts on read, not because I wanted to ignore him, and not because I didn't care, but because I cared too much.

Because every time his name flashed across my screen, my stomach twisted, and my heart lurched into my throat, and suddenly, I felt like I was suffocating all over again.

His messages were never demanding, never frustrated. He was always patient, loving, and kind.

SEBASTIAN

"Thinking about you."

"Hope today isn't too hard."

"Call me when you can."

Not if you can, or if you want to—but when...As if there

was no doubt in his mind that I would. As if he still believed I was capable of reaching for him, but I wasn't.

So, I let the texts pile up, each unread message like a stone on my chest, pressing down, down, down. The ugly truth was that I wasn't avoiding him because of work, or exhaustion, or even a busy schedule. I was avoiding him because he looked at me like I was still me, like I was still the girl he'd loved since we were teenagers, like I hadn't been gutted by grief, like there was still something left of me to hold onto.

I was avoiding him because no matter how hard I tried to ignore the guilt pressing against my ribs, I couldn't stop the way my heart lurched every time I saw his name on my screen.

Because every time I heard his voice, every time I saw his texts, every time I let myself think about how unwavering his love for me has been, I couldn't stop myself from also thinking about what it would feel like if I lost him too, and it killed me.

I loved Sebastian, this much I knew. I had always loved him, but, if I let myself have that, if I let myself fall all the way, love him the way I wanted to, the way I ached too...it would only hurt more when I lost him too. The truth is, people always leave, and love always ends in loss, and I wasn't sure I could survive more, more loss.

So, I let the silence stretch between us, and I let the grief consume me.

CHAPTER 35

Mariana

I knew it was coming, I had been waiting for it. I was the one who let the silence stretch too far, let it grow too thick, until it wasn't space anymore... It was a wall.

A heavy, suffocating wall built brick by brick with every unanswered call, every ignored text, every time I let my phone ring in my hand until it went silent again.

Sebastian had given me time, more than I sure as hell deserved. He had called, texted, checked in, even when I gave him nothing to hold on to.

He had waited for me...fuck, he had waited, for me to come back to him, for me to let him in. He had been waiting all this time for me to stop pushing, stop running, stop letting my grief and my fear swallow me whole.

But I never did, I couldn't, my fear had crippled me. My fear wouldn't allow me to do anything other than choose what felt safe—distance, silence, and escape route.

And in spite of all of that, in spite of everything I've put him through these last few weeks, here he was, still standing on the other side of that wall, still refusing to walk away. And shit,

I am so damn scared of what I have to say, of what I have to do right now.

The knock at the door was sharp, deliberate, and unyielding. A sound that cracked through the quiet of my house, splintering the fragile calm I had spent the last few weeks trying to convince myself was real.

I had been sitting on the couch, staring at nothing, numb from the inside out. But now, with the sound of him at my door, everything inside me locked up, I was frozen.

My pulse thundered in my ears, my breath lodged somewhere between my ribs, my body stuck between fight and flight, knowing neither would save me from what was coming. I stared at the door, heart hammering, waiting for the moment I'd have to destroy him.

"Don't answer it."

"If you don't answer, he'll leave."

But I knew better, Sebastian wouldn't be Sebastian if he just walked away. He wasn't going to just give up...not without a fight.

A second knock came—harder, more urgent. Then his voice, low, rough, frayed around the edges. "Mariana."

I swallowed, my nails digging into my palms.

"I know you're in there."

I squeezed my eyes shut. Sebastian...I knew that voice, the edge of exhaustion beneath the frustration, the ache beneath the anger.

I knew the way his breath hitched when he was trying to hold himself together, the quiet strain in his voice when he was this close to breaking. And fuck, I hated myself, because I was the one hurting him.

But I knew it was better this way, or at least that's what I told myself over and over, like a prayer, like a promise...But it still didn't feel true.

Silence stretched thick and heavy between us. For a split second, I thought maybe he'd given up, that he had left.

One more knock, this time, softer. Then..."Please."

The word shattered something inside me, I hated the way my body responded to it. The way my chest ached, the way my hands trembled, the way my entire being fought against what I was about to do.

I could feel it in my bones, this was the moment. The moment that I knew I wouldn't be able to take back. The moment that would change everything.

Yet, I pushed off the couch, my legs moving before my mind could stop them. I reached for the handle, opened the door, and looked at the love of my life—the man I was about to destroy.

CHAPTER 36
Mariana

Sebastian's eyes met mine, and I felt the impact like a punch to the gut; he looked wrecked and exhausted. For a moment, we just stood there, staring at each other.

Then, voice hoarse, he broke the silence. "Are you going to let me in?"

I hesitated, not because I didn't want to, of course I wanted to...but because if I let him inside, this would become real, and I wasn't ready to face the reality of what was about to happen.

I wasn't ready to face the weight of what was about to happen, the words we couldn't take back, the breaking that felt inevitable. But I stepped aside anyway.

Sebastian entered, and for the first time in what felt like forever, he was close enough to touch, but I didn't reach for him, and neither did he.

The door clicked shut behind us, the sound sharp, final, sealing us inside this moment we couldn't escape, and I knew then, that whatever happened next, we wouldn't walk out of this the same.

Sebastian ran a hand through his hair, exhaling sharply. "I can't do this anymore, Mariana."

I swallowed. "Do what?"

His head snapped toward me, his jaw tightening. "Don't do that."

"Do what?" I repeated, even though I already knew.

"Pretend." His voice cracked. "Pretend that you don't know exactly what I'm talking about. Pretend that you haven't been shutting me out, pulling away, convincing yourself that you don't want this anymore."

My chest tightened, but I forced myself to meet his eyes. "I'm not pretending, Sebastian."

The words landed between us like a slap, a muscle ticked in his jaw. "So that's it?" he asked. "You're just... done?"

I opened my mouth, but no words came out.

Sebastian let out a bitter, hollow laugh, shaking his head. "Fuck, Mariana. I knew you were scared, but I didn't think you'd run again."

"I'm not running."

"Aren't you?" His eyes darkened, something sharp cutting through the sadness. "Because that's what this is, Mariana. You're not just shutting me out, you're running from me. From this. From us."

He stepped closer, and I felt the air shift between us, thick with unspoken words, with everything we were about to lose. "And for what?" His voice was raw. "Because you think it's easier? Because you think if you push me away first, it won't hurt as much if I leave?"

I flinched, because that was exactly what it was, and of course, Sebastian saw through me, like he always did, but it didn't change anything; it simply couldn't.

So I forced steel into my spine, into my voice, into every ounce of me that wanted to collapse. "It's already done, Sebastian."

Sebastian sucked in a sharp breath, his whole body shaking with it, like he was trying to hold himself together but already knew he was losing. "No." His voice fractured, breaking like glass beneath the weight of everything unsaid. "No, I'm not letting you do this."

He stepped forward, close enough that I could feel the heat of him, close enough that if I just reached out, I could hold on, but I didn't, I couldn't. I saw the exact moment he realized it.

His eyes searched mine, desperate, unguarded, wide open in a way I had never seen before. "Mariana, please don't do this."

I couldn't breathe, because this wasn't just a plea, no... this was more than that, this was Sebastian fighting for his heart, for my heart, for us.

"I love you so damn much." His voice broke completely, a sound I had never heard from him before, something fragile, something final.

"You are it for me, Mariana. You are it. You have been since the moment we laid eyes on each other when we were kids." His chest was rising and falling too fast, his hands clenched like he was physically trying to keep himself from reaching for me. "Since the first time I saw you with that ridiculous pink bow in your hair, standing at the edge of the playground like you didn't belong, like you weren't the most beautiful fucking thing I had ever seen."

I clenched my jaw, but nothing could stop the fire from tearing through my chest.

"You have my whole damn heart, Mariana. All of it." His breath hitched, his fingers twitching at his sides like he was seconds away from losing whatever grip he had left. "You don't need to run from this. You don't need to run from me. I promise you don't need to be afraid."

I squeezed my eyes shut. "Sebastian..."

"Look at me," he whispered.

I couldn't, I couldn't fucking look at him, because I know if I did, I would break.

"You can take all the time you need. I won't pressure you. I won't rush you. I will wait, Mariana. I'll wait as long as it takes. I don't care if it's months, years—I'll still be here. I'll still want you. Just... don't do this. Don't shut me out."

My throat burned, my entire body screaming at me to stop this, to tell him I wanted him too, that I wanted everything he was offering me, but I didn't stop it.

"Just don't give up on me, Mariana." His voice wavered, breathless and broken. "Don't give up on us."

I felt myself shaking, barely holding on, because God, he was breaking me too.

"Don't you see? It's always been yours, Mariana. My heart. My love. Every damn part of me." His voice dropped to a whisper, so wrecked, so full of shattered hope that I could barely stand it. "I don't want anything else. I don't need anything else. I don't care if we go slow, if we don't have it all figured out. I don't care about anything except this, except you, except us."

Sebastian took a step closer, his breath shaky, his hands shaking, his whole fucking body trembling. "I just want you to take it."

Tears blurred my vision, my nails digging into my palms so hard I knew I'd leave marks, but I refused to let them fall.

Sebastian swallowed hard, his chest rising and falling like he was seconds away from breaking completely. "Please." His voice shook now, barely above a whisper. "Please just take it."

Finally, I let myself look at him, really look at him, at the way his entire body was trembling from the weight of it all. The way his eyes—his beautiful, brown, love-filled eyes—were pleading with me to just reach for him, to just let myself have this, to just believe that love didn't always end in loss.

Admittedly, for a second, just one horrible second, I almost did. I felt every ounce of love, every piece of his heart he was offering me, and then, I broke it.

"I can't." The words shattered the air between us.

Sebastian flinched, as if I had just physically struck him. My words had landed like a knife, twisting deep, cutting something open inside him that he couldn't put back together.

I watched as his chest caved in, his breath stuttered, his entire body locked up like I had just ripped his heart straight from his ribs.

"You're really doing this." His voice was so empty, like he was already trying to convince himself this was real.

I nodded, because I couldn't trust myself to speak; I knew that if I spoke, I might beg him to stay.

Sebastian let out a shaky, uneven breath, his eyes searching mine, one last time. "I would've waited for you, Mariana."

My chest collapsed. "I know."

"I would've given you time."

"I know."

"I love you."

I squeezed my eyes shut. "Please, don't say that."

"Why?" His voice shook now, splintering apart at the edges.

"Because it makes this harder."

Sebastian's breath hitched, his fingers flexing at his sides, like he wanted to reach for me but knew he couldn't anymore. "It's already hard," he whispered.

I forced myself to look at him. "Then let's not make it worse."

With those final words, something in him broke for good, I saw it happen, I felt it. The way his shoulders stiffened, the way his chest rose with one last uneven breath, the way his face went blank like he was holding back everything he didn't have the energy to say anymore. He was finally done.

Sebastian turned toward the door, and I let him. This was the moment he finally realized he was never going to win this fight. He reached for the doorknob, pausing for only half a second, one last chance for me to stop him, to take it back, to beg him not to go.

I didn't, I let him go.

The door clicked shut, and I collapsed. It was over, and I had ruined the best thing I had ever had. I had loved him and still let him go.

Now, I have to live with it. Alone.

CHAPTER 37

Mariana

I t had been weeks since I let him go, weeks since I stood in my home, arms wrapped around myself like I could somehow hold together the pieces of what I was about to destroy, and told the biggest fucking lie of my life.

It had been weeks since I watched the light die in his eyes, since I heard his breath hitch, since I felt the weight of my words land like a physical blow, one I wasn't sure he'd recover from.

Since I had looked at the man I loved, the man who had given me everything, who had stood in front of me, offering me his entire fucking soul, and told him I didn't want it.

Since I had convinced myself that walking away from love was easier than losing it. I should feel better, I'm supposed to feel better; that's what people always say, right?

"Time heals all wounds."

"You just need space."

"It was probably for the best."

But what if they were wrong? What if time wasn't healing anything? What if every passing day only stretched the wound wider, dug the blade deeper, left me more hollow than the day before?

What if the world kept moving, but I stayed stuck in the moment I let him go?

Autumn had settled over the town. The air was crisp, carrying the scent of burning leaves and woodsmoke, the type of air that used to make me want to curl up inside with a cup of coffee, wrapped in a sweater, tucked against him. Now, it just feels cold.

I walked down Main Street, past shop windows decorated for the season, past people who smiled at me like they didn't know. Like they couldn't see the wreckage I was barely holding together.

The diner was exactly the same. The bell still jingled when the door opened, the scent of bacon and coffee still thick in the air, but without him, it felt different.

There was an empty seat in the corner by the window, our seat. The one where we'd spent countless mornings together, where I'd stolen his toast and he'd stolen my bacon, where our hands had brushed across the table, lingering longer than necessary.

I turned my head before I could look too long, before the ache in my chest could grow sharp enough to cut. But I still saw him....not really, but for a second, I swore I did.

A familiar broad set of shoulders, dark hair, a profile that looked just enough like his to make my breath hitch, and then I blinked, and he was gone...Just like always.

Inside my house, the silence wasn't peaceful, it was suffocating. The heater kicked on, filling the space with warm air, but I still felt cold.

I still reached for his hoodie every night, draping it over my shoulders, inhaling the fading scent of him like I could pull him closer.

I still left the bathroom light on, a habit from when he used to get up before me, when I'd groggily stumble inside and he'd already have my toothbrush ready with a smirk and a kiss.

I still hadn't deleted his messages, or thrown away the half-empty bottle of cologne he used to leave on my dresser, or moved the cup he'd left on my nightstand weeks ago, his fingerprints still faint against the glass. I know I should let go, and that I should move forward.

But every piece of him still existed in this house, in me, and I didn't know how to live without it.

The nights were the worst. The moments between laying down and falling asleep stretched too long, stretched too empty, stretched too goddamn quiet.

The space where he used to sleep was untouched, like some pathetic part of me thought he might come back. I flipped over onto my side, burying my face into the pillow, but the ache in my chest only grew heavier.

I reached blindly toward the nightstand, grabbing my phone before my mind could stop me. I stared at his name, and hovered my finger over it...I could just call, hear his voice one last time, just... say something, anything.

My thumb brushed against the screen, my pulse thudding in my ears, but then reality slammed into me. If I called, what would I say? Would he even pick up? Would he even want to hear my voice after everything I'd done?

My vision blurred, my throat tightening, my chest squeezing like a vice, then, before I could let my heart get ahead of me, I turned off my phone and threw it onto the nightstand. I curled in on myself, blinking against the burn in my eyes, swallowing against the lump in my throat.

I had done the right thing; that's what I told myself. That's what I repeated like a mantra every morning when I woke up alone. Every night when I lay in bed, staring at the ceiling, feeling the weight of the silence press down on me.

I had protected myself, I had made the logical choice. So then why did I feel like I was unraveling? Why did everything feel muted, like the world had dimmed just enough for me to notice that something was missing... That he was missing?

Why did I keep waiting for this ache to pass, for my heart to settle, for time to do what everyone swore it would? I thought letting go would mean moving forward, but I had only been standing in place, waiting for something to change, for something to shift, for something to make me believe that I had made the right choice.

But there weren't any changes, there weren't any shifts... The world kept turning, but I stayed right here. Stuck. I had let him go. It was the right thing to do.

Then why did it feel like I had done the worst thing imaginable? I had broken something that could never be put back together. I had broken him. I had broken myself.

He had forgiven me once before. Somehow, despite everything, he had let me back in.

But twice? No one gets forgiven twice.

CHAPTER 38

Sebastian

I hold on too long, fight too hard for things I should've learned to release. I'm not built for indifference, I'm not built for loss.

But this? This is something else entirely. This isn't just holding on too long. This is drowning. This is waking up every morning with the crushing weight of her absence pressing against my ribs before I even open my eyes.

This is rolling over to a cold pillow, to empty sheets that haven't been touched by her warmth in weeks.

This is gripping those sheets in my fists, burying my face in the fabric because it still carries the faintest trace of her scent. If I close my eyes and breathe deep enough, for just a second, I can almost convince myself she's still here...almost. Then reality sinks its claws in, and I'm left staring at the ceiling, waiting for the ache in my chest to loosen its grip. It never does.

This is standing in my kitchen, staring at two coffee mugs, one for me, one for her, because I still reach for both, every single morning. Every single morning I pick up hers without thinking, my body betraying me, my hands acting on instinct before my mind catches up.

Every single morning I curse under my breath, shove it back into the cabinet like it's something I should've let go of by now. But I never do, because I don't want to.

This is getting in my car, gripping the steering wheel so tight my knuckles turn white, because her scent still lingers in the passenger seat, faint, fading...fading just like she did.

No matter how hard I try to hold on, no matter how many times I inhale too sharply, hoping to catch more of it, I can't do anything to stop it from disappearing, just like I couldn't stop her.

I can't even be angry, even though I really want to be. I want to hate her for leaving, for shutting me out, for making me believe we were something solid and unshakable, only to tear it down.

For making me believe in forever, only to leave me stranded in the wreckage of it. For making me love her so damn much that even now, even after she stood in front of me and shattered my fucking heart...I still can't stop, I still love her.

No matter how much time passes, no matter how much I try to push her out of my head, she's still everywhere. She's in my car, in the way my hand instinctively reaches for hers at stoplights before I realize she's not there.

She's in my apartment, in the blanket she always curled up with, still bunched up in the corner of the couch, untouched since the last time she was here. I should fold it, I should put it away, but I don't, because that would make it real, that would mean she's not coming back.

She's the way I still turn to tell her things, only to be met with silence. She's the way I still hear her laugh even when there's no one around, it happens when I'm least expecting it.

In the shower, where she used to press her cold feet against my legs, laughing when I jerked away.

In the grocery store, when I reached for the snacks she always made me buy but never finished. In my own goddamn reflection, where I see the man she used to love, except now he looks hollowed out, like he's just barely keeping himself together.

She's in my fucking bones. Because Mariana Vargas has never just been someone I love; she's been a part of me. Now, I'm stuck inside a life that still has space for her, still makes room for her, still fucking belongs to her.

And what fucking sucks is that no matter how much it hurts, no matter how much it hollows me out, I don't want to let it go. If I stop reaching for her, stop seeing her in the spaces between silence, stop aching for her...it means she's really gone.

The night stretches long and unforgiving, I can't sleep. I haven't been able to sleep for weeks, but tonight is different, tonight, it's worse. I lie on my back, staring at the ceiling, my breathing uneven, my body heavy with exhaustion that refuses to pull me under. The air in this house is stale, unmoving, thick with the scent of something missing. Her.

I squeeze my eyes shut, fists clenching, breath stuttering as I fight against the sharp, sinking feeling in my chest. The one that says I did this to myself, the one that says I had everything and I let it slip through my fingers.

I reach blindly toward the nightstand, my hand closing around my phone before my mind can catch up. I know what I'm about to do, and I don't stop myself.

Her name is still pinned at the top of my call log...Mariana. I hover over it, my thumb pressing against the screen so lightly that it doesn't register the touch.

I could just call her...the ache in my chest deepens, turning sharp, slicing through bone, because I know she won't answer.

She made that clear, she doesn't want me. The thought makes my throat close up, my breathing unsteady.

I shift my grip, my knuckles going white around the phone. My pulse is in my ears, loud, thudding, drowning out every rational thought telling me to put it down.

Because if I don't call her, what do I do? If I don't hear her voice, how do I survive the night?

My body starts shaking before I even realize it. Not the kind of tremor that comes from the cold—the kind that comes from something inside you breaking, something collapsing in on itself, something you can't fix. I grit my teeth, squeezing the phone so fucking hard my hands go numb.

Just call her.

Just call her.

Just...I exhale sharply and throw my phone across the room. It hits the wall, a sharp crack cutting through the silence before it drops to the floor.

Her name rings out, faint and hollow. "Hey, Seb." I freeze. The sound of her voice cuts through the silence like a blade. I can't breathe.

I turn, my body moving before my mind catches up, my eyes locking onto my phone, the screen still illuminated from where I threw it. It's playing something, something old, something I didn't even remember existed. A voice memo... from her.

I stare at the screen, pulse hammering in my ears, hands shaking so bad I don't think I could reach for it even if I wanted to. Then, she keeps speaking. "You're probably still asleep, but I just wanted to say hi. No real reason. Just... I don't know. I was thinking about you."

A sharp ache blooms in my chest, thick and suffocating, pressing against my ribs like something is caving in from the inside, because I remember this.

I remember this exact morning; it was a Sunday. I had

barely opened my eyes when I saw her name on my phone, a voice memo waiting for me; I had smiled. I had smiled so fucking hard.

She knew I hated voice memos, but she also knew I loved them when they were from her. "Anyway, I know you hate voice memos, but I also know you're probably smiling right now because you secretly love them when they're from me."

My breath stutters out of me, uneven and sharp, because she had been right. I *had* smiled. I had called her two minutes later, voice still rough with sleep, teasing her for leaving me messages when she could've just waited for me to wake up. She had laughed, I can still hear her laughing. "You sound grumpy," she had said.

"That's because you woke me up, Mari."

"Liar," she laughed again. "You love that I woke you up."

She had been right, I had loved waking up to her. I had loved every stupid voice memo, every early morning call, every damn thing about the way she loved me.

Now, she's gone. Now, I'm sitting alone in this apartment that still smells like her, still aches with the absence of her, still feels like it belongs to her. Now, I'm gripping my knees so hard my nails dig into my skin, fighting the sob that's clawing its way up my throat.

"Okay, I'll stop rambling. Just... call me when you wake up, okay? Love you."

Love you.

Love you.

The words ring through the room, through my head, through my entire fucking body. I squeeze my eyes shut, shoving my fists into my hair, fighting the way my whole chest feels like it's caving in.

This is too much.

This is too fucking much.

She loved me.

She loved me, and she still walked away. Not once—twice.

The screen goes dark, and the silence is deafening. In that moment, I realize—I can't stay here. If I stay, this house will destroy me.

I push up from the bed so fast my vision tilts. I need to move, I need to go. I grab my keys, and I leave.

～

It's past midnight when I pull into my sister's driveway. The house is dark except for the glow from the living room window, I don't know why I came here.

Maybe because it's the only place that still feels familiar, or because Analyse is the only person who's ever been able to read me without me having to say a word. Maybe because I'm so fucking tired of being alone.

I kill the engine and sit there, gripping the steering wheel, my hands still trembling, my body still bracing against something that already hit. I take a slow breath, but it doesn't help.

Then, the porch light flickers on. I watch through the windshield as Analyse steps onto the porch, arms crossed, brow furrowed. She doesn't look surprised; I think through some sibling telepathy, she knew I was coming.

I rub a hand down my face, sighing. I don't have it in me to pretend I'm fine. Not tonight. I open the door, step out, and before I even make it up the steps, she's pulling me into a hug.

It's not soft or careful. It's fierce, tight—a hug only Analyse can give, one that says, I see you, I know you, and you don't have to say anything. She doesn't let go for a long time.

When she finally does, she tilts her head toward the house. "Come on, let's go inside."

I drop onto the couch, elbows braced on my knees, head

hanging forward. Analyse disappears into the kitchen. When she comes back, she hands me a glass of water. I stare at it.

"I was hoping for something stronger," I mumble.

She sits beside me, pulling a blanket over her legs. "You need water more than you need whiskey."

I huff a tired breath, dragging a hand through my hair. Neither of us speaks for a long moment.

Finally, she sighs, shifting to face me. "You look like hell, Seb."

I let out a humorless laugh, shaking my head. "I feel worse."

She doesn't argue, doesn't tell me to move on, or that she wasn't worth it. She just waits. The dam breaks.

"I don't know how to do this." My voice comes out hoarse, barely above a whisper. "I don't know how to live in a world where she doesn't want me." Analyse's expression softens, but she stays quiet.

I shake my head, staring down at my hands. "I thought I could handle it, that I could just... exist without her. But I can't." My throat tightens. "I don't know how to let her go."

Analyse exhales slowly. "Do you think she really wanted to let you go?"

I swallow, shaking my head. "She made her choice."

"Did she?" Analyse raises a brow. "Or did she just convince herself she didn't have another option?"

I don't respond, deep down, that's the thing that's been eating at me the most.

Analyse leans forward, voice quieter now. "Seb, I know you. And I know you don't give up on the people you love."

I lift my head, meeting her eyes.

"But love isn't just about feeling it. It's about choosing it."

I flinch, exhaling sharply.

She reaches out, squeezing my arm. "You deserve someone who fights for you."

The sadness shifts, and in its place, anger claws its way to the surface. Not at Mariana, but at myself for waiting, for breaking apart every night, hoping she'd come back, while she's out there pretending I never fucking mattered.

For holding onto her like she's the only thing keeping me whole, when she's the one who let go first. For loving her when she doesn't love me enough to stay.

I inhale sharply, blinking against the burn behind my eyes. Analyse doesn't say anything else. She just lets me sit in the silence—a silence that doesn't crush, a silence that doesn't drown. And for a brief moment, I feel a little lighter.

CHAPTER 39

Mariana

The first knock is soft, patient. I ignore it. The second knock is a little louder. Not urgent, just expectant. I sink deeper into the couch, pulling my blanket tighter around me. Maybe if I don't move, she'll think I'm asleep.

Silence, then...three soft taps, then another. I freeze.

Our childhood pattern. The same way Anna used to knock on my bedroom door when we were little, when she wanted me to come out but knew I'd be stubborn about it. I close my eyes. She's not going to leave.

"Mariana." Her voice is neither forceful nor exasperated, just firm and unwavering.

I stay still, my fingers curling into the fabric of the blanket, gripping it like an anchor. More silence. Then, one final knock.

"I brought you coffee."

My throat tightens. I don't need coffee—I already have a half-drunk, cold cup sitting on the table. But I know Anna... she's waiting. Not pressuring, not forcing, just waiting.

I exhale slowly, forcing my body to move even though it

feels like I'm carrying bricks on my back. My legs ache from staying curled up too long, my chest feels like it's collapsing in on itself, but I still walk to the door and open it.

Anna stands on the other side, arms crossed, her dark eyes scanning my face like she's taking inventory of the damage. Her expression softens, her brows lift, and her lips press together.

"You look like hell."

I huff a humorless laugh. "Thanks."

She holds up a to-go cup. "I brought you coffee."

I glance at it, then at her. "I already have coffee."

She shrugs. "Yeah, but you didn't have this coffee. This one has extra sugar, just how you like it. And it comes with me forcing you to leave your house, which I know you haven't done in days."

I blink at her. "I—"

"Nope." She shakes her head, stepping past me and grabbing my coat from the hook by the door. "Get your shoes. We're going out."

"Anna, I don't really..."

She turns, fixing me with a look so sharp it makes my throat close up.

Then, softer, her voice dipping, careful but knowing:

"Mari, I know you. You're stressed. You're barely eating, barely moving. And I know what that does to you. When was the last time you actually took care of yourself? Stress triggers flares, and you know it."

I swallow hard, looking away. I don't want to talk about that. I don't want to think about my body, about the way I've been ignoring it, about how I've been feeling worse but blaming it all on grief.

"Come with me, Mari. Just for a little while."

I hate how my chest aches at that, because she's not mad, she's not scolding me. She's just asking me not to disappear.

The tightness in my throat gets worse. I look away, and stare at the coat in her hands.

Then, finally, I nod. "Okay."

Anna drives with the windows cracked, letting the cool air slip in. The radio hums softly in the background, some song playing low enough that I don't really hear it.

The streets of Lake City roll by in a blur—small businesses, coffee shops, the bookstore we used to go to when we were kids. She doesn't tell me where we're going or try to fill the silence with small talk, and I really appreciate it.

I keep my hands wrapped around the to-go cup, letting the warmth sink into my fingers, focusing on anything but the weight pressing against my chest.

Then...a very familiar beat starts playing. I freeze.

Oh. No.

Anna's head whips toward me so fast I feel it before I even look.

The opening line comes through the speakers—

"At first I was afraid... I was petrified..."

I groan. "Anna, no."

She claps her hands once, throwing an arm across her chest in a dramatic flourish. Then, she starts singing. Loudly, off-key, and with enough energy to shake the entire car.

"Kept thinking I could never live without you by my side—!"

"Anna, I swear—" I warn, but the corner of my mouth twitches, betraying me despite my best effort to stay serious.

"But then I spent so many nights thinking how you did me wroooong—"

I press a hand to my face, but I'm already smiling.

"And I grew stroooong—"

"Please, for the love of God—"

"AND I LEARNED HOW TO GET ALONG!"

The volume cranks up to full blast. I shake my head, biting my lip to keep from laughing.

Anna smirks. "I see that smile, Mariana."

I turn toward the window, fighting it. "No, you don't."

"Come on, Mari." She nudges my arm. "This is our song."

I roll my eyes. It *was* our song. We used to scream-sing it in Anna's bedroom, standing on her bed like it was a concert stage, using hairbrushes as microphones.

I exhale, shaking my head. "Anna, I'm not..."

"Yes, you are."

"Anna—"

She throws her head back, absolutely butchering the next line.

"DO YOU THINK I'D CRUMBLE? DID YOU THINK I'D LAY DOWN AND DIE?"

Maybe it's the way she looks at me, like she's seeing the girl I used to be, like she's willing me to find her again, or maybe it's just been so long since I've done something this stupid. Either way...I sigh, and I start singing. Badly. Loudly. With no care in the world.

By the time we hit the chorus, we're both screaming the lyrics at the top of our lungs, the wind carrying our voices out the open windows.

For weeks, maybe even months, I haven't felt this light.

But now, a spark of hope flickers—maybe, just maybe, I can feel something other than loss.

When she finally parks, I recognize the place instantly— the outdoor market. The same one my mom used to take us to when we were younger. The one with fresh bread, homemade jewelry, and flowers in every color. The one where my mom would always make us pick out a fruit we'd never tried before, even when we'd whine about it.

My stomach tightens.

"Anna..."

"It's just a market, Mari," she says softly, but we both know she picked it on purpose. She picked this place because it's familiar, because it feels like my old life.

She steps out without giving me a chance to protest.

Without thinking, I follow.

The scent of warm bread and roasted coffee lingers in the air. People move between stands, chatting, laughing, and existing. I hadn't realized how long it had been since I'd been around this many people.

Anna buys a loaf of fresh pan sobao, breaking off a piece and handing it to me without a word; I take it. We walk, passing flower stands and handmade jewelry booths, the kind of things my mom used to love. Something tight pulls in my chest, but I don't let it break me, not here.

"You used to love coming here," Anna says, glancing at me.

I nod. "Yeah."

"You'd always beg your mom for those ridiculous honey sticks."

I let out a small, unexpected laugh. "They weren't ridiculous. They were good."

Anna grins. "Okay, but you never actually ate them. You just collected them in a drawer and forgot about them."

I roll my eyes, but I feel it, the lightness; it's brief but real. We keep walking, and for a while, it feels like nothing's changed, as if I'm still me. As if I'm not someone who let love slip through my fingers, someone who is still drowning in her own grief.

But then, we pass a vendor selling handmade candles, and

one of them...vanilla and cinnamon. It smells like Sebastian's apartment, I freeze.

Anna watches me carefully. "Mari-"

I shake my head, my throat too tight, my chest too full, too raw. I take a step back, desperate for air, even out here, I still can't breathe.

I turn, walking away from the stand, gripping the paper bag with the bread so tightly my knuckles turn white. Anna catches up easily, she doesn't ask what's wrong, she already knows.

We sit on a bench near the edge of the market; I feel the warmth of the sun against my skin, but it doesn't reach the part of me that's still frozen.

Anna lets the silence stretch before finally speaking. "Are you happy, Mari?"

I flinch. The answer should be easy. Instead, it sticks to the roof of my mouth. "I'm fine," I say, but my voice cracks on the last word.

Anna doesn't hesitate. "No, you're not."

Tears burn behind my eyes, I force them down. "I can't..." My voice shakes. I don't even know how to finish that sentence.

Anna exhales. "You can pretend you don't miss him," she says quietly. "But Mari... I've known you my whole life, and I've never seen you like this."

A tear escapes, but I wipe it away quickly—like it was never there. "I don't know how to fix this," I whisper.

Anna nods. "Then start with admitting you want to."

I let out a shuddering breath, I don't say anything else, and Anna just reaches for my hand. We sit in silence for a while, watching the world pass by, lost in our own thoughts.

CHAPTER 40

Sebastian

I haven't slept in a week, not really, not in a way that counts. I close my eyes, but sleep doesn't come, at least not a sleep that heals or replenishes, and definitely not the type that quiets the noise.

Every time I drift off, she's there...Mariana. Laughing, looking at me the way she used to, like I was her favorite thing in the world, as if she had never left, and she had never torn my fucking heart out of my chest and walked away with it.

My dreams of her aren't soft, they aren't gentle, no...they are ruthless. When I wake up, for those first few disoriented seconds, I forget. I forget that she's not here, and that she's not mine anymore.

The realization always hits like a sucker punch, sharp and immediate, knocking the wind out of me before I can even get my bearings. The muscle memory of having her beside me is stronger than my grief.

I roll onto my back, pressing the heels of my palms into my eyes, willing the images away. I exhale sharply, my chest hollow, gripping the edge of the envelope between my fingers.

My hands are unsteady, I don't realize how tight my grip is

until I see the way the paper bends slightly at the corners. I smooth them out with the pad of my thumb, hoping that'll somehow undo the damage.

I haven't opened it, I haven't even been tempted, because it's not mine. It's Mariana's, and it's from her mother.

I swallow hard, my throat tight.

"She's going to need this one day." I hadn't understood what her mother meant when she pressed it into my hands. At the time, Mariana had been happy, we had been happy. She was mine then.

She had let me love her, let me in without hesitation, without walls. She had told me she loved me like it was the easiest thing in the world, like it was as natural as breathing.

Now, she won't even look at me. The weight of that shift is suffocating. If someone had told me back then that this is where we'd be now, strangers standing in the wreckage of what we used to be, I would have laughed in their face.

I would have sworn up and down that Mariana and I were different, that we were unwavering, that nothing could touch us.

But her mother? Her mother had seen this coming. Long before I did, long before Mariana did. Somehow, she had known, maybe in the way only mothers can, that the day would come when Mariana would shut herself away, locking the world out, locking me out, and she had left something behind to stop her.

I drag a hand down my face, exhaling roughly, the weight of it all pressing into my chest. This letter is more than ink on paper, it's a lifeline, a bridge. It's a desperate attempt to reach the girl who once whispered, "I love you," without fear.

If there's even the smallest chance that these words can break through the walls she's built, and can cut through the fear she's wrapped around herself like armor... then I have to try. Even if it kills me, Even if this is the last thing I ever do for her.

Because this isn't about what I want, it's so much larger than that; this is about what Mariana needs. And right now, she needs this letter more than she knows.

~

The porch light flickers once before holding steady, casting a dim, golden glow over Anna's front steps. The night air is cool, crisp enough to sting a little when I inhale, but I barely notice. My hands are cold, but my palms are sweating.

I shift my grip on the envelope, flipping it between my fingers, feeling the worn edges bend and flex under my touch. I've done this too many times—held it, smoothed out the creases, traced the handwriting as if I could pull meaning from the ink without opening it.

I shouldn't be here, I shouldn't be doing this, but I don't know what else to do, so I knock, not too loud, not too soft— just firm enough to be heard over the quiet hum of the night.

A pause, a shuffle of movement inside. Then, the door swings open, and Anna stands there, her hair pulled into a loose bun, an oversized sweatshirt slipping off one shoulder. She blinks at me, confusion shifting into something sharper, something wary.

Her arms folded across her chest. "You look like shit."

I let out a breath of a laugh, but there's no humor in it. "Yeah."

She studies me, brow furrowing, taking in everything—my clenched jaw, my tired eyes, the tension I can't seem to shake. Her gaze drops to my hands, to the envelope I'm gripping like it's the only thing keeping me upright.

Her expression shifts again, caution creeping in. "Come in."

I don't move. That's her second clue, because I always move, I never freeze up. Unless something is really, really fucking wrong.

Anna's stomach tightens. "What's going on?"

I step inside, but I don't sit. I don't shake off my coat. I just stand there, tension coiled in every muscle, the weight of what I'm about to do pressing down hard.

Anna watches me closely, her arms still crossed, her foot tapping once against the floor. She doesn't like waiting, and I don't blame her. But shit, I need a second—just one more second before I do this, before I hand over the one thing I've been holding onto for too long.

I reach into my jacket pocket, pull out the envelope, and hold it out. Anna frowns, taking it. The paper is soft from wear, the edges slightly bent, her fingertips run over the hand-writing, and her face changes. She knows this handwriting. She knows it as well as her own; her breath catches.

She looks up at me, her voice quieter now. "What is this?"

I swallow hard. "It's from her mom."

The air between us shifts. Anna's chest pulls tight, her pulse hammers. I can see it all over her face.

Her eyes drop to the letter, and a quiet breath shudders out of her. "This isn't how she should be getting this." The words are barely more than a whisper, like they hurt to say.

She swallows hard, arms wrapping around herself like she's bracing for impact. "A letter from her mom–" her voice catches, and she shakes her head. "She shouldn't have to read this like this. Not now, Not when she's already carrying so much."

Her fingers twitch at her sides, but she doesn't reach for the letter yet. Instead, she takes a small step back, distancing herself from the letter as if it's a live wire, something too dangerous to touch.

I exhale, my voice rough, uneven. "Her mom gave it to me before she passed."

A pause. A breath. A hesitation.

"She told me to give it to Mariana when she needed it." And now, she fucking needs it.

Anna finally reaches for the letter, her fingers tightening around it. It's just paper, just ink, but it might as well be a bomb. Because once Mariana reads this? There is no going back.

Anna's voice barely makes it past her lips. "Sebastian..."

I shake my head. "I know."

Her voice wavers. "You're asking me to break her open."

My jaw tightens, pulse hammering. Then, my voice drops lower, rougher, but steady. "I'm asking you to help her."

She doesn't move, doesn't argue, she just stares at me. I know what she's thinking. She's thinking about how fragile Mariana is. She's thinking about how hard it's been to watch her shut everyone out. She's thinking about how much damage this could do.

She looks at me, and I realize—This isn't just about Mariana. It's about me, too. Because I still love her, I will always love her, and because I am fucking desperate for a sign that she still loves me, too.

Anna swallows hard. Then, soft, barely above a whisper. "Do you still want her, Seb?"

My eyes snap to hers, and I don't hesitate. "Always."

CHAPTER 41

Mariana

nna's apartment smelled like warm spices and home, not the home we grew up in—but hers.

A place she had made her own, with mismatched throw pillows on the couch, framed pictures of us on the walls, and candles that always smelled like sweet orange and agave.

It was cozy, lived-in, welcoming, yet something about being here tonight felt off. The air carried more weight than it should; it felt like I wasn't just here for dinner.

She moved around the kitchen like she always did—effortless, focused, pulling ingredients from the fridge, chopping onions with quick, practiced movements. The sizzle of garlic hitting hot oil filled the space, mixing with the scent of stewed tomatoes and sofrito.

I sat at the kitchen table, watching her, and she watched me too. Not obviously. Not in a way that would make me call her out for hovering, but she was watching, checking—making sure I was here, making sure I was eating, making sure I wasn't just sitting in this chair pushing food around my plate like I had no appetite for anything anymore.

Anna was observant like that; she had always known when I was hurting, even when I wasn't ready to talk about it, even when I wanted to pretend I was fine.

I sighed, shifting in my chair. "Anna, you didn't have to do all this."

She shot me a look over her shoulder, unimpressed. "You haven't been taking care of yourself."

"I'm fine."

Anna snorted, stirring the pot. "You look like you haven't seen the sun in weeks, Mari."

I rolled my eyes but didn't argue, because she wasn't wrong.

She set two plates down on the table—arroz con gandules, grilled chicken, thick slices of avocado on the side. It smelled exactly like home—exactly like my mother's cooking.

In an instant, the ache I had been trying so hard to ignore wedged itself between my ribs, pressing down hard. I gripped my fork, my throat suddenly too tight.

Anna sat across from me, quiet for once, just watching. She didn't say anything when I hesitated. She just waited, and for some reason, that felt worse, so I took a bite, and then another.

I wasn't sure if I was actually hungry or if I just wanted to prove to her that I wasn't falling apart, that I could sit here and eat a plate of food like a normal person. For a moment, it worked...for a moment, we just...ate.

But suddenly, Anna pushed back from the table. I thought maybe she was going to grab more water or clear the plates. Instead, she reached into her bag, and pulled out something small.

At first, I didn't recognize what it was, but then she set it down on the table between us, and everything inside me stilled. An envelope.

The paper was soft with wear, the edges slightly bent, like

it had been held too many times, passed from one set of hands to another. My name was written on the front, in handwriting I would recognize anywhere. The air shifted. My throat tightened. I didn't move. I couldn't move.

Anna exhaled softly, her voice quieter now. "Your mom wrote you a letter."

Everything stilled; my breath caught in my throat. "What?"

Anna's eyes stayed steady on mine. "Sebastian gave it to me. She wrote it before she passed, and told him to give it to you when you needed it."

Something in my stomach twisted—sharp, unrelenting. I swallowed hard. "Why didn't he tell me?"

Anna didn't hesitate. "Would you have opened it?"

I felt the answer stick in my throat, thick and heavy. No, I wouldn't have. I wasn't sure I could even open it now.

My hands trembled as I reached for it, my fingers tracing over the familiar loops and curves of my mother's handwriting —"For my Mariana."

The air in the room thinned. Tears blurred my vision before I even worked up the courage to slide my thumb under the seal. "I'm going to go upstairs and let you read this," Anna says, setting the letter down in front of me.

I don't move, don't say a word. A moment later, I hear her footsteps retreating, leaving me alone with the envelope, the one I've been too afraid to open.

My fingers hover over it, hesitation curling tight in my chest. But then I slide my thumb under the seal, peeling it open with slow, deliberate care.

The paper inside is smooth beneath my fingertips, the ink slightly smudged in places, like it's been touched too many times. My gaze catches on the familiar loops and curves of her writing, a sharp ache blooms in my chest.

I blink hard, once, twice, then take a slow breath and start to read.

My Mari,

If you're reading this, it means I am gone. And for that, my love, I am so sorry. If love alone could have kept me here, I would have stayed forever. I would have fought the whole damn world just to have more time with you—to see you smile, to hear your laugh, to hold your hand just a little longer. But time doesn't bargain, mi vida. Time doesn't care how tightly we hold on, how much we beg, how desperately we wish for just one more day.

I know you, Mariana. I know you better than anyone. I was the first to hold you, the first to love you, the first to whisper your name against my heart. I have seen every piece of you—the bright, the stubborn, the fierce, the tender. You are made of fire and softness, of wild storms and warm sunshine. You are the best thing I ever did.

I also know how hard you fight to be strong. My girl, always carrying the weight alone, always trying to prove that you don't need anyone to hold you up. You have always been so determined, so fiercely independent, and so afraid to need. You think if you don't let yourself lean too much, if you don't love too deeply, if you don't hold on too tightly, it won't hurt as much when it's gone. But love doesn't work like that, mi corazón. Love is meant to be held with both hands. It is meant to be felt fully—without hesitation, without fear. Love is the only thing worth being afraid of, and the only thing worth choosing anyway.

I know you're scared. I know how loss has shaped you, how it has made you wary, made you build walls you think will keep you safe. But Mari, life without love isn't safe—it's empty. It's the kind of quiet that lingers in the spaces where love should be. It's the ache that doesn't go away, the loneliness that settles in when you've spent too long pushing people away, and I never wanted that for you.

Loving you and your papi was the easiest, most natural thing in the world—like breathing, like the sun rising each morning without question. It was never a choice I had to make; it was simply who I was, wrapped up in the love I had for my family. That kind of love, mi vida, the kind that settles into your bones and fills the spaces between heartbeats, is meant to be cherished, not feared.

I know love can feel uncertain. I know it can feel fragile, it can feel like something that can be taken away in an instant. But that's not a reason to hold back. That's not a reason to shut it out. Love isn't about guarantees—it's *about choosing it anyway, about letting it shape you, letting it remind you that even in the hardest moments, you are not alone.*

So don't let fear steal what is meant to be yours. Love with your whole heart, mi amor, the way you were meant to. Because if there is one thing I am certain of, it's this—you have a heart made for love, and the world is better when you share it.

I am with you. Always.

Con todo mi amor,

Mami

I'm shaking. My hands, my breath, my entire fucking world. Because she knew, Mami had always known.

I spent so long convincing myself that pushing people away would protect me. That if I didn't let myself love too deeply, I wouldn't have to grieve when it was gone.

That if I held my heart close enough, tight enough, no one could ever take it from me. But now? Now, I see the truth.

Because my mom loved me fearlessly. She had loved me without hesitation, without fear, without pulling back to protect herself. She had loved with her whole heart—so much that even now, even in the unbearable absence of her, the love was still here.

It hadn't disappeared, it hadn't faded, it hadn't died with her. Love was never something to be afraid of. I can hear her voice in my head, unwavering and certain, just as it always was when she spoke about love, when she spoke about my father—"Your papi was the love of my life, Mari."

I can still see it, the way her whole face would soften when she said it. The way she would smile, tucking her hair behind her ear like she was seventeen again, falling for him for the first time. "Was it always easy?" she'd say, shaking her head. "No, mi amor. But was it worth it? Every damn time."

She had loved him like breathing. She had loved him even when it was hard, even when it hurt. She had loved him even when they fought, even when they frustrated each other, even when life pulled them in different directions—because she had always, always chosen love.

When we lost him, when grief clawed its way into every part of our lives, she had never once regretted it, she had never once wished she had loved him less, she had never let fear steal her love away.

My breath catches, sharp and uneven, as I press the letter to my chest. It shakes against me, the paper crinkling beneath my fingers as something inside me cracks wide open.

Mami had always told me I was strong, but I wasn't strong when I let fear make choices for me. I wasn't strong when I walked away from the man I loved, convincing myself it was safer than losing him.

I had let fear control me. I had let it steal my love away, but love was never something to run from. My mom knew it, my dad knew it, and deep down, I had always known it, too.

I know what I have to do. I have to fight for the man I never stopped loving. I have to fight for Sebastian.

I have to choose love, even if it scares me, even if it makes my hands shake.

Even if it means stepping into something unknown, something vulnerable, something that could hurt, because my mom was right…love is always worth the risk.

CHAPTER 42

Mariana

I don't run to him, I don't race out the door with my mother's letter still clutched in my hand, tears streaking my face, ready to fall into his arms and beg for forgiveness.

No, instead, I sit. I sit at Anna's kitchen table, the wood cool beneath my fingertips, the uneven grain pressing into my skin like an anchor. The overhead light flickers once, a too-bright thing against the darkness pooling outside.

The kitchen smells like spices, remnants of the dinner I ate, but barely tasted. A faint trace of coffee lingers in the air, mixing with the scent of dish soap. This should all feel comforting, it should feel safe, but right now I feel like I'm suffocating.

My hands are trembling. My vision is blurred, unfocused, hazy around the edges. My breath is coming in uneven, shallow bursts that don't quite fill my lungs.

The letter is still in my hands, creased now from the way I keep gripping it too hard, like if I let go, it'll disappear...like she'll disappear.

I smooth my fingers over the paper, tracing the ink, memorizing the curves of her handwriting. My name, written by her hand, I swallow hard.

The ink is starting to smudge beneath my fingertips, my mother's handwriting delicate but firm, her voice still somehow alive in every loop, every stroke of the pen.

It truly hits me in this moment, she's never going to be here again. The feeling is like a sharp, gutting kind of grief — a visceral pain that twists my stomach, caves in my chest, and makes me want to sob until there's nothing let inside me by hollow space.

But I don't cry. I just sit with it.

I know that this isn't something I can fix in a single night, this isn't something I can patch up with apologies and hope. I hurt him—again. I didn't just break his heart...I shattered it. Twice.

I looked Sebastian in the eyes and told him I couldn't love him the way he deserved. That I was too afraid, too damaged, too unwilling to take the risk. I walked away when all he ever did was fight for me. Now, I have to sit with the mess I made, again.

The silence in the apartment is heavy, but Anna doesn't rush me. She clears the plates from dinner, the sound of ceramic clinking softly against the sink filling the space between us.

She moves quietly, rinsing dishes, wiping down the counter, giving me room to process, to exist, to come apart without an audience. She's always known when I need space, when I need time to untangle my thoughts before I can even say them out loud.

The pressure in my chest builds and builds until it's too much, until my lungs feel tight, until my hands are gripping the edges of the table like it's the only thing keeping me upright.

Eventually, when my throat burns too much and my chest aches too deeply, I break the silence. "I don't know what to do." My voice is hoarse, raw, barely more than a whisper.

Anna doesn't say anything right away; instead, she walks back to the table, sets down a warm cup of tea in front of me, and then sits across from me, wrapping her hands around her own mug, waiting, giving me the time and space to speak when I'm ready.

I swallow hard, my fingers curling around the ceramic, seeking warmth, seeking something solid to hold onto. I force myself to meet her gaze. "What if I've already lost him?"

She exhales slowly, her expression composed, resolute. "Mari, I love you, but you're an idiot if you think he doesn't still love you."

A sharp breath leaves me, half a laugh, half a sob. "I don't deserve it."

Anna tilts her head, considering me. "That's not the point." Her voice is even, unwavering. "The point is, he gave you his whole heart. And yeah, you hurt him, but love doesn't just disappear because of that."

I shake my head, my chest tightening again. "It should."

"But it won't."

The certainty in her voice almost breaks me. I press my fingers against my temples, squeezing my eyes shut. "I don't know how to fix this, Anna."

She's quiet for a moment...then, softer. "You don't fix love, Mari. You choose it."

The words sink in, heavy, unavoidable—I chose fear, I chose safety, and I lost everything because of it. I push back from the table suddenly, standing too fast, my legs unsteady beneath me. "I need air."

Anna doesn't stop me, she just nods. "Do you want me to come with you?"

I shake my head. "No. I just... I need to think."

Anna's gaze holds steady. "I'm here when you need me. You're not alone."

She watches as I grab my coat and step outside into the cool night air, into a town that feels both too familiar and too foreign at the same time.

CHAPTER 43

Mariana

The red glow of the firehouse sign flickers against the pavement as I pull into the lot, my heart slamming against my ribs so hard I have to grip the wheel just to ground myself; I can't breathe.

My hands tighten around the leather-wrapped steering wheel, the material groaning under the force. What the hell am I even doing here? I don't have an answer. I just... ended up here.

The car rumbles softly beneath me, engine idling, headlights casting long, narrow shadows across the asphalt. The garage doors are shut, but with my windows down, I can hear the soft hum of voices inside. Someone's here. A few guys on shift, maybe. Maybe him.

Just the thought sends a bolt of panic straight through me, sharp and unrelenting. I press my forehead against the steering wheel, exhaling shakily, trying to breathe, trying to think, trying to piece together how the hell I got here.

I left Anna's house, the letter folded in my pocket, my mother's words still etched into my ribs. Left with too many

283

emotions tearing through me to sit still, to sleep, to exist in silence.

So I walked, I walked through empty streets lined with darkened storefronts, past the diner where Sebastian and I had spent too many late nights, past the old bookstore where we used to leave notes for each other inside random paperbacks.

Through the town I grew up in but never really felt like I belonged in, and somehow, my feet led me here. To him...or maybe just to the place that built him.

The firehouse looms ahead, bigger in the dark, its presence steady, unmoving. The place that shaped him. The place that made him the man I love, the place I should never have left.

I squeeze my eyes shut, fisting my hands in my lap, my mother's letter still pressed to my chest like a prayer. I can't keep doing this, I can't keep hovering on the edges of his life, watching from a distance, too scared to step in, too terrified to fully let go. I need to do something. I need to fix this.

Before I can talk myself out of it, my hand moves to the door handle, when suddenly...

"You've got to be kidding me."

I freeze. The voice behind me is sharp, rough, frustrated. My stomach knots itself into oblivion before I even turn around. Slowly, I shift in my seat, forcing my breath to stay steady, but the second I meet his eyes, I know that's not possible. Andres.

His arms are crossed tight over his chest, his firehouse jacket hanging open, his uniform underneath slightly wrinkled, like he's been working for hours.

His stance is rigid, shoulders squared, his expression unreadable at first—just flat, distant. The longer he looks at me, the more his face hardens, something sharper flashing behind his eyes. "You've got some nerve, Mari."

The words hit like a slap. I swallow hard. "Andres-"

"No." He shakes his head, stepping closer, his voice like flint striking steel.

"You don't get to show up here and act like this is normal. Like you didn't walk away from him without a second glance."

I flinch, because he's right.

Andres exhales sharply, dragging a hand down his face, his frustration crackling in the air between us. "Damn it, Mari. Do you have any idea what it was like watching him fall apart over you for the second time?" His voice isn't just angry now... it's hurt. "What it was like seeing him show up to every shift looking like he hadn't slept, pretending like he was fine when we all knew he wasn't?"

Guilt digs its claws deep, twisting inside my ribs, my throat, my stomach. "I know I hurt him," I whisper.

Andres lets out a sharp bark of laughter, but it's hollow, bitter. "Yeah? You do?" His jaw clenches, his eyes burning into mine. "You just now figured that out?"

I bite my lip, looking anywhere but at him.

But he's not done. "You didn't just hurt him, Mari." His voice lowers, the words hitting deeper. "You fucking broke him."

My chest caves in. I squeeze my hands into fists at my sides, my whole body tensing, bracing for impact. "I thought I was protecting myself."

Andres lets out a sharp, disbelieving breath. "By what?" he demands, his voice rising. "Destroying him first?"

I squeeze my eyes shut, shaking my head. "I didn't mean to-"

"Didn't mean to?" Andres scoffs, cutting me off. "You think that matters?" His voice is razor-sharp, but there's something underneath it, something raw. "You know, I used to think you were good for him."

The words slice through me like a blade, because I had thought so too—once.

Andres holds my gaze, his jaw tight. "But now? Now, I don't know if you're just here to finish the job."

A sharp, stinging breath catches in my throat, I can't do this, I can't take this. The pressure is too much, the guilt is too much, the regret is too much. "I love him." The words rip out of me before I can stop them.

Andres stares at me. I breathe hard, my hands shaking. "I love him," I say again, stronger this time. "I never stopped. And I...I know I don't deserve him, I know I don't deserve a second or third chance, but I..." My voice breaks, tears burning behind my eyes. "I just can't let him go."

Andres doesn't look away. For a moment, I think he's going to tell me to leave, to walk away, to let Sebastian move on. Maybe, a few weeks ago, he would have.

But then, his expression shifts, frustration melting into something else, something quieter, something knowing. "You better be damn sure about that, Mari." His voice is low, serious. Unforgiving. He's giving me one shot, one chance to prove I mean what I say, because Sebastian deserves better than hesitation. He deserves someone who chooses him. Every. Damn. Day.

I nod, pressing my lips together. "I'm sure."

Andres studies me a moment longer, then lets out a long, slow breath. "Then fight for him."

My pulse stutters.

Andres tilts his head toward the firehouse. "You want him back?" His lips quirk, but there's no humor in it. "Then do something about it."

I look at the firehouse again, my heart hammering. But I already know, I'm not ready. Not yet, not like this. I meet Andres' eyes again, my throat tight but steady. "I will."

He nods. "Good." Then—softer, but with a warning edge —"Don't break him again, Mari. He can't take you breaking his heart again."

"I won't." And this time, I mean it. Because if there's one thing I know for certain— I'm never going to let go of Sebastian Garcia again.

∿

Anna's house is quiet when I walk in. A single light from the kitchen spills into the hallway, stretching soft golden hues against the walls, making everything feel smaller. I toe off my shoes by the door.

Her home has always felt lived in, messy in a way that feels real. There's a blanket draped over the couch, a half-empty glass of water on the coffee table, an old sweatshirt thrown over the back of a chair. It doesn't feel like a place haunted by absence, not like mine.

I make it halfway to the stairs before I hear her voice.

"You okay?"

I turn over my shoulder. Anna stands at the bottom step, her arms loosely crossed, her head tilted just slightly—she already knows the answer. So do I.

I shake my head. "No."

She breathes out quietly, her expression shifting—not shocked, not full of pity, just seeing me. "Did you go see him?"

The question makes my breath catch. I drag a hand down my face, my palm rough against my skin. I wish I could say yes, I wish I had the courage. Instead, I let out a sharp, hollow breath.

"No." I pause, voice raw. "But I saw Andres."

Anna's brows lift slightly, but she doesn't push.

I take a slow step forward, then another. My hands tighten around the wooden banister, grounding me. My mother's letter is still tucked into my pocket, still pressed against my chest like something sacred, something I can't let go of.

I swallow hard. "Mami was right." Somewhere, she's probably smiling—pleased that I finally figured out what she knew all along. She's always right. The words don't just sit in the air, they settle, sink deep. My voice is barely above a whisper, but it carries weight.

I exhale a breath that feels like it carries every ounce of fear I've been living in. Every moment, I convinced myself I was better off alone. Every goddamn excuse I let dictate my life.

"I can't keep running."

It's not a realization. It's a decision.

Anna watches me, waiting, giving me space to find the rest of the words.

I tighten my grip on the banister. My chest constricts, not with fear, but with the truth clawing its way out of me.

"I thought leaving meant I was free of him," I whisper. "That if I moved on, if I built something new, then what he did to me would stop mattering." I close my eyes, breathing through the ache rising in my throat. "But I still hear his voice sometimes, Anna. In the back of my head, telling me I'm too much. Too difficult. Too broken."

Anna's face softens, something sharp and unspoken passing through her eyes. She steps forward, closing the space between us. "Mariana..."

I shake my head, pushing through. "And I let it hold me back. I let him have power over me, even in death. I let him convince me I was safer alone. But the truth is... I wasn't protecting myself." My breath catches. "I was letting him win."

The words leave my lips like an unraveling thread, like something inside me is finally giving way to something new.

Anna reaches for my hand, squeezing it tight. "Mari, you know that's not your fault, right?"

I nod, but I can't speak past the lump in my throat.

Anna inhales sharply, shaking her head. "I hate that he still has space in your thoughts. I hate that you carried this alone for so long." Her voice is quiet but fierce. "But if you're finally ready to let go of him, to stop letting him have even an ounce of control over you—then, Mari, that's the strongest thing you could ever do."

I blink hard, my chest shaking with something that feels a lot like relief.

I lift my chin, forcing myself to say it out loud. "I can't keep pretending I don't love him."

Anna tilts her head slightly, watching me and studying me. Then, quieter now, she says, "So what are you going to do?"

I press my lips together. This time, I don't hesitate, I don't question, I don't let fear answer for me. I straighten, my pulse steady, my chest no longer tight with uncertainty.

"I'm going to do everything in my power to get my man back."

Anna grins, slow and certain. "About damn time."

CHAPTER 44

Mariana

I don't hesitate, I don't second-guess myself, I don't turn the car around halfway there—that alone tells me how much I've changed.

Because two weeks ago? Hell, two days ago? I wouldn't be doing this, I would've let my fear win, but not anymore.

Sebastian isn't just my person—he's Analyse's brother, Maya's uncle, someone who has been woven into so many lives, not just mine. If I want him back, I have to face more than my own regret. I have to face the people who watched him break—because of me.

I park outside Analyse's house, my heart slamming against my ribs so hard I have to press my palm against my chest like that'll do anything to settle it. The lights are on inside, a warm glow spills onto the porch, soft shadows moving inside—her, maybe Maya.

The sight stirs something in my chest, something warm and aching. I used to belong here, but now I don't know if I ever will again.

I step out of the car, force my legs to move up the drive-

BACK TO YOU

way, force myself to breathe through the panic, then, the door swings open before I even knock.

Analyse stands there, arms crossed, brow arched like she already knows, but her voice isn't warm when she speaks; it's cool, measured. "Are you here to hurt him again?"

It takes everything in me not to flinch, because I deserve that. I force myself to meet her eyes, to hold my ground. "No," I say, my voice steady despite the storm inside me. "I'm here because I love him, and because I need to make this right."

Analyse studies me for a long moment, her expression unreadable; she exhales sharply and steps aside. "Come in."

I walk in, and the faint scent of coffee lingers in the air. Maya's tiny shoes sit by the door, and a handful of toys are scattered across the floor, abandoned mid-play. I don't sit, I can't sit.

The air feels too heavy, pressing down on my shoulders, making it impossible to stay still. I stand in the center of her living room, my hands clenching at my sides, fingers digging into my palms. If I don't hold onto something, anything, I might come apart.

Analyse leans against the arm of the couch, watching me carefully. "So what exactly do you want, Mari?" she asks. "Because if this is just about you feeling guilty-"

"It's not." The words leave my mouth before she can finish. "I mean...I do feel guilty. I feel like the biggest fucking coward in the world. But this isn't about that." I take a breath. "This is about fighting for the man I love, the man I never stopped loving."

Her jaw tightens. "Then why did you leave....again?"

I look away, pressing my lips together. Because fear convinced me I was safer alone, because I thought the distance would shield me from the pain because I believed that pushing him away would make the loss easier to bear.

I lift my gaze back to hers. "Because I was wrong."

Something flickers in her expression. Not forgiveness, not yet, but something close to understanding. I swallow hard, reaching into my jacket pocket and pulling out my mother's letter.

"This is why I'm here," I whisper, voice thick. "My mom wrote it before she died. She gave it to Sebastian. She knew I would need it...and she was right."

Analyse hesitates, then, cautiously, she steps forward and takes it from my hands. Her gaze drags over the familiar hand-writing, over the creased edges from where I've been holding onto it too tightly. She doesn't say anything for a long time, then, quietly, but not unkindly, "So what are you going to do?"

I lift my chin, something fierce burning in my chest. "Everything."

I wake up before the sun. For the first time in weeks, I don't wake up feeling hollow. I don't wake up with that crushing weight on my chest, the ache of absence wrapping itself around my ribs like something alive. I wake up with something else, restlessness, determination.

I stare at the ceiling, my pulse steady but strong, my body buzzing like my mind is already three steps ahead of me. There's no more debating, no more wondering if I should fight for him. I already know I will, I just have to figure out how.

The house is still quiet when I push back the covers and sit up. The air is cold, and I pull Sebastian's hoodie tighter around me before making my way downstairs. I don't even realize I grabbed it when I left my house, but it's been with me every day since. The sleeves are a little too long, the fabric worn soft, the faintest trace of his scent still clinging to it.

In the kitchen, I move on autopilot, filling the kettle with water and setting it on the stove. My mind is already spiraling forward. I need to prove to him that I'm not going to run again, that I won't let fear win. I lean against the counter, arms crossed, staring at the steam rising from the kettle like it holds the answers. What do I do? What does he deserve? I don't even hear Anna walk in until she speaks.

"Didn't expect to see you up this early."

I glance over my shoulder. She's still in her pajamas, her hair tied up in a messy bun, her voice thick with sleep. "I couldn't sleep," I admit.

She hums, padding over to the coffee maker and pressing the button to start brewing. "Thinking about him?"

I exhale sharply. "Thinking about how the hell I'm supposed to show him that I mean it this time."

Anna leans against the counter, studying me over the rim of her coffee mug. "So you're done running?"

I nod. "Completely."

She tilts her head. "Good. Now what's your plan?"

My stomach tightens. I stare down at my hands, my thumb running over a loose thread in the cuff of Sebastian's hoodie. "That's the problem. I don't know."

Anna doesn't say anything for a moment, then—"Well, what are you trying to tell him?"

I glance at her. "That I love him."

"Okay, but he already knows that." She sets her coffee down on the counter. "He didn't let you go because he didn't think you loved him, Mari. He let you go because you didn't choose him."

The words hit hard. I knew that , of course. But hearing it out loud makes me feel heavier.

Sebastian had always been steady, always sure, always willing to fight for us, and I had let fear decide for me. I swallow, pressing my hands flat against the counter. "Then that's what I have to show him. That I'm choosing him."

Anna nods. "So what's your version of a grand gesture?"

My mind starts flipping through every memory I have of us. The late nights at the diner, the way he used to grab my hand at stoplights, squeezing once, twice, three times like a secret message only we understood.

The way he would look at me, like I was something sacred. We had so much, so much that mattered. Suddenly, it hits me...a moment, a memory, a promise I never kept. I straighten, my breath catching in my throat.

Anna notices immediately. "What?"

I look at her, my pulse kicking up. "I know what I'm going to do."

She raises an eyebrow. "Yeah?"

I nod, heart pounding. "I'm going to prove it to him."

CHAPTER 45
Mariana

I have a plan, a real plan, not just words, not just a half-hearted apology—because words can be empty, words can be said in a moment of desperation and taken back just as easily.

Sebastian deserves more than that; he deserves proof, he deserves action. He deserves to see that I'm not just saying I won't leave again—I'm showing him. I'm choosing him, with every single step, with every single breath.

I drive through town with my heart lodged in my throat, gripping the wheel so tightly my knuckles ache. It has to be perfect. It's late, but I know where he'll be. The firehouse. He's always at the firehouse on Wednesdays.

The hoodie sitting in the seat beside me, his hoodie, the one I never gave back. The one I've kept through every mistake, through every lonely night, through every moment I tried to convince myself that walking away was the right choice.

The book tucked into my bag, his favorite one, with the note I wrote inside, the one he left on my nightstand after the first time he told me he loved me.

The words I've been rehearsing in my head over and over again, the things I should have said before I ever let my fear win. I don't just want to tell him I love him. I want him to feel it. I want him to see it in the things I kept, in the pieces of him I never let go of, in the way I'm standing here now, ready to fight for him. This is more than just an apology, it's a promise.

I swallow hard, my pulse roaring in my ears as I turn onto his street, the firehouse coming into view...the bay doors are open, the station alive with movement.

A few trucks are parked outside, their reflective decals catching the glow of the overhead lights. Through the window, I can see movement—firefighters checking gear, talking, laughing at something I can't quite make out. The kitchen light is on, a warm glow against the night. But he's not there.

This doesn't make sense. Sebastian is always here on Wednesdays.

My heart stutters, panic clawing its way up my throat.

No.

No, no, no. This wasn't the plan.

I slam the car into park and all but stumble out, my breath coming too fast, my pulse hammering like a war drum against my ribs. The cold air slices through me, but I barely feel it. I was supposed to find him here. I was supposed to pull him outside, tell him everything, make him believe me.

I push open the firehouse doors, the scent of smoke and coffee hitting me instantly. The warmth of the station wraps around me, the hum of familiarity pressing in from all sides.

Boots thud against the floor, voices carry, the radio crackles faintly in the background. This place has always meant home to him. It's supposed to lead me to him, but it doesn't.

I grip the strap of my bag, my fingers clenching tight, my breath unsteady; this wasn't how it was supposed to go.

Mateo is the first one to see me, his eyes flick over me, taking in the urgency, the desperation, the sheer fucking panic.

"Where is he?" I ask, breathless.

His brows furrow. "Not here."

The air leaves my lungs. "But he—" I shake my head. "He's always here."

Mateo crosses his arms. "Not tonight."

I press a hand against my chest, trying to keep my racing heart from breaking free. I swallow hard. "Then where-"

Mateo exhales, rubbing a hand over his face, like he's debating whether or not to tell me, then, reluctantly, "Try the lake."

My stomach twists. The lake. I don't thank Mateo, I don't say anything. I just run.

∾

By the time I get to the lake, the sky has opened up. The downpour is relentless—thick sheets of rain hammering against the truck, my windshield wipers barely keeping up.

My stomach churns as I throw the door open and step into the storm. I should be scared. I should be second-guessing myself. But I'm not, because I see him.

He's standing by the water, hands shoved deep into his pockets, head tilted toward the sky like he's waiting for it to tell him something. My chest constricts, a desperate hope clawing its way to the surface—please don't let me be too late.

"Sebastian!" I shout over the storm, my voice ragged from everything I've been holding in.

His head snaps toward me, eyes wide with surprise...and concern. "Mariana?" His voice cuts through the rain, sharp and worried. He starts toward me, his brow furrowed. "What the hell are you doing-"

"This is not how it was supposed to go!" I cut him off,

laughing and crying all at once, my hands shaking as I pushed drenched hair out of my face.

Sebastian slows, eyes scanning my face, his own expression unreadable. "Are you okay?"

"No!" I bark out another wet laugh, because this—this was supposed to be perfect. But it's not. It's a fucking mess, but it doesn't matter, because he's here, I love him so much.

I step closer, not letting him get a word in. "I had a plan," I tell him, forcing the words past the fear lodged in my throat. "It was a good plan. Solid. Thought-out. Romantic as hell."

A flicker of something crosses his face.

"But nothing about us has ever gone according to plan, has it?" I whisper.

Sebastian stays quiet, his chest rising and falling too quickly.

I reach into my bag and pull out his hoodie. The old, worn one I stole from him when we were in high school, the one I've refused to throw away. The one that still, somehow, smells like him. Sebastian's breath catches. I shove it against his chest.

His fingers curl around the fabric instinctively. "Mari, what-"

"I kept it," I whisper. "This whole time, I kept it. Even when I left, even when I swore I was moving on. I kept it because-" I shake my head, choking on my own confession. "Because I was never moving on. Because I never stopped loving you."

His throat bobs. Hard.

I take another step, closing the distance between us, and forcing him to look at me. "I was scared, Sebastian." My voice is shaking. "I was scared of needing you too much. I was scared of loving you too much." I press a fist against my chest, over my heart, over my mother's words. "But I lost you anyway, and it wrecked me."

Sebastian's jaw clenches, like he's trying to keep himself together.

I grab his face, my fingers trembling, my thumbs brushing against the faint stubble on his jaw. "I don't want to be scared anymore," I whisper. "I want to be brave." The words pour out of me, raw and desperate, carried by the storm raging around us. Rain soaks through my clothes, clings to my skin, drips from my lashes, but I don't care. I have one chance to get this right.

I step closer, my pulse hammering, my hands shaking at my sides. His expression is unreadable, stunned, wary, guarded in a way that guts me, but I don't stop. I can't stop.

"I choose you," I tell him, my voice breaking, my breath unsteady. "Every damn day." My fingers curl into fists. "No matter how scary it gets. No matter how much it hurts. No matter how much my brain tries to tell me to run, to protect myself, to keep my heart safe." I exhale sharply, shaking my head. "I don't want to be safe anymore, Seb. I want you."

Thunder rumbles overhead, a deep, vibrating pulse that shakes the ground beneath us, but it's nothing compared to the way my world tilts, the way everything inside me cracks wide open. "You are it for me, Sebastian Antonio Garcia," I whisper, my voice fierce, unwavering now. "It's always been you. It's only ever been you." My throat tightens, tears mixing with the rain as I take another step toward him, bridging the distance, reaching for him even though I don't know if he'll let me.

His chest rises and falls unevenly, his eyes dark and unreadable beneath the dim glow of the streetlights. He hasn't moved, hasn't spoken, hasn't given me any indication of what he's thinking, or whether I'm too late. Fear creeps in, but I shove it down.

"I am never leaving you again," I swear, my voice thick, fierce with the weight of the promise. "Not because I need you to fix me, not because I don't know how to be without you, but because I love you. I will fight for you. I will fight for us. Every single day, for the rest of my life."

Silence stretches between us, thick and charged, the rain pounding against the pavement, our breaths the only thing cutting through the storm. And then...something breaks, his control, his hesitation, the last of the walls between us. Because suddenly, he's moving—a sharp, desperate pull forward.

A crash of bodies, heat and cold colliding as his hands grip my soaked clothes, his fingers curling into the fabric like he's afraid I'll disappear if he lets go. His mouth is on mine—fierce, claiming, aching. It's not soft or careful, it's raw, it's wrecked, it's everything. I gasp against him, but I don't pull away, I press closer.

I let him feel every inch of my promise. Every breath, every heartbeat, every ounce of certainty. I fist my hands in his shirt, pulling him closer, anchoring myself to him, to this moment, to the only thing that has ever felt this real.

This time, I'm the one who's sure. This time, I'm the one who's fighting. This time, I'm never letting him go.

CHAPTER 46

Mariana

We sprint toward the car, laughter tumbling between us, breathless and wild. Rain clings to our skin, drips from our hair, and soaks through every layer, but none of it matters.

Our hands stay locked, fingers tangled, as we stumble through puddles, shoes splashing, hearts pounding. The cold is there, biting at the edges, but it never quite reaches us—not with this, not with us.

The car door slams shut, sealing us in, muting the storm's fury outside. Rain streaks down the windows, distorting the world into a blur of lights and motion, like something out of a dream. Inside, the air hums, charged and heavy, every drop of water, every ragged breath amplifying the energy crackling between us.

I barely have time to catch my breath before his hands are on me, warm and desperate, threading into my soaked hair, pulling me closer.

Our mouths crash together, feverish and unrestrained, the taste of rain still fresh on our lips. There's no hesitation, no second-guessing—only need, raw and overwhelming, surging between us like a live wire.

His hands are everywhere at once, leaving trails of fire across my skin as he peels away my rain-soaked clothes. I fumble with his shirt buttons, desperate to feel his bare chest against mine. Our lips clash again, hungry and insistent, as we tumble into the backseat.

The leather is cool against my back, a stark contrast to the heat of his body pressing me down. He hovers above me, eyes dark with desire, chest heaving.

For a moment, time stands still. Then, like a dam breaking, we're a tangle of limbs and gasps and fevered touches. His mouth blazes a path down my neck, across my collarbone and along the curve of my breast.

I arch into him shamelessly as he takes one hardened nipple between his teeth and sucks hard enough to make me moan. His hands roam over my body, leaving trails of heat in their wake as he explores every inch of me.

I can feel his hardness pressing against me, a delicious friction that makes my stomach clench with need. He groans as I grind against him, his hands gripping my hips tightly. I roll us over so that I'm on top, straddling him. His eyes are dark with desire as he runs his hands up my thighs, under my shirt, and finally cupping my breasts.

I lean down to kiss him again, but he pulls away slightly, a teasing smile playing on his lips. "Slow down," he whispers breathlessly.

I pause for a moment, looking into his deep brown eyes. I see the same longing and passion mirrored in them that I feel in my own heart.

We both want this—each other—more than anything else in this world. With that thought in mind, I lean down to capture his lips in another searing kiss. Our bodies move together with a primal urgency, our breaths mingling and hearts racing.

He flips us back over so that he's on top again. His lips leave mine to trail hot kisses down my neck and along my collarbone. Goosebumps break out all over my skin as he moves lower and lower.

When he reaches the waistband of my jeans, he pauses and looks up at me for permission. I nod eagerly and help him remove the jeans along with my underwear. His gaze roams over my exposed body hungrily before settling between my legs.

"I want to taste you," he growls before dipping his head between my thighs.

His tongue flicks and teases, driving me closer to the edge with every skillful stroke. I'm panting and moaning, completely lost in the moment as he brings me to the brink of ecstasy. I can feel his lips curve into a satisfied smile against my skin as he pulls away from me.

His gaze meets mine again, filled with desire and a hint of mischief. Just when I think I can't take it anymore, he pulls away with a smirk. "Not yet," he says, his voice low and husky.

I groan in frustration, but he quickly makes up for it by kissing his way back up my body. When his lips meet mine again, there's a desperation in our kiss that wasn't there before. We both want release—but we also want to savor every moment of this shared pleasure.

"I need you," he says in a low voice.

He positions himself at my entrance and slowly enters me, inch by delicious inch. I gasp at the feeling of him filling me completely, my body responding eagerly to his touch.

He moves slowly at first, building a steady rhythm that has us both moaning and writhing together. As our bodies move in perfect sync, I feel myself being consumed by pure and unadulterated pleasure.

His hands roam over my body, caressing every curve and sensitive spot, adding to the intense sensations coursing through me. Our pace quickens as our passion reaches a fever pitch.

I wrap my legs around his waist, deepening our connection and urging him on. He thrusts harder and faster, each movement sending shockwaves of pleasure through me. I arch my back, pressing my chest against his and holding onto him tightly, not wanting this feeling to ever end.

I feel myself getting closer and closer to the edge, my body trembling with anticipation. He senses it too and moves faster, his movements becoming more urgent and desperate as he chases his own release.

With one final thrust, we both reach our peaks, crying out in ecstasy as we climax together. Our bodies shudder and tremble with the force of it, leaving us both completely spent and breathless.

We cling to each other tightly as we come down from our high, our hearts beating in perfect unison. We stay like that for a few moments, catching our breaths and basking in the afterglow of our lovemaking.

He leans down to kiss me again, this time with a tenderness I haven't seen before. "I love you," he whispers against my lips.

CHAPTER 47

Mariana

The morning light spills through the windows of my bakery, warm and golden, casting soft shadows along the floors. It catches on the flour-dusted countertops, glints off the glass display case, and stretches lazily across the wooden tables.

The air is thick with the scent of honeyed almonds, caramelized sugar, and warm butter, curling around me in a way that feels like home.

It's an hurried morning, the soft rhythm of dawn settling into the space before the world stirs to life. The scent of fresh espresso drifts in from the back, mingling with the sweetness in the air.

The low hum of the oven fills the space, punctuated by the soft clatter of trays being set down, the rustling of parchment paper, the quiet scrape of a spatula against metal. I breathe it all in, letting the warmth settle deep in my chest.

This place, *my* place, my sanctuary—a space where my hands know exactly what to do, where every scent, every sound, every flicker of morning light belongs.

The best part of it all is that Sebastian is here.

He's behind the counter, sleeves rolled up, forearms dusted with flour, looking like he's belonged in this space all along. My chest tightens at the sight, my heart stumbling over itself, caught between the sheer familiarity of him and the quiet wonder of seeing him here, in my world.

His brows knit together in concentration, his hands working the dough with an ease that shouldn't make sense—but somehow, it does. There's no hesitation in his movements, no second-guessing.

His fingers press, fold, and knead with a rhythm so natural it feels like he's done this a thousand times before. I don't even think he realizes it—like muscle memory, like second nature.

It's effortless, unthinking, as if this kitchen, this moment, this *us*, is exactly where he's meant to be.

"You know," I say, leaning against the counter, watching him work, "for someone who swears he doesn't bake, you sure look like you know what you're doing."

He glances up, his mouth twitching into that half-smile that always gets me. "I grew up with you, Mariana. I absorbed some things by osmosis."

I roll my eyes, but warmth spreads through my chest. *This.* This is what I never thought I'd have again—this easy rhythm, this laughter woven into the everyday moments, this quiet kind of love that doesn't have to ask for permission to exist.

Sebastian wipes his hands on a towel, walking toward me, his gaze soft, searching. "You okay?"

I nod, but I know he sees through me. He always has.

He leans against the counter beside me, his body close enough that I can feel his warmth, even with the space between us. "You've been quieter today."

I exhale, rolling a loose thread on my apron between my fingers. "I think I'm just... taking it all in. This place, us, how different everything feels."

Sebastian studies me for a moment before nodding. "Yeah," he murmurs. "It does feel different."

Different, because I'm here. I'm present. I'm not stuck in my head, waiting for the worst. I'm standing in my dream bakery, beside the man I love, in the life I chose. And it's not just something I let happen—it's something I fought for.

He reaches out, tucking a strand of hair behind my ear, his touch lingering. "Do you regret it?"

I shake my head without hesitation. "Not for a second."

His throat bobs slightly, his fingers ghosting over mine. "The letter... I know it wasn't easy to read."

A lump forms in my throat, but I nod. "It wasn't. But I needed it. I think..." I pause, finding the right words. "I think she knew I wouldn't let myself face certain things unless she forced me to."

Sebastian watches me carefully, his brows drawn. "Like letting yourself be taken care of?"

I huff out a soft laugh, shaking my head. "Like learning how to stop running."

His eyes darken, and for a moment, I see every ounce of hurt I caused him. He doesn't throw it in my face, doesn't weaponize it—but it's there, unspoken, lingering in the space between us.

"I can't do this again, Mari," he says quietly, his voice steady, sure. "I love you. I always will. But if you ever decide to run again, if you ever decide to push me away instead of letting me in..." He swallows hard, his fingers tightening on the edge of the counter. "I won't chase you."

My chest aches, but I understand.

"I don't want to be that person anymore," I whisper. "And I won't promise you that I'm perfect, or that I won't have moments where I falter. But I *will* promise you that I'm done running. I'm here. I choose you, Sebastian."

His exhale is slow, measured, but his eyes soften, the steel in them easing just slightly. "I choose you too. But, Mari... if you ever need space, if you ever feel like you need to leave—just talk to me first, okay?"

I nod, my throat tight. "Okay."

A slow smile spreads across his face, and before I can process what's happening, he's pressing his flour-dusted fingers against my cheek.

I gasp, jerking back. "Sebastian!"

His grin is unrepentant. "What? You looked too clean."

I stare at him, my jaw dropping. "You did not just—"

He lifts a brow, daring me.

Challenge accepted.

Without thinking, I grab a handful of flour from the counter and toss it straight at him. It lands square on his chest, a puff of white exploding between us.

For a moment, we just stare at each other.

Then, he lunges.

I shriek, trying to escape, but I have no chance. He's faster, stronger, and entirely too smug about it. His arms wrap around my waist as he lifts me onto the counter, trapping me between his body and the shelves of ingredients behind me.

I'm laughing so hard I can barely breathe, my hands bracing against his shoulders as he grins up at me, his face inches from mine.

"That was a mistake, princesa," he warns, voice full of teasing threat.

I giggle, squirming, but he tightens his hold. "Let me go!"

"Never," he says easily, his fingers sneaking to my waist, squeezing just enough to make me squeal. "You start a war, Mariana, you gotta be ready to finish it."

I twist, half-heartedly trying to break free, but he only lifts me higher, holding me like I weigh nothing. A breathless laugh escapes before my legs instinctively tighten around his waist, my fingers curling into his shoulders for balance. His hold is firm, unyielding, a silent promise that he has no intention of letting me go—not now, not ever.

The laughter fades, replaced by something deeper, something that hums in the space between us. Our breaths come slow and measured, the heat of his body sinking into mine, wrapping around me like a second skin. His eyes drop to my lips, lingering, knowing, and my pulse stutters.

If I move even an inch closer, if I let the pull between us win, we'll be kissing.

"I love you," he murmurs, like a vow, like a promise.

I close my eyes, my hands curling into the fabric of his shirt. "I love you too."

Now, saying it isn't a risk—it's a certainty.

CHAPTER 48

Mariana

T he midday sun streams through the blinds, painting soft lines of light across Sebastian's kitchen. The scent of coffee lingers, mixing with the fresh crispness of laundry and the faint trace of his body wash—the one that somehow always smells impossibly good.

It's been a couple of weeks now, and for the first time in a long time, I feel like I can breathe. Like I'm not waiting for the other shoe to drop.

Things between us have been... easy. Natural. The way they used to be, but somehow different, too—stronger, more certain. I don't feel like I'm walking on a tightrope anymore, bracing for the fall.

Instead, I feel grounded. Safe. *Home.*

Maybe that's because I've finally started letting myself believe that I deserve this. That I don't have to carry everything alone anymore.

Therapy has helped.

It's strange, talking to someone who isn't family, isn't a friend—someone who doesn't already know all the ways I've built my walls. But it's also... freeing.

I don't have to soften the truth for a stranger. I don't have to pretend I have it all figured out. I can just say things out loud, things I've buried for so long, and let them exist without the weight of guilt pressing on my chest.

I cradle my coffee mug in both hands, my fingers curled around the warmth, letting it seep into my skin. Across from me, Maya swings her legs from her seat, a piece of toast in one hand, her curls bouncing with every excited movement.

Sebastian leans against the counter, scrolling through his phone, still in his worn athletic shorts and a loose T-shirt, his hair tousled from sleep. He's completely at ease, unhurried, like there's nowhere else he needs to be.

Something in me loosens at the sight, a quiet warmth unfurling in my chest.

Therapy hasn't erased the past. It hasn't magically made the grief or the scars disappear. But it's given me something I didn't even realize I needed—a way to move forward.

"Tío Sebaaaaa," Maya drawls dramatically, dragging out his name like it's a royal decree.

"Hmm?" Sebastian barely looks up from his phone, but there's a ghost of a smirk on his lips, like he already knows where this is going.

"You promised we'd go on an adventure today," she reminds him, her tiny hand smacking the table for emphasis.

Sebastian sighs, finally setting his phone down. "Did I?"

"Yes!" she insists, eyes wide with determination. "And you can't break a pinky promise. Ever."

I bite back a smile at the absolute seriousness in her little voice. Across the table, Sebastian makes a show of scratching his chin, feigning deep thought.

"Hmm. Are you sure I promised?"

Maya gasps, outraged, her tiny brows furrowing. "TÍO SEBASTIAN," she scolds, pointing an accusing finger at him.

"You said we were gonna do something fun today, and that means we have to do it."

Sebastian winces dramatically. "Ah, well, if the pinky promise is involved..."

I shake my head, unable to hold back my grin. "Well, it just so happens that I was also thinking an adventure sounded fun today."

Maya gasps again, eyes darting between us. "Really?"

I nod. "Really."

Sebastian leans down, resting his elbows on the table so he's at eye level with his niece. "Alright, bebecita. What kind of adventure are we talking about?"

Maya taps her chin, thinking hard, her little face scrunched up in concentration. "Something big," she decides. "And fun."

Sebastian tilts his head. "How big? How fun? Like, going to the park fun? Or like, jumping out of an airplane fun?"

Maya's jaw drops in horror. "Nooo, tio, that's too scary! Mommy would be so mad at you."

I snort into my coffee. "Lyse would murder you."

Sebastian chuckles, shaking his head. "Alright, alright. No skydiving. How about the lake?"

Maya's entire face lights up, excitement bursting through her tiny frame. "YES! Can we bring snacks? And my floaties? And can we catch real fish?"

Sebastian reaches over and ruffles her curls. "We can bring snacks, definitely bring floaties, and—" he shoots me a look "—maybe we leave the fish alone, huh?"

I nod solemnly. "Sounds fair."

Maya beams, bouncing in her chair. "That. Sounds. AWESOME!"

Sebastian leans back, shaking his head. "You're so easy to impress."

Maya shrugs. "You're just that cool, tio."

I laugh as Maya takes another triumphant bite of her toast, already planning out the details of our little trip. She's talking a mile a minute—listing the exact snacks we need to bring, debating whether or not she should wear both of her floaties or just one, because she's a big kid now, after all.

Sebastian just listens, nodding along with the occasional uh-huh and good idea, but every now and then, I catch him sneaking glances at me—taking this in, holding onto it, fully present in the moment, just as much as I am.

Sebastian meets my gaze from across the table, something soft, something sure in his expression. Like maybe this, these mornings, this quiet kind of happiness, is what he's wanted all along.

I set my mug down, exhaling slowly.

"You know," I say, voice quieter now, more thoughtful, "my therapist asked me something the other day."

Sebastian raises a brow, intrigued. "Yeah?"

I nod. "She asked me if I believed I deserved to be happy."

Sebastian's expression shifts, something unreadable flickering behind his eyes. "And what did you say?"

I glance down at my coffee, tracing the rim with my finger. "For a long time, I didn't. I think I got used to expecting the worst. To bracing for impact. But... I don't want to live like that anymore."

Sebastian leans forward slightly, his gaze unwavering. "And now?"

I lift my eyes to his, my chest tightening. "Now, I think I'm starting to believe it."

His lips part like he wants to say something, but instead, he just reaches for my hand, threading his fingers through mine. He doesn't have to say anything. I feel it.

For once, I'm not caught up in the what-ifs or the ticking clock of what happens next. I'm just here, with him, with Maya—and *damn*, it feels good.

CHAPTER 49

Mariana

The drive to the lake is easy, the winding road flanked by towering pines, their scent mingling with the crisp morning air. The distant shimmer of water peeks through gaps in the trees, a quiet promise of the day ahead.

Sunlight filters through the branches, casting shifting patterns across the dashboard — golden light that makes everything feel softer, slower.

In the backseat, Maya swings her legs, unable to keep still, her tiny hands clutching her backpack like it holds something precious. Every so often, she bounces a little, barely containing her excitement, and I catch her in the mirror, her face alight with anticipation. It's impossible not to smile.

"You're really excited for this adventure, huh?" I tease, glancing back at her.

Maya gasps dramatically. "Yes! But no questions, Titi Mari! It's a secret adventure!"

Sebastian chuckles beside me, shaking his head, his fingers tapping absently against the steering wheel. He's been quiet since we left, but it's not the kind of quiet that makes me uneasy. It's easy, settled, yet beneath it, something hums, something just beneath the surface that I can't quite put my finger on.

Maya, for one, hasn't stopped giggling. She tries to stifle it, pressing her lips together, but every few minutes, another little burst of laughter escapes, like she's carrying some secret too big to keep in.

I glance at Sebastian, but he keeps his eyes on the road, his fingers tightening briefly on the wheel before relaxing again, his jaw ticking like he's fighting the urge to smile.

Something feels... different. Not wrong, not unsettling, just—charged. The air crackles around me, sending a shiver down my spine, my skin prickling with something I don't quite understand.

It's like standing on the edge of a moment I don't yet know is coming, like a shift is about to happen and I'm the only one who hasn't been let in on it. I push the thought aside as we pull up to the lake. When suddenly, I see it...

My breath catches. My heart slams against my ribs, hard and fast, as the world narrows down to the scene in front of me. I freeze, my mind struggling to make sense of what's right there—waiting for me.

The lake is stunning, as always, the water reflecting the sunlight in golden ripples, shifting and glimmering like liquid light. The air smells crisp, clean, tinged with pine and the faint scent of blooming wildflowers. But none of that is what steals my breath away. It's everything around the lake.

String lights are woven between the trees, delicate and twinkling even in the daylight, as if the stars themselves have been pulled down just for this moment. They guide the way, a glowing path toward the water's edge.

And there, standing against the backdrop of the endless sky and shimmering lake, is a wooden arch draped in soft, flowing fabric that catches in the breeze. It's adorned with roses, lilies, and delicate white blooms that look almost too perfect, like something out of a dream.

Just beyond it, nestled in the sand, is a picnic blanket, carefully arranged with flickering lanterns casting soft, golden light over everything.

A chilled bottle of champagne sits in an ice bucket, tiny beads of condensation glistening in the sun. A small speaker plays softly, the familiar melody curling around me like something warm and safe, something that makes my chest tighten in a way I don't fully understand yet.

And then...there's them.

Anna. Analyse. Mateo. Ruth. Hilda. Andres. Nathan. Our people. All standing there, waiting. A lump forms in my throat as my eyes dart between them, confusion crashing through me.

"What..." My voice comes out barely above a whisper, shaking. "What's everyone doing here? I turn to Sebastian, searching for answers, and my world tilts, because he's not standing beside me anymore...He's kneeling.

The breath rushes out of my lungs so fast I feel lightheaded. Sebastian is down on one knee, the sunlight catching in his dark hair, casting soft glints of gold.

His eyes are locked onto mine, deep and intent, holding me in place as if nothing else in the world exists. But my gaze drops to what he's holding.

A small velvet box and inside—my mother's ring. The same ring my father gave her all those years ago. A sob breaks free before I can stop it, my hands flying to my mouth, my entire body trembling.

Sebastian's voice is even, but emotion clings to every word, thick and unshaken. "When your mom gave me this ring," he says softly, his fingers tightening around the velvet box, "she told me it belonged with you. That one day, when the time was right, I'd know."

He exhales, slow, measured, but I can see the way his chest

rises just a little too fast, the way his jaw flexes as he swallows hard. His grip on the box tightens, like he needs to ground himself, like this moment is as overwhelming for him as it is for me.

"Mariana," he continues, his voice dipping lower, rougher, "I knew the moment you walked back into my life that I was never letting you go again. But the truth is... I knew long before that. I knew from the moment I met you." He lets out a soft, almost breathless laugh, shaking his head slightly. "And then I made the mistake of letting you leave." His eyes lock onto mine, steady, unyielding, filled with everything he's never said aloud.

"The moment you walked back into my life, I promised myself I wouldn't make that mistake again."

His words land deep, settling into the very core of me, unraveling something I didn't even realize I'd been holding onto.

The world around us fades—just the two of us, the lake stretching behind him, the sky wide and endless above.

Tears slip down my cheeks, my vision blurring.

Sebastian smiles—crooked, nervous, perfect—the kind of smile that's always felt like home. But this time, there's something else woven into it, something deeper—vulnerability, a love so big it barely fits inside him.

"We've taken our time," he says, his voice thick with emotion, filled with every battle we've fought, every scar we've mended, every piece of us that we've rebuilt. "We've learned each other again. We've grown together. And through it all, Mariana, I've never stopped choosing you."

His thumb brushes over the edge of the ring box, a tiny, unconscious movement, like he's holding something sacred in his hands—like he's holding us. He exhales, his breath shuddering just slightly before he continues, softer now, but with a certainty that settles deep into my bones.

JASMINE AHMAD

"I know what it's like to lose you, Mariana." His gaze locks onto mine, unguarded, stripped bare, filled with the weight of the years we spent apart, the ache of every moment we weren't this.

"I know what it's like to wake up every day with an emptiness that nothing could fill. To carry your name in my chest like a prayer I wasn't sure would ever be answered." His fingers tighten around the box, knuckles paling as he swallows hard. "And now that I have you, now that I have this second chance, I'm never making that mistake again. Never."

His voice dips lower, raw, trembling with the depth of what he feels. "I don't ever want to live in a world where you're not by my side. Not for a second, not for a day, not for a lifetime."

He shifts, steadying himself on one knee, his free hand reaching for mine, his touch warm, solid, grounding me when I feel like I might float away under the weight of this moment. "You are my heart, mi vida—my home, my safest place. You are the love I have never, not for one second, stopped believing in, and I want forever with you. If you let me, I will spend the rest of my life proving to you that love like ours doesn't fade, doesn't break, doesn't end." His thumb strokes over my fingers, his grip unwavering.

"So what do you say, princesa?" His voice is barely more than a whisper now, but it holds everything. Every promise, every memory, every piece of him that has ever belonged to me. "Marry me?"

It's not just a question. It's a promise. A forever. A love story written between every glance, every touch, every moment that led us to this.

My heart slams against my ribs, my entire body trembling from the weight of this moment, from the sheer force of him. The way he's looking at me, like I'm it for him, like I have been since the very beginning nearly brings me to my knees.

For a moment, I am still, frozen between the past and the future, between the love we lost and the love we found again. This is everything.

The boy who once held my heart. The man who never let it go. The one who fought for me, even when I couldn't fight for myself. My best friend. My home. And the ring—Mami's ring. She knew. She always knew.

A shaky laugh tumbles out, tangled with my tears. I don't think, I just move, dropping to my knees in front of him, my hands find his face, cupping it, grounding myself in the warmth of him, the realness of him—of this, of us.

"Yes," I whisper, my voice breaking. "Yes, yes, yes!"

Sebastian lets out a breath of relief, something like a choked laugh, something full of so much love I feel it in my bones.

He slides the ring onto my finger, his hands shaking as much as mine, and the second it's in place, I launch myself into his arms, knocking him back into the sand as our friends erupt into cheers around us.

His mouth finds mine, a kiss full of promise, of forever, of every moment we've ever lost and every moment we'll have ahead.

And in the middle of it all, Maya squeals, clapping her hands. "BEST. ADVENTURE. EVER!"

Epilogue

The world is quiet. Finally, blessedly quiet. For the first time in what feels like a lifetime, everything slows—no noise, no rush, no chaos. Just the steady beep of the monitor, the rhythmic rise and fall of my breath, and the overwhelming, all-consuming weight of love pressing down on my chest.

It's everywhere, filling the spaces between my ribs, curling into the deepest parts of me. I feel like I've run a marathon and somehow floated into a dream all at once.

My body is wrung out, aching in ways I never knew it could, my limbs too heavy to move. But my heart—my heart is light, full, more than it has ever been. It swells in my chest, stretching wide, big enough to hold this moment, big enough to hold them.

Sebastian is beside me, his grip firm but careful, holding my hand like it's the only thing tethering him to this moment. His thumb moves in slow, soothing circles over my skin, grounding me, steadying me, as if he's afraid that without the constant touch, this might all slip away.

When I turn to look at him, my breath catches. He looks

wrecked, in the most beautiful way. His curls are damp, clinging to his forehead, his jaw clenched like he's fighting to keep himself together.

But his eyes are what break me; they are shining, red-rimmed, utterly, completely undone. Every barrier he's ever had is gone, stripped away by the weight of this moment.

He blinks, his chest rising in a shuddered breath, and I watch him lose the fight to keep his composure as a single tear slips free.

Because she's here. Our daughter.

A sob wells up in my throat as I look down at the impossibly small baby curled against my chest. She's warm, soft, the tiniest thing I have ever held, and yet, she is the biggest thing I have ever known.

Her little mouth puckers in her sleep, her delicate fingers curled into a fist against my skin. A white cap covers the dark curls already peeking through, and I know, I just know, when I take it off, she'll have his hair. She is the most perfect thing I have ever seen.

Sebastian shifts closer, his hand moving to her back, his fingers barely brushing over the fabric of her blanket, like he's afraid she might disappear if he touches her too quickly.

His breath is shaky when he finally exhales. "You did it," he whispers, his voice hoarse, reverent.

A wet, breathy laugh escapes me. "We did it."

His lips press to my temple, lingering there like he's trying to hold this moment in place, like he needs to memorize it before time moves again. When he pulls back, his jaw is tight, his throat bobbing.

"I don't think I've ever loved anything more in my life," he murmurs, voice breaking at the end.

Tears prick at my eyes again as I reach for his face, brushing my fingers along his stubbled jaw, feeling the way his breath shudders beneath my touch. "Me neither," I whisper.

Sebastian leans in, resting his forehead against mine. The weight of it, of him, of us, settles deep into my bones. Our baby stirs in my arms, a tiny whimper leaving her lips, and we both freeze.

I hold my breath, waiting, but she settles again just as quickly, her tiny body warm and safe against me.

Sebastian exhales a soft, disbelieving laugh. "She already knows how to keep us on edge."

I smile, never taking my eyes off her. "She's ours."

His fingers tighten around mine. "Ours."

The door opens softly, and a nurse steps in, her voice gentle. "How are we doing?"

Sebastian answers for me. "Good." His voice is strong, but when he looks down at our daughter, his face softens. "Perfect."

The nurse smiles. "She's beautiful. Have you decided on a name?"

I glance at Sebastian, and in that second, we know. It isn't a decision. It isn't even a choice. It was never a question. It's been in our hearts from the moment we knew she existed, from the moment we dreamed of who she would be.

Sebastian reaches for my hand again, squeezing it tight, his eyes locked on mine, full of love, full of certainty. Together, in the same breath, we say it. "Lucia."

The nurse's smile widens, her voice soft. "That's a beautiful name."

My throat tightens as I press a trembling kiss to our daughter's forehead, letting my lips linger against her warm, delicate skin. Because she is beautiful. Because she carries more than just our love—she carries her love. My mother's love. The love that never left, never faded. The love that still lingers in every sunrise, in every whispered prayer, in every moment of warmth I feel deep in my soul.

Sebastian's fingers trail over our daughter's tiny hand, his voice low, steady. "Your abuela would've loved you so much."

Tears slip silently down my cheeks, but this time, they don't come from grief. They come from love, from gratitude, from everything.

Sebastian wraps his arm around me, holding us both close, and in the quiet of this hospital room, in the golden glow of our daughter's first moments in the world—I know we've found forever.

THE END

Acknowledgments

Thank you so much for reading *Back To You*! This book holds a piece of my heart, and the fact that you took the time to read it means more than I can ever put into words. These characters, their journey, and everything in between have lived in my mind for so long, and seeing them find a place in the world—on the page, in your hands—is a dream come true.

To my incredible support system—I could not have done this without you.

To my sweet husband, who has listened to me talk about these characters for hours on end, never once making me feel like I was rambling too much (even when I absolutely was). You have been my sounding board, my rock, and the person who stepped in to handle admin tasks the second I made the decision to self-publish—without hesitation, without question, just unwavering support. With you, every dream feels possible.

To my sister, who never let me give up on my self-imposed deadlines, who pushed me to keep going even when I felt stuck, who celebrated every milestone like it was her own. Your belief in me has been an anchor through every doubt-filled moment.

To my mom, who is always the ear I need, the voice of reason, the steady presence reminding me that I can do this. Your support has meant everything.

To Jenny—sorry, not sorry for the middle-of-the-night texts. You always respond, always encourage, always remind me that I'm not alone in this. I appreciate you more than words can say.

To my editor, my alpha readers, and every single person who let me ramble about this book, these characters, and every idea that popped into my head—thank you for listening, for offering your insights, for being as invested in this story as I am. Specifically, Kylie—your voice notes, your feedback, your push to step outside my comfort zone...it all meant the world. This book is better because of you.

And finally, to every single reader who picked up this book, who got lost in these pages, who connected with these characters—thank you. You make all of this worth it.

About the Author

Jasmine Ahmad is a romance author who writes heart-wrenching, emotional love stories full of heart, depth, and swoon-worthy moments. She loves exploring the messy, beautiful complexities of relationships, personal growth, and a love that lingers long after the final page.

A proud Latinx writer, Jasmine holds a Bachelor's degree in Psychology, which gives her a deep appreciation for human emotions and the way people connect. That insight finds its way into her storytelling, bringing her characters and their journeys to life in a way that feels real and deeply felt.

Originally from Queens, NY, she now lives in Southern California with her husband and children. When she's not writing, you can usually find her chasing after her little ones, lost in a good book, or advocating for mental health and chronic illness awareness. She believes stories have the power to heal, to inspire, and to remind us that even in the darkest moments, we are never beyond hope, love, or the chance to begin again.

Connect with Jasmine:
Instagram: @AuthorJasmineAhmad

TikTok: @AuthorJasmineAhmad
Website: www.authorjasmineahmad.com

www.ingramcontent.com/pod-product-compliance
Lightning Source LLC
Chambersburg PA
CBHW030246120726
47903CB00005B/1646